His Heart

by

Sheila Kell

HIS Series

Cover Art by *Lea Schizas*

The Wild Rose Press, Inc.
PO Box 708
Adams Basin, NY 14410-0708
Visit us at www.thewildrosepress.com

Publishing History
First Edition, 2025
Trade Paperback ISBN 978-1-5092-6047-8
Digital ISBN 978-1-5092-6048-5

HIS Series
Previously Published: Cunningham Publishing 2017
Published in the United States of America

Dedication

To Debi Rodriguez
I love you more, Sis—the end.

Chapter One

Another damn family wedding he'd had to attend. Matt Hamilton smiled and wished the happy couple the best. Christ, he wanted his family to be happy, but would it never fucking end? The sappiness of all the couples nearly drove him insane.

Matt had suffered through four brothers and his sister getting married to the one they couldn't live without. His father, U.S. Senator Blake Hamilton, was now tying the knot after too many years alone. Everyone had their fucking happy ending except him. And his twin, Brad.

He exhaled a long breath. If only he could go back and do things differently....

Dammit, his future still looked bleak without the woman he loved by his side. After all these years, all he wanted was for her to forgive him, even though he'd probably never forgive himself, or welcome him back. It was his fault tragedy had struck her. If only....

A hard slap on his shoulder brought him back to the present festivities. "Hey, man, how you holding up?" Brad's question was filled with concern. He knew Matt's aversion to weddings and the harsh memories they evoked. Like when they were young, he and his twin had few secrets between them.

"I'll survive." Taking the focus off him, he issued a sly grin before he spoke next. "Pity there aren't any bridesmaids for you to chase today." Their father's bride—their new stepmother—only had one attendant who wasn't married, and she was old enough to be their mother. Of course, knowing the horndog Brad was, that might not be a roadblock to him.

"Don't I fucking know it. Hell, I'm off to The Square. Want to come? We can hit up the new pizza joint on the Square, then grab a beer somewhere. There're lots of college girls hanging out at the bars." Brad waggled his eyebrows in emphasis.

Unfortunately, the lure of the entertainment hub of Oxford, Mississippi, didn't bolster him. The burden he carried was too great, and being in Oxford, where he'd fallen in love and then had his heart destroyed, weighed on him. "No. I'll pass." Matt raised an eyebrow in question. "Aren't you a bit old for college girls?" he joked. Hell, they were thirty.

Brad ignored his question and gave him an inquisitive stare before shaking his head. "Shit. This is about Caitlyn, isn't it?" He didn't wait for an answer. "Every fucking wedding has brought you to this brooding mood. I don't know whether to be pissed at you for hanging on to her memory for so long or feel sorry for you for doing the same. Listen, you're here, so why don't you visit her father, find out where she lives, and go see her?"

"It's not that simple and you know it." Nothing had been simple with his and Caitlyn's parting.

"Yes, it is," Brad stated hotly. "You're just too much of a fucking pussy to settle this shit."

Anger surged through Matt. He shoved his balled fists in the front of the pockets of his khaki pants to keep from swinging at Brad. How dare his brother—his twin of all people—tell him to settle this shit? He knew what had happened and how Matt had been at fault.

Eight years ago, Matt was engaged to be married, and the thought of his wedding had made him happy beyond all means. His heart sank at the thought and rolled around there to crush the joy he'd once felt. But things had gone horribly wrong, and Caitlyn Robinson had called off the ceremony.

Before blasting back a reply, Matt's gut churned. Brad was right. Hell, he needed to salvage a future worth living, which meant he needed to settle things with Caitlyn. But he wasn't sure he could handle her rejection one more time. Not from her…the woman who was still the only future he wanted.

Saying he could just forget the reason for their estrangement and move forward was impossible. Her final words had held him captive all this time. Sure, he'd dated—though he used that term loosely—during the intervening years, but no one came close to replacing Caitlyn in his life or, most importantly, in his heart.

"Hey, guys, what's up?" AJ, the youngest Hamilton brother, approached, holding his nine-month-old son, Alex, in his arms and grinning like everything in the world was perfect. Since he'd become a father, AJ's smile had grown twofold and remained permanently in place.

"Just planning single guy stuff. Remember that? The fun? The women?" Brad mocked as he wiggled his eyebrows playfully.

AJ narrowed his eyes at Brad, but his smile didn't falter. "Maybe you aren't familiar with the married stuff—a great woman in your bed every night and children who bring joy to your life."

"Someone criticizing you. Someone always telling you what to do. Someone always in your business," Brad retorted like they were playing an I'll-one-up-you game he planned to win.

"What's going on?" Jesse, the eldest of the brothers, joined them. Not expecting a wedding when Matt and his siblings had made the family trip at their father's insistence, most weren't prepared for the dress attire a wedding usually required. Not Jesse though. Seemingly prepared for just about anything, he'd packed a blazer in his luggage. Who the hell wanted to wear a blazer in this summer heat? Not Matt. Luckily, his father and the bride hadn't wanted to wait until they all were dressed to the nines; they wanted everyone to come as they were for their wedding in the gardens of the Oxford family home.

Matt shrugged and nodded between the two of his brothers, who were dressed similarly to him in khakis and a short-sleeved polo shirt. Golf attire. That'd been their plan anyway until the ceremony changed their schedule. "They're arguing married versus single life." Although watching from the sidelines, Matt crossed his arms over his chest and widened his stance as if to dig in for a good, long fight. "They just got started slinging mud, so this should be good."

"There's no contest. Married life kicks ass," Jesse offered, wearing a broad smile. "It won't be long before you two"—he pointed to Matt and then Brad—"tie the knot."

"Fuck no," Brad answered forcefully. "No way would I give up my freedom for some chick. There's too much pussy to go around, especially now that you guys are off the beat, leaving much more for me."

"Watch your language," AJ commanded while rubbing the back of his sleeping son, whose head lay on AJ's shoulder.

"Shit, sorry," Brad apologized in a low-pitched voice.

Heads shook in hopelessness, but no one bothered to inform Brad that he'd cursed in his apology for cursing in front of Alex.

Matt didn't respond to Jesse. Once, he'd been willing to give up his freedom, but he wasn't sure he saw marriage in his future. From experience, Matt knew that if the right woman came along, Brad would jump at the chance to marry her and make her his. His twin just hadn't fallen in love yet. It'd happen. Matt hoped sooner rather than later, though. He'd like to see Brad as a father.

Fuck. How could he let it escape him that if Brad fell in love, that would mean another wedding? He didn't think he could endure it, because he was confident Brad would ask him to be his best man. They had promised to do that years ago. Christ, they'd still been in high school. Like him, Brad would remember and ask him to stand up with him. A shiver of dread snaked up his spine.

The crazy number of weddings taking place in the last two years did nothing but drive home that he'd been too chickenshit to resolve what stood between him and moving forward. He'd never searched for Caitlyn, but her moving away had always been on his mind. Yet there he stood—a big, bad, former Navy SEAL who wouldn't confront his past.

Releasing a sigh, he scoffed at himself for the

internal emotional rant. Yeah, he'd been thinking like a big, bad former SEAL who needed a kick in the ass.

Resolved to take whatever hits Caitlyn gave, he made up his mind. He'd find her and apologize one more time. Then he could close that door and move forward. Maybe. But he hoped it wouldn't come to that.

First, the team had a job scheduled for when they returned from this short family retreat. He hadn't been involved in the planning, but surely someone could replace him from the mission. "Hey, Jesse, if you can spare me on this next assignment, I've got someplace I need to be."

Jesse eyed him suspiciously, and Matt tried to keep his facial expressions neutral—unreadable—like he'd learned long ago in the navy. Granted, Matt had never backed out of a mission before, so he expected the curiosity. He just hoped he didn't get any questions. Sharing why he wanted the time would open too many other inquiries from Jesse and his brothers, if they found out. Brad would keep it quiet, so best he kept it between them for now. Then, if things went well, he'd share the happiness with everyone. If they didn't, he wouldn't have their pity any more than he had eight years ago.

"Yeah, we can make it happen." His older brother paused for a moment, still studying Matt. "Anything you need help with?"

Matt shook his head. "Nah, just some hunting I need to do." Hunting was precisely what he'd be doing because after Caitlyn had dumped him, she'd disappeared, and her father had kept her location secret. After his brother Devon's wedding and advice, Matt up on Adam Robinson's doorstep amends. e hadn't been able to face Caitlyn's father after everything had happened.

Adam had stated he'd never blamed Matt and wished he'd been visiting all along, because he missed his company. His card playing too. Years ago, they'd sit and play gin rummy while Caitlyn did her college coursework on days or nights when Matt just needed to be near her.

God, he still missed her terribly. Her smile. Her scent. Her laughter. All of her.

With a nod, Jesse said, "Well, we're here if you need us."

A lump formed in Matt's throat. Now that they all worked together at Hamilton Investigation & Security, he and his brothers remained tight like they had when growing up together. They had each other's back at HIS and in their regular lives. However, he had to do this alone. He had to face it without his family watching, no matter how much he wanted them with him. "Thanks."

They shook hands, and before any could ask questions, Brad exclaimed, "Good. It's settled. I'm out of here." He dipped his head in farewell, then turned and strode away.

"I think I'll get going also," Matt echoed, ready to be away from the celebration. But, like a dutiful son, he once again congratulated the happy couple before climbing into one of the minivans rented in town to drive the family from the small private airport. He'd need to get his own vehicle if traveling would be involved in finding Caitlyn. He wouldn't leave his brothers and their families high and dry without transportation.

Leaving the Oxford family home, he exited the

magnolia and oak tree-lined driveway. Some had grown large enough that their branches almost touched across the top of the drive, creating a canopy of shade and coolness. Lord knew they needed a bit of cool in July down south, so he cranked down the temperature for the air conditioner.

Driving west on MS-6, he approached the Water Valley exit, his nerves jumping through his system. Visiting Caitlyn's father was one thing, but asking him her whereabouts was something he'd avoided in the past, because he couldn't bring himself to hear again that she didn't want to see him when every part of his broken heart wanted to see her. No longer. He would find out where she'd gone into hiding and show up on her doorstep, like he had Adam's.

After the things she'd said to him—blaming him— he wasn't sure what to expect from her. Yet he'd try. Hell, it could only go one of two ways—she'd forgive him, or she'd kick him off her property, maybe with a weapon. He'd prepare himself for all possibilities, knowing that she could be a different person since he hadn't seen or spoken to her in eight years. No. He wouldn't believe she would've changed from the sweet and caring woman he'd fallen in love with.

As Matt pulled up to the old wood, A-frame house desperately needing a coat or two of paint, and parked, two years of memories in the house rushed at him. She'd been his from the moment he'd caught sight of Caitlyn at her freshman orientation. Although he couldn't say for sure when he realized how much he loved her, he believed it was pretty much love at first sight. Corny as fuck, but true in this case.

A shot rang out, and he reacted instantaneously.

Hand on the door handle, he was out of the minivan and at the front door in seconds.

With blood pumping like wildfire through his veins, Matt slowly eased the front door open and peered inside to assess the situation, hoping like hell that what he found didn't require a weapon since he was unarmed. His heart nearly stopped. Adam lay on the floor while a man aimed a handgun at his prone form. Adam lay bleeding, his light-colored shirt turning crimson.

Biting back his desire to charge in, consequences be damned, Matt crept up behind the man with the weapon and tackled him. The handgun flew through the air as they grappled to reach it, each tossing a punch at the other when a hand was free. Pain ricocheted through his skull, and his head snapped back from a direct hit to his face.

Motherfucker, Matt's mind screamed and his blood raced through his veins.

It took a moment before he came back to himself. Angrier than a hornet's nest, he rolled on top of the gunman and pinned the guy's arms under his knees. Matt's hands were at the attacker's throat for just a moment before he suddenly slumped forward, stunned and dazed, losing his grip. The gunman took the advantage and kicked Matt off him, grabbed his weapon, and bolted out the door.

Struggling to his hands and knees, Matt shook his head, trying to clear it. He had no idea what had just happened to him, but fuck, he didn't like it. The shooter had escaped, and Matt wasn't in a frame of mind to chase him. He could barely keep himself from being too dizzy to stand.

Once he grasped his wits, he focused on Adam and getting him the needed help. Matt removed his cell phone from his pocket and dialed 911 before he made it back to Adam's side and began applying pressure to the gunshot wound. He couldn't do anything about the obvious torture the man had suffered. It appeared some of Adam's fingers were broken. Also, there were knife slices over the exposed flesh of his arms. Christ, how long had he endured this? For what?

"Talk to me, Adam," Matt urged.

"Don't tell her that it happened like this," Adam rasped as blood trickled from the cut on his lip.

His gut clenched at the beating the man had taken, but he made no promises. It had been damn lucky Matt had come to visit when he had. Hell, a few minutes later, Caitlyn's father might've been dead at the hands of the shooter.

Matt mentally kicked himself. He should've come sooner instead of pretending to enjoy the wedding. Yet how could he have known something like this was happening? Crime existed in Water Valley, but not typically to this level of attempted murder. The sheriff had to catch the shooter before he tormented someone else, or worse, killed them.

"Who did this?" Matt probed calmly. It was what he was known for—his calm in the face of a storm, his peacefulness amidst the horror. His brothers and SEAL buddies had dubbed him "the peacemaker." Yet Matt's blood boiled and temper rose, belying any semblance of internal peacefulness and calm as he stared down at Adam's battered body.

The 911 operator responded just as Adam slipped into unconsciousness. "I need an ambulance. I have a

10

gunshot victim…." He relayed the information and address before dropping the phone and reapplying pressure to the bleeding wound on Adam's side. It hadn't been in the heart or gut—a possible mortal wound. The fucker had still been toying with him by just inflicting more pain.

Hours later, finally free of the sheriff deputies and their questions, he drove to the hospital, wondering again what had happened to Adam. He had no idea what the shooter had wanted, but the asshole had been pumping Adam for something.

Picking up his phone, he called his twin. Thank the fuck Brad had pretty much goaded him into coming now. When his brother answered, his voice had almost been drowned out by the loud music in the background. "If you've chickened out, I'm coming to kick your ass." Matt knew he wouldn't actually do that, but he'd continue to prod until Matt made a move on seeing Caitlyn again.

"You drunk yet?" Matt asked.

"On my way, and I've got two pretty co-eds hanging on my arms."

Matt didn't doubt it.

"Hang on, Matt, while I go someplace quieter." With the phone away from Brad's mouth, Matt barely discerned, "Excuse me, ladies. I'll be right back." A shuffling noise sounded as the background noise dropped. "Well, did you get her address?"

"No, and I didn't ask. Adam was being attacked when I arrived."

"Holy fuck." Matt could hear the outrage in his brother's voice. "What the fuck happened?"

Matt relayed the information, ending as he entered

the hospital emergency room parking lot, and felt like a weight had been lifted. He still held the concern of Adam's attack and finding Caitlyn, but knowing his brother knew always made him feel lighter. It sounded girly, but it was a twin thing. At least, that was the excuse he'd always used.

"Do you want me there?"

Did he? He internally shook his head. Not for this, at least not yet, but he appreciated his brother had asked. "No. I've got this. Thanks, man." He hesitated. "Brief Jesse for me." It was early, but inside, he knew he'd need support of some sort—just the family or a team. He'd call his oldest brother later once he found out exactly what had happened and the identity of the threat to Adam.

They ended the call and before he could step out of the minivan, Caitlyn came to mind.

Hell, she needed to know about her father, but he still didn't know how to contact her. She'd go ballistic that this happened. Adam had been his only hope in finding her. Maybe when Adam came around, he'd be helpful. However, it wasn't how he expected his reunion with her to be. *I missed you, but oh, by the way, your dad had the shit beat out of him and then was shot.*

But life sometimes sucked. He'd learned that lesson on many occasions—losing Caitlyn, losing friends in combat, losing some of himself…. He'd tried to run away from the loss of Caitlyn when he'd joined the Navy and then, eventually, qualified as a SEAL, where he'd run into a world that guaranteed success and failure. And he'd experienced both. Hell, he'd been on the team that had brought down a prominent terrorist leader, but he'd also been on a team that had been ambushed and lost half of its members. He swallowed hard at the memory that never faded and shoved it away. He couldn't go down that road right now.

He'd learned to deal with life. At least as best as he could.

After too many worrisome hours to count, Adam's surgery had been successful. Once he was out of recovery, Matt sat at his bedside, hoping the man would wake and tell him everything. He'd woke a time or two but had been too drugged to maintain a coherent conversation. If the sheriff's department was going to find out who Adam's attacker was, Adam had to survive and tell them. Hell, the deputies had been by once already and were eager to learn what Adam knew. Matt hadn't had much to offer, except a description, but a shaggy hair and beard had covered most of the guy's features. The description was vague since Matt really hadn't gotten a good look at him. The thing was, from that flash of his face when Matt had his hands around his throat, the man had seemed familiar, but he couldn't place him. He didn't share that with the deputies, knowing they'd hound him for more until Matt was sure to snap.

"Catie." Matt heard the faint word coming from the bed. It was the nickname Adam had given to Caitlyn when she was a baby. Well, then it was Catie-bug, but Caitlyn had told Matt that her father had finally dropped "bug" when she'd entered college. Matt had quickly put together that she liked the endearment, and in her mind, her father could do no wrong.

He leaned closer and watched as Adam's eyes fluttered open, nearly clear of the drugs that had put him in a deep sleep. "Adam," Matt acknowledged, hoping to gain the man's attention.

Caitlyn's father turned his head toward him. "My Catie, he's after her."

Fear sliced through Matt at the thought of anyone hurting Caitlyn. "Who's after her?"

"Travis Ripley's brother, Luke Ripley."

Son of a bitch. He wanted to scream to the heavens. Now he knew why the guy had looked familiar. He'd been the brother of her rapist. He'd seen him in the courtroom of the trial. How could he have not noticed? Granted, Matt had only slipped into the trial for one day since Caitlyn had told him to stay away. How could he have allowed a threat to Caitlyn to get away? *Fuck!* He wanted to roar and rip the place apart.

He took a deep breath and held it for a moment before he released it with a steady sigh. *Calm*, he reminded himself. "Does he know where she is?" That would explain the torture. But had Adam caved? Matt guessed not since the shooter had still been there interrogating Adam, but he could've been just taunting him like his brother had supposedly done to Caitlyn during the trial.

"I didn't tell him."

Kicking himself for not noticing the scratchiness in Adam's voice earlier, he reached for the pitcher beside his hospital bed, poured a cup of water, and then pushed the button to lift the bed. He held the plastic cup to the man who had almost been his father-in-law's lips. "Drink. Slowly," he directed.

Fuck, all he wanted to do was run out of here, grab Caitlyn, and race for the hills. But he still didn't know where the hell she was. And if Adam hadn't shared her location, she was safe for the moment. Matt was well aware though that Ripley had already taken extreme measures to find Caitlyn, so there was no telling what else he was capable of.

"You've got to warn and protect her," Adam demanded.

"Okay." His response was automatic.

Adam's face registered surprise at Matt's quick agreement. Maybe he'd expected Matt to fight him on it, but that would never happen regarding Caitlyn's safety. "You didn't even ask why he wants her."

Matt shrugged. "I figured you'd tell me."

"Well, I would. I am. Travis is up for parole again, and if Catie testifies, he won't get out. By the sounds of what Luke kept saying, they don't want her there and will do whatever it takes to ensure she doesn't make it."

"When's the hearing?"

"A few months out. They're obviously preparing early."

"They?" Matt asked, surprised.

"I could be wrong, but I thought someone else was in the house."

"I didn't see another person."

"I didn't either, but like I said, I could be wrong. If I'm not and they got into my office and found her address...." He let the words trail off.

Fuck me. This just kept getting worse. "Do you want me to look through your office?"

Not addressing the question, Adam turned to hold his gaze. "I don't know how she'll feel about you just showing up, and you can't tell her how bad I am," he instructed, wincing as he spoke.

She'd probably be pissed off to see him, maybe

throw something at him. No, that would be a massive underestimation considering how they'd parted, but no matter how she reacted, no way would he lie to her. "Let me worry about how she feels, but, Adam, I won't sugarcoat your injuries. You could've died if I hadn't arrived. Hell, they had to remove a bullet. Sure, it wasn't a serious wound where it hit anything vital, but that's no walk in the park. I'll try to wait and let you tell her, but I won't hold back if I need to tell her so she understands the depth of this threat. She needs to know that fucker is out and looking for her."

Adam appeared to think it over for a moment. "Just don't bring her home."

Matt countered with a shake of his head, and a laugh tried to push its way out. It wasn't an appropriate time to laugh, so he held it close, but telling her she couldn't come home was laughable. "As much as I want to, I can't guarantee that." Adam had to know Caitlyn would want to be by her father's side. At least the Caitlyn he knew would. And if she remained as tenacious as she used to be, nothing he could do would stop her. Short of tying her up and locking her away. That wasn't the way to go if he also sought her forgiveness.

"Just protect her," Adam pleaded. "Promise me."

"I can't do that until you tell me where she is."

"She's going to kill me for sharing, but"—Adam turned back, pushed the button to lower the bed, and then looked at the ceiling as if contemplating his next words, before continuing—"she's in Winchester, Kentucky."

"Winchester? What the hell is in Winchester?" He hadn't even heard of the place. Had she just dropped a pin on the map and moved to where it landed? Oh shit, had she married? He hadn't considered that possibility, but he had to explore it. It had been a long time, and they weren't engaged any longer, no matter how much he wanted that to be the case.

All he knew was that over the years he'd realized they'd had something special. A love that existed for eternity. No matter how he changed or how he perceived her changing, that love would only grow. Yeah, he knew it sounded like a sissy talking, but his heart still beat for her, and no matter who she was now, he'd still love her.

Adam turned back to him. "It doesn't matter. Just get there and protect her."

That, he could promise. Now that he knew where to find her, he wasn't letting her go so easily. He should've fought for them the first time instead of allowing guilt to lead his actions. "I'll do everything I can to keep her safe."

"Don't let that bastard get to her. She suffered enough because of his brother."

"I won't." He'd failed her once where that fucking family was concerned—hell, twice now for letting that asshole escape tonight—but he wouldn't fail her again.

Chapter Two

Luke fucking Ripley, whose brother had ruined both his and Caitlyn's lives with a single, reprehensible act. Caitlyn's life had been irrevocably changed, and Matt had failed to do anything to protect her. He had no clue what Luke's plans were once he had Caitlyn and could only assume the worse.

The fallout of that fateful night swam in his head. While Matt had experienced a hangover, his fiancée had rested in the hospital, broken and brutalized. She'd turned into a shell of her original self, which had destroyed him. In his next stored memory from when she was out of the hospital recovering at her home, she'd blamed him and later disappeared.

He wanted to scream at the injustice of it all. She hadn't deserved to be raped and beaten. It wouldn't have happened if Matt had been where he was supposed to be. That "if only" slipped back into his mind, and he wanted to rip it out and strangle it until it couldn't breathe life around him.

The past was the past. He couldn't change it. He couldn't forget it either. But, like he'd already convinced himself, he could move forward and change his future direction. He had a chance to make things up to her by protecting her this time. His heart pounded, and his gut churned. Nothing could happen to her. He wouldn't allow it.

Changed into jeans, a black T-shirt with the HIS logo and claiming his tennis shoes, Matt finished tossing his clothes into his suitcase, uncaring if they wrinkled. He didn't need much for his trip to Winchester, but he wouldn't return to the family home for a while. It now belonged to his sister, Emily, but it was still dubbed and used as the family retreat, as it always had been.

Adam had finally coughed up Caitlyn's address in Kentucky. The man's fear had dictated breaking his promise of secrecy to his only daughter. He wanted Matt to keep her safe, no matter what was needed.

Hell, Adam wanted all of HIS to be there for her. Something Matt wished also but knew it wasn't possible. The team had assignments. But, he'd speak with Jesse about the few team members who weren't going out in the next couple of weeks. All the brothers and his sister were partners, but Jesse still mostly ran HIS. They needed a person who kept track of who was where and made any quick decisions on behalf of the family. Jesse fit that bill 100 percent.

Showing up and convincing Caitlyn that he was there to provide protection would be easier said than done. She might kick him out on his ass before he even had an opportunity to explain. And she'd have every right to do so.

No matter how she felt about him, Matt had to get her to understand and let him help keep her safe.

Sitting on the edge of the bed, Matt placed his elbows on his thighs, then sank his head into his hands, his fingers in his hair. He'd fucked up so badly in the past. No matter what people said, her rape was on his shoulders. She'd been right to blame him...to run from him. How the hell could he convince her he was sincere and wouldn't allow harm to come to her this time?

Hearing a noise in the open doorway, he looked up at his twin. Brad studied him before he walked into the room they shared. "You're thinking about it again, aren't you?"

He knew "it" referred to the rape. His twin knew him well. Too well. With a heavily burdened sigh, he nodded. "I should've been there. Christ, I was drinking with my friends instead of being where I was supposed to be with Caitlyn. She waited for me—" He sprang from the bed, his nerves on edge. "If I'd been there, it wouldn't have happened."

Brad narrowed his eyes and nearly bore a hole in Matt's skull. "According to Caitlyn, Ripley had a weapon when he cornered her. What would you have done?" He didn't give Matt a chance to answer. "You didn't have your SEAL training then. You were just a college kid. Plus, you'd been drinking. What would've happened is that you'd have gotten yourself shot. And then it still would've happened. Hell, she could've been killed."

Matt's back straightened, ready to launch a defense. "That's because he got scared off."

Brad snorted. "Yeah, you and your drunk buddies happened to come by. None of you noticed him as he slipped away. So tell me, how would you have stopped it if you didn't even see him after he attacked her?"

Anger surged through him like a volcano getting ready to erupt. Only Brad had ever pushed him to lose his calm. "Stop it!" he shouted. "She had every right to blame me." He forcefully gestured with his thumb to his chest so Brad didn't misunderstand.

Brad sighed and his shoulders sagged. "She was distraught, Matt. It was easy to blame you, and you took it all. You wallowed in your self-pity and left her without a fight. I feel she won't feel that way when you see her. Caitlyn was too good of heart. She'll come to her senses. Probably already has set things straight in her mind."

If only Brad were right. It was a fucked-up feeling being pulled in two directions—craving forgiveness and not deserving it—neither giving him the freedom of his hell that he sought. The hell that had started when he'd agreed to another round of shots with his college buddies, who were celebrating their upcoming graduation, and ignored the time he was to meet with Caitlyn for their date, knowing she would ask for him to repay her for that time with more loving in bed that night.

Needing to focus on now and not the past, he shook his head to clear what had been. "I've got to speak with Jesse about a team. I'll see you later." Not waiting for Brad to respond or try to give him more advice, he exited the room, descended the stairs, and walked into the large family room where he found Jesse and his family lounging on the sofas.

"Jesse, can I speak to you for a minute?"

His older brother whispered something in his wife, Kate's, ear, then stood and approached Matt on the other side of the room, which was surprisingly void of people, considering how many had packed themselves into the house.

"I'm going to see Caitlyn," Matt stated matter-of-factly.

Jesse nodded but didn't mention Matt had already

told him that when he'd filled Jesse in on all that had happened earlier with Adam to include his concerns for Caitlyn's safety. "You want a team when she visits her dad? Because we both know she'll demand to visit him."

His brother had read his mind and knew Caitlyn well. Hell, they'd dated for almost two years before he'd gotten up the courage and asked her to marry him. His brothers had teased him incessantly. As for protection, there'd never be enough as far as he was concerned. But he'd take what was available. "I do."

With a thoughtful look, Jesse held out his hands to count on his fingers. "I can spare Boss, Ballpark, Romeo, and Nemo." He held up four fingers on his right hand. "They can fly in today and be ready for when you return. That should be enough."

"I'm coming, too," Brad interjected as he bound into the room. "No way would I leave Matt out there without me at his back. No telling what the fuck would happen to him."

Even at the stab to his manhood, relief slipped into his bloodstream. Brad may be cynical and try to piss him off from time to time, but he was still the best friend Matt had. While he'd be happy for any of his brothers to have his back, he'd prefer Brad beside him in danger.

Danger. God, he hoped there wouldn't be any danger.

Luke Ripley hadn't extracted Caitlyn's address from her father during the torture session. But bringing her back here worried the hell out of him. While Adam's attacker could be in hiding since he had to know that Adam identified him, he could be sitting and waiting. Maybe Matt could convince Caitlyn not to visit. He groaned. Who the hell was he kidding? Even though he hadn't met the woman she was today, he knew without a doubt that she would still want to visit her father. The two had been close. Hell, she was closer to her father than he was to his old man. He and his father had a good relationship, but nothing like Caitlyn and Adam.

"Where do you want them?" Jesse's words interrupted his thoughts. He really had to start paying more attention and not allowing his mind to run away on that broken train track it kept finding.

Great question. He thought for a moment before responding. "I think here, protecting Adam to start. Ripley doesn't know where Caitlyn lives, so I can travel and collect her without him knowing. Hopefully, I can convince her to stay home, and then we can bring half the team there to help."

Jesse snorted. "Unless she turned into one cold-hearted bitch—which I wholeheartedly doubt—she's coming to visit her dad in his condition. I don't see her staying away. No matter how long it's been."

Matt nodded. "That's why I want them waiting here. Plus, I don't want Adam attacked again."

"I can get a second team here in a few days," Jesse added thoughtfully, "so take a team with you when you take her home. If that bastard has any sense, he's in hiding far away from here. But if he's watching for her to come here, we can nail his ass to the wall."

"Good." Matt's emphatic response left no room for confusion of his position.

"What did the deputies have to say?" Jesse asked.

Shaking his head in disgust at the sheriff's

department in Adam's county, Matt responded dryly, "They've knocked on a few doors and have an APB out on him but aren't holding their collective breaths that they'll find him."

"I still can't believe Luke would try this now. This isn't Travis's first parole hearing," Brad stated.

"I overheard two deputies talking. After they'd finished, I asked for confirmation, and they reluctantly gave it to me. They talked to Travis Ripley's son, who was paroled after ten years in prison. While incarcerated, the kid bragged that when he was released he'd get his dad out of prison. Don't get excited. He has an alibi for when the incident occurred. He must've hit up the uncle since he had no resources, and he's playing his parole cool."

Caitlyn wouldn't be expecting anyone to be after her. She wouldn't be prepared for danger, for a possible attack. Hell, Luke had already shot her father. He might try to do what his brother promised when he'd raped her—to kill her.

"Jesse, I'd like a team trying to track him down," Matt asked. "Adam thought someone else was in his home, so the son and brother could be working together." Knowing resources were limited due to the scheduled workload, the worst that could happen was his older brother said no.

Jesse slowly shook his head. "I wish we could, but we can't do it. There are too many assignments. I'm already bare-bonesing them to give you two teams, and they're only short-term."

Matt started to shake his head in disagreement.

"Don't shake your head. You'll need two teams until he's captured. Now, what we can do is put Devon on it. If he finds something, then we'll reevaluate. The uncle might slip up. For groundwork, we may send one person from Adam's security detail now to investigate, but we won't pull the entire team from Adam or Caitlyn until Luke Ripley is captured and we're sure the son is clean in this."

Warmth flooded him at the love Jesse was showing with his actions. He didn't use the words, but making sure Matt and those he loved were protected said it all. They'd had to do this so many times in the past two years with women the men fell in love with. He could only hope he had the same happy ending they had.

Dammit, he'd had her heart once, and he'd have it again. He would not stop until he was confident it couldn't happen. This time, he wouldn't allow their current circumstance to stand in his way. He was a big boy and needed to act it when they reunited.

Remembering Jesse had spoken to him, he nodded. "Okay. Thanks." What else was there to say? He had what he needed. Sure, he wished they had a team tracking the bastard down since he doubted the sheriff was putting his limited manpower on just Luke Ripley, but Jesse was right; it was best to be in place to protect Caitlyn and Adam. Who knew? The asshole might come back to them, and HIS could capture him.

Matt could only hope.

"I'd best get on the road. I'm driving since it'll take nearly as long with security and transfers and then renting a car when I connect flights. Plus, I don't want to deal with the hassle of transporting a weapon, and I won't have her with me without them. So, I've got about seven or eight hours to drive."

"Christ, you'll get there in the middle of the night

and freak the shit out of her," Brad stated unnecessarily.

"I plan to get a hotel nearby and see her in the morning when she's awake." When he wouldn't have the possibility of getting shot as an intruder. Growing up where Caitlyn did, he could almost guarantee she had a weapon at home. Hell, she could shoot him if she was still pissed at him, but he'd gamble on her not being—that the years had made her wiser. He expected her to hold some resentment still, but shooting him? He didn't think so but could never understand a woman's mind.

Jesse nodded. "Smart move."

"Listen, say goodbye to everyone for me." Matt's statement contained a question about his brother's acceptance of the task.

"I'll do it," Brad piped up.

Matt shook his head with vigorous force. "Oh, hell no. You'd just as soon punch everyone in the mouth."

"Fuck you," Brad retorted. "I love this family. It's the rest of the world who can kiss my fucking ass."

Matt internally shook his head. That about summed up his identical twin. One day, they'd work to overcome his problem. But not today. Today, Matt had his issues to tackle.

Safe in the rental car delivered to him, he cranked up the air conditioner, inhaled the new car smell it still had, and drove. Once he merged onto MS-7, his mind took its route of times when he and Caitlyn had been planning their wedding. She'd been so excited about having it in the garden at the Hamilton Oxford house as his father had just done.

Caitlyn had even picked out her dress and had refused to allow him to see it. She'd said it would be bad luck if he saw it, so he hadn't pushed, even though he didn't believe in that tradition or supposed consequence for breaking it. They'd only been three short weeks away from their wedding. Sure, she'd still be a college student, but he'd have graduated the week before they married and started his new job in Oxford. They hadn't cared about being so young. They'd only wanted to be together.

He passed a home with dozens of pink azalea bushes lining the front yard near the road. Pink. Not bright pink, but closer to a pastel pink. That'd been the color she'd had for her bridesmaids' dresses, flowers, men's cummerbunds, and bowties for the men's tuxedos. Brad and Matt's friends grumbled but agreed because they'd had a look at the bridesmaids and couldn't wait to meet them, spurred on by the thought of hooking up.

When blue lights flashed behind him, his mind returned to the present, and his pulse raced. *Shit!* He didn't have a permit to carry his weapon in Mississippi. Since Devon, one of his older brothers, always handled administrative things, like clearance to carry weapons, Matt had never learned the rules associated with what states required extra paperwork. Except for rescuing Elizabeth, they hadn't needed for their weapons down South until today. He'd have to call Devon and find out if he was good—something he probably should've done before this moment. The question was whether he was good if he was pulled over by this state trooper.

A whistle of remembrance blew through him at his answer to his question. Mississippi, Kentucky, and Maryland did have reciprocity laws, but he'd rather not test his theory. If Matt got caught and had needed something other than his Maryland permit, he could pull his father into the situation, but he wouldn't do that to his father's stellar reputation. He slammed his hands on the steering wheel and slowed, easing the car to the shoulder of the road. *Fuck.* He'd just see how it played out.

Relief whooshed through him as the cop sped by, leaving Matt alone. After calming his breathing, he pulled back on the road. He had to pay attention to his driving. This time his thoughts were of nothing but getting to Caitlyn without a stop by a state trooper or, heaven forbid, being arrested. He'd do neither of them any good if his butt were in jail.

"Caitlyn," he said out loud, "I'm coming, whether you like it or not."

Chapter Three

"How can this possibly be?" Caitlyn Robinson murmured. Sitting at the scarred, second-hand break room table at Helping Paws, the service-dog training organization she'd founded, she reviewed the financial statement before her. Taking a sip of her lukewarm coffee, she grimaced, looked at it, and stood. Putting her free hand on her lower back, she arched her spine and stretched before throwing the coffee into the sink and refilling her cup from the fresh pot.

After adding a teaspoon of sugar and cream, she stirred the coffee while her mind whirled. *Where had the money gone? Had they really spent so much?* Damn. She'd thought donations were steady. What would the board of directors think? More importantly, what would they do? The thought of them asking her to step down for her failing flitted through her mind. The idea of a disappointing performance pushed courage through her veins to combat that possibility. The organization was still good for a long while, just not where she thought they'd be at this time.

Helping Paws, a nonprofit charity, relied on donations to stay afloat. She'd done more than enough begging—her term when she asked for money—and thought she'd pulled enough to last them for much longer than the projections she'd just reviewed showed.

Maybe Rick had it wrong. When she'd hired Rick

Marsh a few years ago to help train the dogs, she'd been impressed with his accounting background. With her inability to make heads or tails from accounting worksheets—her worst subject while earning her degree in business through an online university—she convinced him to take over the finances. She'd even convinced the board of directors to give him the lofty title of Financial Officer and pay him a higher salary than they could really afford.

He'd simplified the statements for her so she could see what kind of trouble they would soon be in if she didn't pull in more money. And that was her primary job—keeping them in enough money to operate. While the consensus of this type of organization was that it cost nearly $25,000 a year to train a dog—and they could take up to two years to train—she'd lowered their cost per dog to $21,000 per year. Her goal was to slide it down to $17,000 per year per dog, like the organization she'd trained with before she began this leg of her journey in life.

She took a sip of coffee and allowed the warmth of the beverage to seep into her system. She didn't relish doing another fundraiser or going door-to-door to collect funds. Hell, the reality was despite a fundraiser taking money to arrange, they drew the right people who were able to donate, plus the payoff was incredible. If you had the right people ripe for the picking. She grinned at that saying. Her Aunt Kathy had said it often enough.

She could make this happen. First, she needed a grant writer to take on her cause. While she'd muddled through small grants, like the Wal-Mart Community Grant, she'd pulled in quite a number of donations. But they were small potatoes. The Wal-Mart grant was $2,500. She needed complicated federal grants and had never pursued that avenue before because she knew it would take a professional grant writer to get them through it. Besides, the money had always been there. Second, there was a group of devoted supporters who sent monthly checks like clockwork. She'd check on if they fulfilled their commitments.

Rick poked his head into the room.

"Are these accurate?" She gestured to the papers now strewn across the table in no discernible order.

He fully entered the break room and closed the door behind him. "I'm afraid they are."

"It just seems we should have more there. Even the monthly donations appear to be down."

"Converting that space to a new set of pens for the dogs ran over budget, and so did the roof repair." He shifted. "Maybe you should stop paying me extra. I'd help for free. Besides, you've been picking up the more complicated financial analysis sheets better than before."

If it were only that simple that getting rid of his salary would make the difference, she'd consider it for the sake of the organization, but only for a moment, because she couldn't do that to an employee, no matter their situation. She shook her head. "No. You earn that money. I won't have you volunteer for financial services, but I appreciate the offer." Deciding upon her best course of action, she asked Rick for copies of the monthly donations lists and then added reluctantly, "Have Tonya come see me. I'm adding searching for a grant writer to my too-long to-do list, but in the meantime, we need another fundraiser."

Tonya Beck, her only other full-time dog trainer, majored in marketing and PR and knew how to create events that drew people to donate their money. Her payment was a small percentage of the overall take, which probably worked out better financially for Tonya. Not carrying another increased salary like Rick worked well on a daily basis for the organization.

Caitlyn had lucked out with those two employees. Not that she discounted the volunteers who'd arrive sporadically, but Rick and Tonya were more invested in the success of Helping Paws.

He nodded. "I can do that. Anything else?"

She took another sip of coffee and told herself to focus on the now. She'd take care of the finances later. She'd research the donation list. Someone had to have forgotten to send money like they'd promised. Trying to change her train of thought, she asked, "How's the training coming with Cooper, Bella, Sadie, and Gabe? I saw most of their future handlers here last week."

The veterans who scheduled to receive a dog were encouraged to visit and work with some of the pups after they'd returned from their six-month foster care, where the pups received basic socialization skills before their official training could begin. This allowed Helping Paws to pair the best match of dog and future handler. Once they'd been chosen, the veteran was encouraged to work with the trainer and the dog to be more comfortable with each other. It also strengthened the bond between the veteran and the dog before they were alone. It wasn't a requirement, and some vets lived too far away to regularly come in regularly, but most of the future handlers found a way.

While she managed the overall training, she'd

allowed her two employees to take the lead on these four dogs because they were closest to being ready. It had almost killed her to step back. She trusted them to do a good job but also missed working with the dogs at that level herself. Because she couldn't completely step away from training the dogs, she'd already started working with the younger ones who were still in the early stages of their development.

"We need a few more days to ensure they're good and ready. Then the new handlers can do their formal instruction with them."

By formal, it meant a ten-day block where the trainer made sure the handler could manage the dog and that the dog would respond properly. It didn't matter if they'd been working with their dog all along because Caitlyn required this final schooling since it provided the final evaluation of ownership.

Their dogs received instruction on working with veterans who had PTSD, traumatic brain injuries, and a host of other disabling injuries. Some had lost limbs; some had lost their hearing or their sight. There were just so many, and it broke her heart each time she had to deny someone because they didn't have enough dogs ready or enough money to train them. It's been why she'd only focused on one group—veterans—for her dogs. Her delivery chances were better than if she dealt with a broad group needing service dogs. Of course, she always referred them elsewhere, to a larger organization, so they might get the required help. If only she could snag a whale of a donor, she could then expand and help close the gap between need and availability.

A girl could dream. And this girl always did.

After her rape, she'd been adrift, not sure what she wanted to do with her life. Being a fashion designer no longer appealed to her. She didn't like being around people she didn't know, and trust became an issue. A shiver snaked up her spine at the thought.

In the beginning of her life post-rape, many times she'd thought about ending her life. Then she'd met Brent Timms in a group meeting for people suffering from PTSD. The war vet had raved on how his service dog—lying quietly at his feet—saved his life. The more he spoke, the more she realized what she wanted to do…what she needed to do.

As a little girl, she'd always loved dogs and had trained all of hers. Yet, she knew she'd need specialized instruction before beginning her own operation. So, she volunteered at a service dog facility and learned all she could. After significant on-the-job experience and homework to learn the ins and outs from all angles, she felt ready to expand the program with her own operation. With money and Tonya, she branched out and opened Helping Paws, a 501C, with a slogan of "Working Pets for Vets."

The land had been bestowed upon her—the first significant donation she'd received—so she only had to worry about taxes for the land, but each year when she went to pay them, she discovered someone had anonymously paid them for her. It always warmed her soul with the much-appreciated generosity of strangers.

She didn't promote her operation—it was too small. She already had more interest than she could ever hope to fill. Occasionally, she and the board of directors had turned down veterans due to concern that they wouldn't care for the dog properly. She took choosing a match for her client to heart and investigated every possible aspect of the dog's life once it left her care.

Drunks, those strung out on drugs, and plain old mean suckers got her concern and prayers, but they'd never get one of her dogs. Her latest reject—Neil Holbrook—had issued all kinds of vile threats against her. She shuddered at the hatred he'd spewed. His behavior only confirmed that she'd made the right decision to deny him access to one of the animals. The dog would've probably lived in fear, and she couldn't have that.

Of course, in reality, she still lived in fear, even knowing her attacker was in jail. She'd told her staff to watch for Neil but didn't know what else she could do. She went to the sheriff to tell them about the threats, but he pretty much blew the situation off. The deputy she spoke with assured her they'd do extra drive-bys of her place, which meant they'd do absolutely nothing. A fat lot of good that would do if Neil decided to show up and do her harm. She had to remember that unlike in the city limits with the police department, the sheriff's department had limited resources and a large area to cover. Heck, when she'd called once for a possible prowler, it'd taken them eighteen minutes to arrive. It turned out to be a stray dog that jumped up on the windows, but still, it had been a long, fearful wait for the cavalry.

But she couldn't let it stop her from working or living her life. Neil could just be a blowhard. They had clients relying upon them, and she'd never missed a deadline. Her team knew what they were doing. They were some of the best and loved what they did.

Trying to remember the thread of conversation she'd been having with Rick and being pleased he didn't mention how long she'd spaced out on him; she sipped her coffee to appear as if she'd just been mulling over the topic and not letting her mind wander. Training. A few more days. That was right. "That's fine. I'll get them scheduled so reservations can be made, since two vets live too far away to drive back and forth each day." She set down her coffee cup. "I like this group of clients. I think our dogs are going to excellent homes, and they'll be able to do a lot of good to improve the lives of these veterans."

Rick nodded. "I'll let Tonya know that you want to see her."

And he was gone, leaving her alone with her random thoughts. They flitted through her mind, giving her a worry or two, then moved along, leaving a sense of foreboding in their wake.

She shook her head to clear it. She needed to focus. She needed to be with the dogs, who soothed her.

Putting her coffee cup in the sink, she turned and cleaned up the paperwork from the table, stacking it neatly. After glancing to ensure she had collected everything, she went down the hallway to her office. It wasn't fancy with its second-hand furniture, but she'd painted the room in warm colors and added artwork she'd purchased before she decided to be poor—she took a sickening low salary for her position—but happy.

Noticing more paperwork on her desk that she meant to file the day prior, she sifted through it and collected it all to put away. It was her least favorite job. She'd take cleaning a dog's pen over filing any day.

Most people would consider her "poop over paper" philosophy backward, but she didn't care. She hated filing.

With her back to the door, she squatted behind her desk and opened a lower drawer on the four-drawer, black metal file cabinet in the corner. A floorboard creaked. Thinking Tonya had arrived, she swivelled toward the door. "Tonya, can you—" Her breath caught. She froze and her heart felt like it skipped a beat before it erupted into an erratic rhythm. *Oh my God. He's here. After all these years....*

Images of them together—laughing, holding hands, and making love—flashed in her mind. This man stirred her to hope for impossible things, and she'd ruined everything. With a racing pulse, she tried to appear unaffected by the hunk of a man standing at her doorway. The man she'd done wrong. He'd changed in the years since they'd been apart. His T-shirt showed that he was still broad-chested, but his muscles were more defined than when in college. It's possible she drooled looking him over.

His face looked more masculine if that were possible. Lord, he still took her breath away. Then she gazed into his gorgeous golden-brown eyes. It was all she could do not to melt into a puddle right on the spot.

She slowly stood and put the papers on her desk, leaving them damp from her sweaty palms. "Matt—" She cleared her throat from the croak his name had sounded. "—what are you doing here?" How did he know where to find her? Only her father knew, and that tossed the contents of her stomach. Something had to be wrong. Her father wouldn't have sent Matt to her just so they could see each other again.

"Caitlyn," he started as he walked into her office as if he owned it, "it's good to see you again. I'm here for two reasons. One, your dad was injured."

Fear rocketed through her, setting off tiny sparks of panic. Her initial suspicion had been right: Her dad was hurt. She opened her mouth to ask what happened and how badly, but Matt forestalled her.

He put up his hands to ward off her questions. "He's okay, but he sent me to you. You're in danger, and I'm here to protect you."

Danger? Protect her? Had he heard about Neil Holbrook? Surely not. Protect her. Had he lost his frickin' mind? This had to be some scheme to get near her. Maybe her mind wasn't thinking logically with all that information tossed at her at once. How could a person embrace that in two seconds? But her dad? Ignoring the second reason he was there, she asked, "What happened to Daddy?"

He put his hands in his front jeans pockets, making him look vulnerable. "He was beaten up pretty badly and then shot."

"Shot?" she squeaked, her blood running cold. She grabbed the edge of the desk for balance.

He nodded. "He asked for you to stay here instead of going to see him."

Some strength jetted back in her at that statement. *Is that right? Humph.* Her dad should know her better than that. Not go see him? Impossible. She loved him, and he was hurt. "Well, he can ask all he wants. I'm going to see him," she informed him.

Matt flashed that grin she'd once loved. "I figured you would, so I'm here to escort you, and I have a team already at Adam's, ready for your arrival."

Confused and still a bit flustered at his being there and all that he was saying, she shook her head. She needed space from him. He affected her too much. "I can drive myself. I've done it plenty of times."

"Not with Travis Ripley's brother looking for you."

This time, she was sure her heart stopped for a moment. A tremble she couldn't control began to take over her body. "What—what do you mean? Why would he look for me? I don't know the man, nor do I want to know him."

With a shake of his head, Matt seemed sincere when he answered, "He's the one who hurt your father because he's looking for you."

"Oh God, oh God." She slipped into her office chair before her wobbly legs collapsed on her, and she embarrassed herself. *No. No. No.* This couldn't be happening. She wanted Matt to be wrong. Very wrong. Only, he appeared stoic and resolute. Strength radiated from him.

He was beside her, handing her a water bottle that he must've pulled from the mini fridge in her office, where she kept plenty of beverages for her and the staff.

Her hands shook so badly she almost had the water sloshing over the top, but it did feel good going down. After two swigs, she calmed a little. Maybe it was Matt rubbing his hand up and down her back soothingly. As if suddenly realizing he was touching her, she stiffened and jumped from the chair—away from him. Holy cow.

"Thank you for…the water," she stumbled to say. What the hell was wrong with her? She'd gone all this time not being able to accept a man's touch, and she'd allowed Matt to soothe her like old times and put his hand on her. She shuddered at the idea of a man touching her. One man had ruined her life that way, and it hadn't been Matt.

Not moving from where he'd parked himself behind her desk, he said, "Now you understand why I'm here."

"But you didn't help last time" almost popped out, but she stopped the vile statement. He didn't deserve it when it was only her anger leading her thoughts. Instead, she took a deep breath and responded, "Again, I can do this myself."

Maybe if she said it enough, even she'd finally believe it.

Matt started to speak, and she held up her hand. "But I'm smart enough to know that until this gets sorted out, I—" She cleared her throat, preparing herself for her following statement that would surely please him unless he really listened to what she actually said. "I agree that I need help protecting Daddy and me."

Having admitted it, her body felt lighter, but she worried about more than her safety.

Chapter Four

Matt stood behind a desk he assumed was Caitlyn's and had to fight the overwhelming urge to reach out, pull her tightly into his arms, and comfort her. She'd been okay with him until she'd realized he was touching her. Then she'd freaked and couldn't put the distance between them fast enough. Was her aversion to touching relegated to him in particular, or men in general? There was a time when she asked for his touch. It seemed a lifetime ago, but it had been the case. And he'd always enjoyed giving her even a whisper of a touch anytime she was near.

Standing apart from him in her snug jeans and loose-fitting, blue T-shirt with Helping Paws imprinted on it, she was a sight to behold. She'd filled out a bit more than when they were in college. Back then, she'd had college girl slender curves, and now she had womanly curves. He swallowed hard. He enjoyed the sight of her mature body. Now, there was something to hold on to. Not that he'd complained about her body before this maturing of her figure.

Trying to get his dick under control as his jeans tightened, he examined the rest of the woman he'd loved for ten years. In the eight years since they'd been apart, he'd wondered what she looked like, and his imaginings didn't do justice to the woman in front of him. With her brown hair streaked with blonde flowing down near the middle of her back and those memorable bluish-green eyes wide, he wanted to jump to her, take her in his arms, and show her how much he missed her. She'd changed from a beautiful coed to a remarkable woman who could still affect him by just being around him.

Handling her was the last thing he wanted to do, but on the trip up, he'd decided to do it if necessary. She'd thrown him by agreeing to travel with him, so he quickly had to rethink his plans and practiced arguments to get her to agree. "Good," he stated firmly, since she'd taken all his bluster by saying "Yes."

She fidgeted, and that bothered him. She obviously hadn't forgiven him. He was damn lucky she'd even allowed him in the same room. Of course, he hadn't really given her a chance to toss him out. When he'd arrived, a male employee greeted him and pointed him to the office. He'd convinced the guy that he was an old family friend. He'd chuckle at how easy it was to get to Caitlyn if they didn't have a serious fucking problem where shitty lack of security could get her killed.

She appeared to fight with her emotions for the next minute or two. He saw anger and fear cross her face—she'd never been good at hiding her emotions—before a "don't even try it" mask appeared. He almost wanted to applaud her for making that happen but didn't figure she'd appreciate it.

"Matt," she said with that slight southern accent he so loved. Then she released a sigh. "I appreciate you coming all this way to tell me about Daddy, but next time just use a phone. I could've hired someone to travel with me for protection."

An actual slap in the face would've felt better than

her statement. He slammed both hands down on her desk and watched her jump. Crap. He hadn't meant to scare her, only grab her attention. That was when the light bulb in his head went on, and he realized that she'd agreed she needed protection but never agreed it'd be him. *Well, fuck me.*

"Look. Did you not hear that your attacker's brother is the one who hurt your father?" Okay, he'd told Adam he wouldn't share that unless he had to, but dammit, she needed to know the truth or she wouldn't listen. "He was looking for you."

She wrapped her arms tightly around her body. Her bluster waned and she looked like a frightened rabbit. "Why is he after me?"

He swiped his hand down his face. He hadn't slept much the night before, anxious to see her again. Not for this reason though. "It's got something to do with the next parole hearing. Caitlyn, your dad wants me to protect you."

"I get that I need protection, and I'll somehow get it for both me and Daddy. My question is, how did it end up being you that my dad chose?" Her soft words almost sounded like a plea.

A heavy sigh slipped past his lips. "I found your father." His insides churned. "I ran off Ripley and got Adam medical help. He asked me because I was there, and he's worried about you."

"But—"

"No buts. Listen, there's a lot you don't know about me, but protecting people is what I do for a living. I *will* protect you, Caitlyn." There had to be quite a bit he didn't know about her either, and he looked forward to the road trip to catch up on what she'd been doing all this time. Admittedly, it was opportunistic, but he needed all the help he could get.

She narrowed her eyes but didn't get a chance to speak.

"Oh my God, Caitlyn," a blonde woman said from the doorway.

Hell, he'd been so focused on Caitlyn that he hadn't noticed the woman slip up and eavesdrop on their conversation. That was bad. Very bad.

"If what he says is true, you've got to take his protection."

That was better but interesting. It sounded like the woman knew about Caitlyn's past. She must be close to her.

"And you are?" he asked calmly while his insides screamed at her for needing to be more careful than to sneak up on someone. He could've perceived her as a threat and subdued her.

He wondered if he'd put on deodorant that morning since she and Caitlyn kept their distance.

Caitlyn answered for the woman he'd just made fear him. "That's Tonya Beck. She works here."

He swung his gaze back to Caitlyn, keeping Tonya in his periphery. "She obviously has some sense."

In an instant, Caitlyn's hands made it to her hips, and her nostrils flared. Oh, he loved an arguing Caitlyn. While he hadn't wanted to argue with her, he'd hoped to see her in this mode at some point. "Are you saying I don't have any sense? I said I'd get protection. Is it wrong if it's not you?"

He wouldn't get roped into some stupid argument with her that he'd never win because, face it, men never really did. "All I'm saying is she understands the importance of my being close." Refusing to allow her to counter, he continued, "How long before you want to go? I filled the gas tank on my rental, so it's ready. Your dad will be released later today." Then, to really throw her off balance, or at least he hoped, he walked toward Tonya and thrust out his hand. "Matt Hamilton." He added, "Old friend of the family." He had no idea what type of secrets Caitlyn may have shared with this woman, so he wouldn't call himself an ex-fiancé or the loser who had been drinking with his friends instead of taking care of his woman. Both descriptions fit.

Tonya smiled. "It's nice to meet you, Matt. I'm, well, like Caitlyn said, Tonya Beck. I sure am glad you're here if someone is after Caitlyn." Her eyes widened. "Do you think he'd come here? Should we get guards or something? Bodyguards?" She looked him up and down with a hungry gaze. She turned to Caitlyn. "Like him?" she asked hopefully.

Glancing over his shoulder at Caitlyn, who'd moved away when he'd approached Tonya, he noticed her slide behind the desk and plopped into her desk chair. With her head hung low, she looked defeated. He couldn't tell whether it was the situation itself or his offering to help. Hell, he didn't offer. He did what Hamilton men were apt to do—he dictated.

"Why don't you let me discuss this with Caitlyn, and we'll go from there? Right now, I believe you're safe because he doesn't know her location."

Nodding her agreement, Tonya left as quietly as when she'd entered. He'd have to keep his eye out for her. She might sneak up and scare the shit out of him without even trying.

Caitlyn plopped her elbows on her desk and

dropped her head in her hands. "I can't believe it," she murmured.

He moved to one of the two armchairs facing the desk and sat, waiting for it all to sink in. There had been a time when, if she'd had devastating news, she'd rushed into his arms and held on tightly until she sorted out her headspace. How he wished it could be that way now.

Still not keen on her going to her father, he silently hoped she'd do the smart thing and remain here where he knew her to be safe. No, he'd never push her not to see her father. Hell, he'd have been on the first plane out had it been his father—danger be damned.

Which is why he was here. She'd go, and he'd be with her, no matter what she wanted. He wouldn't push if she'd actually been afraid of him, but she wasn't scared. What was she?

Angry?

Disappointed?

Repulsed?

It was too hard to figure out, but luckily fear hadn't been an emotion she'd shown him, except when he'd slammed his hands down. He could avoid that or anything like it. It stood to reason she'd have some reservations about a man who displayed a temper and violent tendencies. Luckily, that didn't fit him. Normally. Working on this case just might flip some of his good intentions, though.

"Is he really okay?" she asked with her head still resting in her hands so he couldn't read her emotions.

He leaned forward in the chair and rested his forearms on his jean-clad thighs. "Yes, he'll be okay. He'll need a bit of time to recover, but he said his sister would help him."

"Aunt Kathy?"

"That's what he said."

"And you're sure it's that monster's brother, and he's after me."

He wasn't sure if she meant that as a statement or as a question. He thought it best to be honest. "That's right."

She looked up. "I'm still going to see Daddy."

He decided not to mince words. "We figured you would."

"What did you mean you had a team there? What kind of team?"

Finally, they could talk this out. "My brothers and I opened HIS—Hamilton Investigation and Security." He sat up straight. "It's a group of men and women with military or law enforcement backgrounds who do whatever it takes to get the job done. As for jobs, we do just about anything—kidnapping cases, hostage rescue, embezzlement, personal protection, and more—for the government or civilian world. Anyhow, I have a team of five at Adam's house watching out for Luke Ripley in case he returns. They're at the hospital now, but they'll be at the house when he's released. Plus, we wanted protection in place for when you visited."

She nodded, almost as if in a trance, which bothered him. It twisted up his gut. "Okay. That's good."

What part was actually good? Since he wasn't sure he wanted to know the answer, he decided not to ask and plowed ahead. "After you visit, a team will come here with you. We'll do everything we can to ensure we aren't followed back to your home."

"What about Daddy? He won't have protection. I'd rather he have it than me."

God, he loved this woman—still. Of course she'd put someone else above herself. "Before we return, there'll be a second team, so you and Adam are covered."

"Okay. So, I ride down with you and back with this team," she stated, even though it was clearly a question.

He wanted to chuckle but kept it inside. He saw what she was doing, and it wouldn't fly. "No. You ride down with me and back up with me."

She shook her head and said, "But the team will be fine. I mean, I'm not sure yet how I'll pay for it, but we'll make it work. But you don't need to spend your time driving me. I'm sure you have better things to do."

Better than being around her? Not likely. "You're not paying a dime for the protection, so I don't want to hear about it." He almost blurted out that, even with all the years apart, she was too important to him even to negotiate protection. "This is something we're doing for Adam's sake."

"But all those men will need to be paid. There's no telling how long they'll have to stay." Then, as if an afterthought, she asked, "How long will they stay?"

"Until Ripley is caught. As for the men, they want him as badly as I do, so they'll do anything to capture him. And that means protecting you because we fear he will find a way to you, Caitlyn, which is also why you aren't getting rid of me." He continued his mini-rant by shoving his foot in his mouth. "I may not have been there before, but I'll be damned if I'll let another asshole near you again." His voice was tainted with anger, something he rarely allowed to escape.

He froze. Holy shit. He'd thrown it down on the table. He hadn't meant to bring up the incident or the part he'd unknowingly played. But part of him needed to let her know he'd be there, no matter what.

She sat back in her chair and sat ramrod straight, her face ashen.

Christ. Look what he'd done. He'd brought those horrible memories to light. Now, she'd fight him again.

Surprising him, she stood. "I need to pack and talk to my staff. I'll be ready to leave in an hour." Then she walked around the desk and out the door without looking back at him.

It wasn't forgiveness, but she also didn't turn him away. He'd take every win he could get.

Chapter Five

Why was her world spinning out of control? She'd worked hard to put it back together after the horrific incident in her life, and she'd succeeded. Sure, she'd been lonely, but other than that, everything had been merry. She'd had her friends, her dogs, and a life she enjoyed beyond all measure.

Now Caitlyn's foundation needed money, her dad was hurt, a man was supposedly after her, and her ex-fiancé was at her door. She fisted her hands to her side. She had to control something. Something had to be going well. Her dogs were her first positive thought.

Thank God the dogs were safe. The organization currently had sixteen of them—labs and golden retrievers—on the premises, each at various stages of training, plus the four in foster care. Would the dogs and her employees be safe? They had to be. She couldn't accept putting their lives in jeopardy.

Remembering what Matt had said, she breathed a sigh of relief. Security would come back with her. Surely, they'd protect the entire area, not just her and the small house she lived in on the property. The dogs were housed in an old, converted barn with concrete floors and large kennels that were inside and had an outside run for the dogs. The area they were given to play outside was fenced so they couldn't get lost, or any predators make their way in.

Walking into her bedroom to pack, Caitlyn's mind flitted back to the dark-haired man sitting in her office. Or was he still there? Maybe he'd followed her into her home. How frickin' observant was she? While she hated the idea, having a bodyguard might not be a bad thing. But it didn't have to be Matt Hamilton, did it?

As a woman on a mission seven and a half years ago, she'd taken many self-defense classes because she wanted to know everything she could about protecting herself. Working hard, she'd vowed never to be a victim again.

Hearing the sucking noise of the seal on her refrigerator door as it was opened, she figured Matt had followed her back to her house and made himself at home. Tonya and Rick would've knocked before they entered, out of courtesy, something Matt seemed to lack.

"I may not have been there before, but I'll be damned if I'll let another asshole near you again."

Thinking of his words was like a sucker punch to her stomach. It flooded her with a myriad of emotions—both positive and negative. She tried not to remember that evening and, therefore, Matt's unwitting role in it.

Forgiveness, she reminded herself. She had to issue forgiveness. He hadn't planned on being late. He hadn't asked her to wait near the dark alley. As much as she blamed him initially, she knew it wasn't his fault. She'd learned from tons of counseling that it wasn't her fault either. While she could've stood elsewhere, she'd waited for Matt in that exact spot plenty of times and had never had an issue.

A weary sigh escaped her. She'd been wrong to

send him away after the rape had occurred, blaming him and lashing out like she had. Especially at a time when she'd needed him the most. And what had she done? Drove him away. She'd thought it was for good, which had broken her heart. But her life had changed, albeit not her broken heart. Unfortunately, she didn't know how she felt about his finding her and pretty much telling her he'd be her shadow. To be honest, if she had to have a man follow her that closely, she was glad it was Matt. But how to tell him that without giving him any signals that she wanted more? Because she didn't want more. Did she?

God, she was so damn confused. She had no idea why she was thinking about Matt like that. Hell, he could be married for all she knew. Caitlyn thought back, trying to remember if she'd seen a wedding ring. Nausea sat heavily in her stomach at the possibility before she fought hard to shake it away and concentrate on packing.

Retrieving an overnight suitcase from her closet, she pulled clothes out to pack for her short trip. She wouldn't need anything fancy to see her dad, which made the packing ordeal short and sweet. Jeans, shorts, blouses, underclothes, pajamas, and socks were tossed haphazardly among toiletries she'd snatched from her bathroom. She wanted to get on the road. Her dad wouldn't care if her shirts were wrinkled.

She wheeled her suitcase into the living room, where Matt waited patiently on the couch. "I'm packed." She dropped the handle of the suitcase. "I just need to speak with Rick and Tonya so they know I'm going and what to do while I'm away."

He stood to his full height of six foot two inches in

one fluid motion. His eyes twinkled at her. "Okay. Let's get moving. How well do you trust them?"

"They're in the training center"—she pointed to the converted barn where he'd met her in her office—"and I trust them completely." She didn't mention that they knew everything about her. Well, except that she'd been engaged to Matt. But she'd shared that she'd once been raped, explaining to them why she didn't wish to be alone with an unknown male. They didn't get many visitors, but when they did, one of them always provided a feeling of security by accompanying her. Until Matt. They'd left her alone with him. Curious.

They walked into the training center, and she immediately went to her office first and then hesitated before she grabbed her laptop to take with her. Her focus would be on her dad and his recovery, but maybe she'd get some work done when he slept.

Sliding the laptop into the carry bag, she walked into the break room, encountered Rick, and asked him to find Tonya. Tonya already knew most of what had happened, but Caitlyn wanted the three of them together before she explained everything. After Rick returned with Tonya and Matt hovering in the background, she described to them what she knew had occurred.

"I want you to be careful while I'm gone. This man doesn't know where I am, but I don't want you to take any chances."

"We won't," Tonya agreed.

"We'll hold down the fort here," Rick stated. "You take care of your dad."

"While I'm gone, you can start planning the fundraiser. Rick, please help Tonya however you can."

"Speaking of fundraising, a Tate Hart called this morning about making a significant contribution." Rick shrugged. "His words, not mine. Anyway, he wants to see the facility and meet you to ask some questions."

God, she could use significant cash infusion in the next few months. Although what one person called significant, another might call a pittance. "We'll set up the standard tour and meeting when I return." Thankfully, at Tonya's insistence, she'd already put together a dog-and-pony show for prospective donors who showed up unannounced. It ensured that what they wanted a potential donor to see was shown. Not that they had many who visited the site. Most relied upon the website, literature Tonya had created, and word of mouth.

She needed more word of mouth. Then again, what organization didn't?

"Speaking of showing potential donors around, if you have a second before you go, I have an idea," Tonya said hesitantly.

Caitlyn wanted to rush for the door and make Matt floor the car, but she knew she needed to give her staff a moment before she just rushed off, leaving them with a story of danger that might come to the door. Her dad was safe and in the hospital. Matt would get her there in plenty of time once her dad was released and at home so she could take this moment—a brief one.

Curious about Tonya's idea, Caitlyn raised an eyebrow in expectation.

"What if we have the fundraiser here? In the training facility." She held her hand up to ward off Caitlyn's words. "I can have this place transformed for about thirty guests. We keep the main training area open, and the dog pens are back against the wall. We can show them some of the moves of our best-trained dogs. We could even coincide it with graduation so the veterans can participate if they'd like."

If the transformation could happen, that would be a brilliant idea. If potential donors saw the dogs and what they could do, those in attendance would surely want to help Caitlyn expand the operation. She already had volunteers in mind that she'd like to hire full-time, give them formal dog trainer training, and set them free with Tonya and Rick.

"I think it's a great idea. It'd be a smaller fundraiser than I'd pictured, but if we invite the right people…." She trailed off, thinking about the best and potential donors to invite. Her mind whirled with the possibilities now that Tonya had planted the seed. She probably knew that would happen, considering how well she knew Caitlyn. "We could showcase Bella and Cooper."

"I'm sorry to interrupt," Matt said, pushing off the wall, "but if we're going to make good time before it gets dark, we'd best leave."

Christ, she'd let the conversation go on too long. Matt's words were her slap to reality and her injured dad. She liked this idea and knew Tonya could run with it without her. She needed to leave and care for her waiting dad.

"You're right." Smiling, she turned back to her employees. "I'll be back in a few days. Until then, stay safe." She stood and approached Matt, who led her to the front door. Once outside, he took her suitcase, and her breath hitched when their hands slightly brushed each other. She had so many incredible memories of the two of them together that had never left her, however that touch had brought them all flooding to the forefront of her mind.

Oblivious to her distress, he loaded her suitcase in the rental car's trunk, a nice sedan that didn't fit the style of the man she'd once known. She'd expected something like a 4-wheel drive pickup. Then again, it was from a rental agency; he might not have had much choice. Or, he could be a completely different person now.

Even though he'd just driven to her from Water Valley and she knew the way, Matt set up the GPS in the car to her dad's address before they left her sanctuary. The only place she'd felt safe in a long time. A chill crept down her spine. That vicious, despicable, violent—she couldn't even find the right word for him—man hurt her dad to draw her out. She knew that. And she was playing right into his hands. She hoped Matt was as good as he professed to be.

Her mind went unwillingly back to that horrible night eight years ago. While Travis Ripley had raped her, he'd promised to kill her. She'd taken it as the ravings of a lunatic. Had his brother taken up the promise? Why hadn't she brought her gun? She'd definitely feel safer with it. Maybe Matt had an extra.

"Do you have more than one gun?" she blurted out, breaking the uncomfortable silence that had weighed between them.

He glanced at her incredulously, like she'd asked the world's stupidest question. "Of course."

She going to follow up on where he hid them. "I want one," she stated matter-of-factly.

He shook his head emphatically. "No."

"Why not? You know I'm a good shot. I've been shooting since I was ten years old." What Mississippi country girl hadn't?

"First, I'm not giving up one of my weapons. Second, you won't need it. You'll have me and the others protecting you."

She crossed her arms over her chest and almost pouted. "Then turn around. I'll get my .38 from under my pillow."

The car swerved momentarily before it righted itself back between the lines. "You sleep with a .38 under your pillow?" He said it more as a question than as a statement it was.

Wondering whether this was a trick question, she hesitantly said, "Yes."

Matt's fingers tightened on the steering wheel, and his knuckles began to turn white. She wondered if she'd done that to him. It was odd. They acted as if nothing had happened to their relationship so long ago. They weren't acting like they were in love or anything, but they were talking like ordinary people who hadn't had their worlds torn apart. Maybe she should apologize to him now when he might listen.

"Why the hell do you feel the need to sleep with a weapon under your pillow?" he growled.

She shrugged off his question, answering only, "I live out in the middle of nowhere. It's just to make me feel safe. No other reason." There. That should end it. He didn't need to know she never felt truly safe out there alone.

Too many fears held her back from doing what needed to be done, which is why her organization was still so small. But she wanted the organization to grow and had to overcome all that held her back from pushing for more money, seeking out the big donors for her type of organization, and making it a priority instead of waiting until it was needed.

That worry of being alone with a man had to stop. Thank God she didn't feel that with Matt, or this would've been one uncomfortable ride. She almost snorted out loud. Who was she kidding? It was an uncomfortable ride.

Seemingly satisfied with her answer, he asked, "Tell me about Helping Paws."

That was something she enjoyed discussing. Pride filled her, and her body relaxed.

She told him how she'd learned about organizations that trained dogs, although she didn't tell him she was at a meeting for people with PTSD. She'd just "met" Brent Timms. She'd talked about all her training and how she'd worked to finish her business degree online, so it would help her. Then she got to how the land with the home and barn had been donated.

"Someone just gave you all of that?" he asked in astonishment.

A happy smile split her face. "Someone did. While getting it adapted for our use, I found four puppies and immediately fostered them out."

"Why foster?"

She explained the need for fundamental social skills and the length of time spent before they returned to the organization. The ease of talking with Matt about her passion surprised her. It seemed so natural, like an end-of-the-day conversation between a couple who'd been together for a long time.

"It takes about two years to train them?" he

exclaimed in a bewildered question.

"One and a half to two years. These dogs can learn up to eighty-five tasks, which doesn't even include specializing them to their future handler so they can interrupt nightmares or other things that are distressing to the vet." There had been times when she wished she had a dog to interrupt her nightmares. However, now, her nightmare might be coming true. Ripley's brother was after her. She shuddered inwardly at the thought.

"Wow. I can't wait to see your operation. It fascinates me."

"Me too," she thought aloud.

"When we return, we have to talk about safety there. Heck, Rick just allowed me to come to your office alone."

Somehow, she guessed Rick was within earshot of her meeting with Matt. He'd never have left her completely alone. Then again, Tonya did appear and had heard almost everything. Not wanting to talk about herself, which was where the conversation was headed, she turned the tables. "Tell me about your family."

He paused for a moment before answering. Whether he had to think about it or whether he realized what she'd done didn't matter, the focus was off her. "Let's see. Dad just got remarried. That's where I was before I visited Adam."

"Wow, it took him a long time to find someone, didn't it?"

A ghost of a smile lit his lips. "He's really happy. Let's see what else. Since you saw us last, Jesse lost his wife, but not before they had a little girl." He turned to her. "You'll love Reagan. She's a little spitfire. He's got his hands full with that one."

"Oh, Matt. I'm so sorry to hear he lost Jen." She'd liked the woman, even though she'd only met her a few times while Caitlyn and Matt had been dating since Jesse and Jen lived in Maryland, and she and Matt were going to college in Mississippi.

"He found someone new. Kate was an FBI agent who *he* decided needed his protection." This time, a smile did split his face. "Danger withstanding, that was hilarious watching them come together and fight it simultaneously. Anyhow, they're married now and adopted a teenage boy named Jason."

Married with kids. She guessed that should be the oldest Hamilton son. But, dammit, that should've been her. She mentally slapped herself. She'd called off the wedding. It was her fault Matt had left. Her eyes slid to his hand on the steering wheel. No ring. That triggered elation shooting through her body.

"AJ got married and has a son. Devon got married. Oh, and Emily and Jake got married to each other, and they have a little girl also."

"Yeah, I figured that would happen one day. Whenever he finally got his head out of the sand and saw what was before him." It had been obvious Emily worshipped the ground Jake walked on, yet he rarely gave her the time of day.

Matt chuckled. "It's a long story."

"We've got a long ride."

"Oh, the family secret here—Trent is actually our half-brother, and he's married now also with a kid."

Shock hit her. "What? Trent McKenzie? He's your brother?"

"Another long story. They all are. There's a common thread, though."

"What?" She really wanted to know the answer. So much had changed with the Hamilton family, but it had been eight years. She couldn't expect it to be the same.

He turned to her and spoke before refocusing on the road. "They were protecting the women they eventually married."

She swallowed hard. What did that mean for Matt protecting her?

Chapter Six

"Yeah, Trent's now a rancher in Montana," Matt told Caitlyn as he finished his story about how they'd found out Trent was their brother and how he'd almost died—twice since they'd found out. It appeared becoming a Hamilton could be dangerous to one's health, although that wasn't the reason for any threats to Trent.

She shook her head slowly. Amazing what the men and women had been through and what he insinuated by their falling in love during danger. The stories of his brothers and their wives were amazing, almost unreal. She felt more comfortable with the team that she hadn't even met yet waiting for her. "You guys don't play around, do you?"

He shook his head. "Nope. You hungry?"

It took her a moment to realize she was and to catch up with the change of topic. The time on her watch surprised her. They'd been talking for almost four hours. *Wow, he'd made time fly by with his family's tales.* Good. She wanted to see her dad. She'd never have moved so far from him if she hadn't been deeded that land for Helping Paws. Her initial thought had been to find some land near home. But who could turn away free when you worked on a shoestring budget?

"I could eat. But can we drive through? I want to

get to Daddy as quickly as possible."

"I don't drive and eat."

She laughed. "Since when? You always ate on the way to my place."

He flashed a grin at her. "I've got some sense now."

She rolled her eyes. "Oh, good Lord. Will you do it this time?"

He glanced at her. "Eat in the car?" Nodding, he leaned across the seat close to her and whispered near her ear, "This time."

A delightful shiver raced across her body. She fought to get herself under control. Satisfied when she could think and speak coherently, she looked at signs from the highway for the upcoming exit. "EATS?"

"That's fine."

Her body might tell her it was hungry, but she had little appetite or taste for anything in particular, so any ole place would do.

They made it through a drive-thru line that Matt constantly complained about how slow it moved and were back on the road. Immediately, she scarfed down her fries while they were hot. Her chicken sandwich was disappointing, but she ate as much as possible to keep her energy level up. If Matt expected trouble, she wanted to be prepared. Damn…she wished she had her gun.

Once she put their trash in the fast food restaurant bag and tossed it on the back floorboard, she questioned him again for two reasons. One, she didn't want him asking her questions, and two, she was that curious.

"What about you? What did you do after college, or did you and your brothers start your business then?"

What she really wanted to know was if he married. It wasn't her business, but she still wanted to know. He didn't wear a ring, but not all men did nowadays.

"No, we started HIS a few years back. It started with Jesse, Devon, and me, but Jesse had a grand idea all of us would be part of it, so we planned for it. Hell if he wasn't right. One by one, everyone joined in, including Emily."

"Your baby sister Emily? She runs around carrying a gun?" She shook her head in disbelief. "No. I can't see it."

Matt laughed. "No. She's a forensic accountant and is damned good at what she does. She's a pro at finding embezzlement links."

"So you didn't go pro?" She knew the answer because she'd checked each of the NFL draft picks to see if he'd made it.

"No," he bit out.

"Did you ever tell your family that coaches in the NFL had spoken with you?" Matt had wanted to keep it secret from his family that he'd been approached about playing professional football. At the time, he'd been waiting to see if Brad also got a visit, but when he didn't, Matt had clammed up about the whole thing.

"No. They don't need to know. It's done and over with," he said tersely.

Realizing she'd pushed too far on that topic, she returned to her original question. "What did you do after college?"

"I joined the Navy." His matter-of-fact tone gave her the impression he couldn't believe she'd think anything but that.

"The Navy?" She didn't see the man she'd been

about to marry being a military man. Definitely the man sitting beside her now, but not then. Of course, that meant they'd turned him into the man he was today. Still, she almost snickered at thinking he might have his name slapped on his butt. Did the Navy even still do that to uniforms?

"It gets worse." He leaned across the seat and whispered, "I eventually became a SEAL."

Shocked didn't even begin to describe what she felt. Matt a SEAL? Sweet, kind, caring Matt able to do what she heard SEALs did, like kill a guy with one finger? Not possible. He had to be pulling her leg. "Haha. Very funny."

He straightened in his seat. "I'm dead serious."

She stopped laughing. Wow. That brought the quality of her protector's abilities up several notches. Several. Of course, there'd never been anything average about Matt. Why should she expect it different now?

Christ, she had a former Navy SEAL at her side. No wonder she felt safe in his presence. No way would Travis's brother get near her. She settled back in her seat and sighed in relief. Yeah, he wouldn't get past Matt.

Thinking of Matt in an all-white dress uniform, cap and all, turned her on. The stirrings of desire—something that had disappeared eight years ago—were there. Just a little bit, but nonetheless there. Her stomach did a nervous flip. She didn't know whether to appreciate the yearnings or be worried they'd returned. There was too much between them for something like burning up the sheets again to happen.

Caitlyn still didn't think she could actually do it. Have sex again. On the few dates she'd been on, she could barely stand to be kissed and couldn't bear a man's hands on her. However, so far, she'd been fine with Matt's touch, and now she wanted him touching her, loving her. It was all very confusing. Yet, refreshing to know her healing had progressed.

Even with the light connections they'd made—his touch, his whispering in her ear—the weight of the reason they'd split rested on her shoulders, and that weight seemed to permeate the car's atmosphere. She couldn't see or physically feel it, but she held back, and so did he. She needed to clear the air, especially now that she realized she might still have sexual feelings for him. Then, if he forgave her for sending him away and something grew between them, they'd be free to pursue it. But would either of them? She'd settled into living her life out at Helping Paws alone, but always wishing she had Matt with her. Maybe that was why none of her dates made it.

"Matt," she said hesitantly before blurting out, "I'm sorry for blaming you."

****

Matt nearly slammed on the brakes in the middle of the highway, heedless of the traffic. Caitlyn had shocked him that much. Instead, he slowed the car and pulled to the corner of a gas station parking lot. After scanning the area, he turned to her with a pounding heart, praying she'd said what he thought. "Want to repeat that?"

She fidgeted with the edge of her T-shirt that hadn't been tucked into her jeans. "I said—" She cleared her throat. "—I'm sorry for blaming you. It wasn't your fault."

It was what he'd been longing to hear for many

years. So why didn't he feel relief or had the weight been lifted? It made him feel more like shit than he already did. He hadn't committed the crime, but if he'd been there, he'd have found a way to stop it. He didn't care about Brad's logic; he'd have found a way, even going up against a weapon in his drunken state. He'd rather have died protecting her than leaving her on her own as he had. That startling revelation hit him square in the chest, and he found breathing hard.

As a Navy SEAL, he'd known he was putting his life out there for someone else, an ever-changing group of people. But knowing he would be doing it for Caitlyn was almost overwhelming. Feelings were intertwined between them. It made it goddamn different.

"Caitlyn, you were right to blame me. It was my fault you were all alone. I'm so very sorry." Thank the fuck she brought up the topic. He hadn't known how to apologize without mentioning a subject she might wish to ignore. He'd asked for her forgiveness eight years ago, but she hadn't listened. Not that he'd felt he'd deserved anything from her.

"There's nothing to forgive, Matt. You may have been late, but I could've had someone wait with me. I didn't. When it first happened, it was easy to lash out at you…to blame you. But," she hurriedly added, "none of it was your fault. I'm sorry for what I said to you. I just wanted you to know."

The angry and hateful words she'd said after she'd been released from the hospital had stuck with him. *I blame you for this. It's your fault that bastard raped me. This happened because you weren't there for me….* He'd deserved every one of them.

He'd come not only to protect her but also to hear her words of forgiveness. Just because he didn't get the relief he'd hoped to have didn't mean he needed to reject her offer. It had to have taken a lot for her to issue absolution. He wanted to know how long she'd fretted over telling him she didn't blame him and why she hadn't tried to contact him and deliver that apology, but he wouldn't ask. At least not now. Things were just repairing between them. He didn't wish to fracture any new ground they'd laid together.

"I accept your apology." He swallowed past the lump in his throat. His body hummed with the possibility of a new beginning with Caitlyn. He turned back to the front of the car, put it in drive, and pulled back onto the highway. "But, know that I'll never forgive myself."

She sat quietly, and he wondered what her mind was pondering. There weren't any more words needed to clear the air. They'd done it quite simply. Now, he wanted to move forward with what they were facing. "Let me tell you about the security detail."

As he turned off the Water Valley exit, his nerves tightened. Would that asshole be lying in wait for her? Maybe he should've had her wear a Kevlar vest. He'd have one of the women's vests brought back with the second team since it'd fit her small frame.

"Brad will be there."

"How is Brad? You haven't said anything about him. Is he married with kids?"

At that image, laughter bubbled up, lifting his mood. "I don't see that for a long time for my twin. After graduation, he went into the Secret Service and then joined us at HIS."

She giggled. "I could see Brad strutting around protecting the president."

Strutting would be about right. "Yeah well, he won't talk about if he did protect the man at the top. He's not the same Brad you knew in college. He's jaded."

"I remember Brad as being nice to me but a bit cocky to everyone else."

"Something happened while he was with the Secret Service. Before you ask, I'm not sure what exactly, but it made a cynic out of him." He'd just lied to Caitlyn and wanted to kick himself for it. Not the best way for a new beginning. He knew exactly what had messed with Brad's attitude, but it wasn't his story to share. He'd been pulled into the strictest of confidences when Brad told him the horrible thing that had happened. The family knew he left the Secret Service in disgrace. They just didn't know the how and why. Hell, Brad didn't know the why.

"That's a shame," she declared softly.

Matt cleared his throat. "Well, Ken Patrick will lead our teams when we're in the field. He's who I'll work with for your protection."

"Wait a minute, what about Brad or you? Wouldn't one of you work with him since you're both in charge of HIS? Didn't you say you all owned and ran it?"

"Yes and no. Since we—my brothers and me— don't go on all the assignments, we have a field team leader for consistency, and so at times like this, Brad and I don't have to flip a coin. To make it standard for the men, we allow Ken, or Rob, in Ken's absence, to run things when we're out in the field. Mostly. At times, like when my brothers fell in love with the woman in trouble, they took the lead, and Ken kept everything working like the well-oiled machine the men are. Now, as for Ken being in the lead," he said with a smile, "that doesn't mean we don't drive him crazy interfering somewhat." He didn't add that he'd be taking command of this one since it was Caitlyn. No one would argue with him on that decision either.

She shook her head and chuckled. "That poor man."

"Oh, I wouldn't call him that. He's bigger than I am and could give me a run for my money in the ring. He's a former Army Ranger who likes to wear a ponytail and ride a Harley. He'll also 'ma'am' you to death."

"So, you have some heavy hitters on your team. Who else do you have? The world's strongest man?" she joked.

Since he wanted her to grasp how serious the situation was, he didn't show her how much he enjoyed having fun with her. Instead, he furrowed his eyebrows and tried to be serious. "Of course not."

"Okay, so besides your team, what about the sheriff? Sheriff Brown's still there, isn't he?"

Matt nodded. "He is." The crotchety old bastard that he was. Matt had only spoken with him briefly at Adam's house when they'd made him stay behind and answer questions while Adam had been raced to the hospital. The sheriff had been concerned about Caitlyn's return to the area and whether this was about her. He didn't, however, offer protection.

"Your dad filed assault charges, but you'll have to notify the county where you live of the verbal threat. I've already called and checked. They'll let you file a report, and that's about all they'll be able to do besides some extra drive-bys." Wanting to keep things positive, he pressed on as if the sheriff hadn't been mentioned. "Let's see, we still have the rest of the team there. Danny Franks and Steve Smith will also be protecting you, and then Neftali Navarro will be set up as a sharpshooter."

"Why do I need one of those?" Her voice held a quiver.

Matt shrugged. In his mind, the assigned team wasn't enough to effectively protect Caitlyn from the threat. He'd love enough expert shooters to cover every blind spot near her organization. It would already be a bitch for Neftali to see it all without being on top of the barn. "Better safe than sorry."

She rubbed her hands up and down her arms and said, "You've got me a little scared. Good grief, all of you are needed to protect my daddy and me. It's…surreal."

Matt reached over, took her hand, and inwardly pumped a fist when she didn't yank it back. "All I ask is that you listen to us. We'll keep you both safe."

He turned to her and caught her staring at him. "I trust you," she admitted.

As far as he was concerned, that was enough for them to start toward a future.

Chapter Seven

When they arrived at her dad's house, Caitlyn wanted to bolt from the car and rush in to see him. Matt wouldn't allow it. Safety, he'd told her. That gave her the chills. So she sat in the vehicle while Brad met with someone at the front of the car. They spoke where she couldn't hear their conversation and imagined it had to do with security. That still chapped her ass that they had to go through this because of another Ripley. She wanted to run out there and scream, "I'm not scared of you," but the truth was that she was petrified, no matter what she told herself or anyone else.

Matt finally opened her door. "Remember to do exactly as I or any of the men say. No hesitation. No questions."

Once she'd nodded her agreement, he moved aside, and she stepped from the vehicle. The men must've felt her urgency because they moved at a fast pace to the front door where a rather large man with tattoos streaming down his arms, wearing a shoulder holster with a gun on each of his sides, opened the door, looked around, and then moved to allow them entrance.

"Caitlyn, this is Ken Patrick," Matt said, then turned to the man. "Ken, this is Caitlyn Robinson."

He thrust out his hand. "Nice to meet you, ma'am."

A smile flitted on her lips. Matt had tagged that one right. "Nice to meet you." She turned back to Matt. "I

72

want to see Daddy now," she requested.

Ken spoke up. "He's resting in his room. He'll be glad to see you, but expect an earful about you actually coming." He shook his head and led the way. A route she knew by heart.

Her dad must think highly of these men, at least Ken, to tell the agent something like that. When she grew up with just her and her dad—she'd lost her mother to a car accident when she was three years old—she'd learned he liked to keep family business in the family. It kept them even closer.

Ken stopped outside her dad's door, and she almost bumped into him. He turned to her. "He's not as bad as he looks." With that, he stepped aside and allowed her to enter the room.

Mentally preparing herself, she vowed to keep whatever emotion grabbed her off her face so she wouldn't worry her dad. She should've learned by now that was impossible. When she walked into the room, she almost collapsed and, by the look on her father's face, her expression showed her shock and fear.

With her hand to her mouth, she stood there, shaking, while he smiled through a swollen jaw, split lip, and two black eyes. She noticed a splint on his hand and his color was a bit gray. Good God, what had that bastard done to her dad?

She took a step forward and tried to appear unaffected. "Hi, Daddy."

"My Catie," he said weakly.

She asked the question that gnawed at her most. "Should you be out of the hospital?" Really, would they allow a man so gravely ill—that's how he looked—out of the hospital early?

"It was a splint and a couple of stitches."

"But Matt said you were shot."

"Turns out the bullet went through. I was one lucky bastard and only needed the holes sewn up. That's it, sugar." He shifted on the bed and grimaced. "Now, didn't Matt tell you that you shouldn't've come?"

Knowing she had to be strong, she straightened, took a fortifying breath, and moved beside him. After kissing him lightly on the cheek, careful of where she placed her lips, she responded, "Of course I should've." She fussed with his covers until he told her he was fine.

"I'm glad to see you, but I wish you weren't here. Only because it's not safe."

Caitlyn forced a smile. "Of course it's safe. Several armed men are keeping watch, so both of us are protected."

"Thank God for Matt," he murmured. "Give me some water, please."

Taking a cup from the bedside table, she checked to ensure it had water and handed it to him. As he drank thirstily, she scanned his body again and noticed his arm that had been stitched. Heck, the closer she looked, she saw it wasn't the only one.

Damn that fucking bastard's soul to hell.

Her dad returned the cup to her, and she placed it where she'd collected it. Patiently, she waited for him to answer her.

"I bet you're wondering why I sent Matt."

"The thought had crossed my mind, but I understand he was here to help you." She didn't want to throw out that he surely had to remember she'd never wanted to see Matt again in her life. But, now that he had shown back up—when she'd probably needed him the most—she wasn't as upset as she thought she'd be if that happened. Odd.

He held up his good hand to forestall her speaking more. "Yes, and because I wanted you to have protection when you came home. I didn't want you to come home—not because I don't love you, but because I worried Luke Ripley would be hiding in wait for you."

"Well—"

"Now Matt," he continued as if she hadn't tried to speak, "and his brothers protect people for a living. They do more than that—lots more—but I knew they would protect you if you got stubborn and came home." He looked at her and smiled. "Like you did."

"But, Daddy, I could've hired someone near where I live."

He continued and considering his words, he didn't believe her statement. "And, if you couldn't have found someone? You'd have come alone, and what would've happened if you came to the house and that asshole was in the front bushes just waiting? What would you have done? I don't care what kind of self-defense you've taken. It's not a risk I wanted to take."

Her heart expanded at the protectiveness of her dad. "But why Matt of all people? There are plenty of people who provide protection."

"Because he was here—" Adam coughed, breaking off his words, spiking her concern about what else could be wrong with him. Once finished, he responded, "And because I trust him with your life."

She plopped down in the chair that was beside his bed. That put her in her place. She could not argue with that statement since if she hired an unknown firm to protect her, she'd never feel that safe. The thing was, she did feel safe, even though she hadn't wanted to admit the truth until now. She truly did feel safe with him around. She did with the others also, even without meeting them all.

"I take it that Matt told you everything. He grilled me at the hospital."

Caitlyn shook her head. "No. He did say he'd promised you he wouldn't tell me everything, but he did admit to telling me stuff you didn't want me to know, but he never promised to hold back. For example, he didn't tell me the extent of the damage."

Adam sighed. "It's not too bad. I'll be good as new in a day or two."

She winced at his bald-faced lie. That explained why she was unable to lie well. "What happened?"

He grimaced. "I came home and he was in the house. I don't know how he got in, but he did."

She wished she'd have convinced her dad to buy a security system. He lived in a safe neighborhood where a resident could probably still leave his or her door unlocked, although the homeowners would rather not test that theory. But no one in the little cul-de-sac had a security system—at least as far as she knew. Her dad had talked about getting one when she'd first returned home from the hospital, but she'd left so soon after that there hadn't been a desire.

"I worried he'd found a letter from you. I keep them all in my office." He shifted in the bed. "Anyhow, he had a gun, so I was pretty much stuck. I couldn't see a way to run from a bullet. Only, he didn't use it at first." He paused. "Look, I don't want to tell you about this. Suffice to say, I have a couple of broken fingers, some stitches, bruises, and two new scars from the bullet holes. I was very lucky. He didn't shoot to kill."

He said everything so casually that it took her brain a moment to catch up. *Lucky? Lucky?* she wanted to screech at the top of her lungs. Even in her mind, her volume rose with each word.

Before she could find the proper response, her dad interrupted her thoughts. "Help me out of this bed. I've rested enough today."

Knowing it would be dark soon and time to return to bed, she didn't argue. At first. "Okay." She stood and watched him struggle to move to the side of the bed. Color had leached out of his face, and he panted his breaths. "No, Daddy. I think you should still be in bed."

"Ken," he belted out.

The burly man lumbered into the room and moved to Adam's side. "The chair or the living room?" he asked her dad. Apparently, they'd done this before.

"The living room."

With an arm supporting him, Ken helped her dad shuffle to the living room. She followed behind with tears in her eyes at the pallor of her father's skin and the small grunts he tried to hide from her.

Through bleary eyes, she watched in bewilderment as her dad, in his blue plaid pajama pants and white T-shirt, settled in his recliner, and the big, bad warrior leaned it back and then draped the afghan her mother had made on her dad's lap. "Did you want anything?" Ken asked quietly.

Her dad shook his head. Exactly how long had these guys been here? The incident just happened, but you'd think they'd been doing this for a while now. And wasn't that Ken guy supposed to protect her dad, not play Nursemaid? Thank goodness Aunt Kathy was coming. She wanted Ken out there keeping her dad safe from that asshole who thought to ruin her life. Again.

With a smile, she dropped onto the couch. "Ken seems to be a big help."

Adam nodded. "He has been. So has Brad."

From what Matt had said about Brad, that statement surprised her. Maybe he was still a big softie after all. "Aunt Kathy will be here tomorrow, won't she?"

"Yeah. I think my sister is happy to have someone to care for. She's lonely, but she won't admit it."

Her aunt never had children, and since her only niece—Caitlyn—hadn't had children yet for her to spoil, she had no one but her brother and Caitlyn. She kept in touch with her aunt regularly and had a soft spot in her heart for her, even though Aunt Kathy had moved away with her husband, who'd died a few years ago. From what Caitlyn had gathered, her dad had tried to get his sister to move back to Water Valley, but Aunt Kathy had refused.

"I spoke with her last week. She started going to Bingo." Caitlyn laughed. "Can you see her with all the blue-haired ladies who usually go? I mean, she and I went a time or two when I was in high school, but we were always the youngest women there, and they asked us to leave because we were giggling so much."

"She needs something to keep her busy. Being retired at her young age isn't working for her, but she knows trying to get hired at her age won't be easy. She's at a crossroads."

"Maybe you can convince her to move back here now."

"We."

"What do you mean we?" she asked.

"You should still be here when she arrives, so you can help me talk her into it. She listens to you."

Caitlyn laughed at that absurdity. "Listens to me? I'm still a kid to her. You're her brother." She knew all this talk was to keep her off the main topic of Luke Ripley and what had happened, but she couldn't allow it to continue indefinitely. Her dad was already tiring out. "Daddy, I'm not sure how long I should stay." She rushed to add, "I mean, I want to stay as long as you need me, but Matt…."

Matt hadn't said how long they would remain in Water Valley, but she thought it was a quick trip. She would love to see her aunt again. Some of her most enjoyable memories while growing up involved aunt-niece days. Like when she'd check her out of school, and they'd go to the movies where they had the theater all to themselves. Daddy didn't really appreciate her aunt checking her out of school, so those stopped once he'd found out. But there was more that didn't involve her being checked out. Instead, Aunt Kathy would agree to pick her up from school. Her heart would always race when she saw her aunt's car in the school pickup lane because she knew they'd have some type of adventure.

They'd go to the fair, paint pottery, go to the candy store, or go to the arcade, but they always got something sweet that usually ruined her dinner. It was a sad day for her when her aunt moved away with her husband, although they always did something when she returned for a visit, always building great memories.

"Ken," her dad said.

The man appeared. Christ, where did he hide that large frame, and how did he move so quickly and quietly? That's right, he was a former Army Ranger.

"Yes, sir?"

"Would you get Matt, please? We need to talk."

Ken nodded and turned from the room. The next thing she knew, the door opened and Matt and Brad entered. Brad smiled, opened his arms, and said, "It's good to see you, Caitlyn."

After a moment's hesitation, she jumped from the couch and rushed into Brad's arms. She missed the camaraderie she'd had with Matt's twin. Of course, she was also glad he'd left off his typical endearment for her. He used to call her "Brat," and she hated it.

"It's so good to see you, Brad," she said on his shoulder. Before she settled into the comfort too much, she pulled back and broke free. She hadn't cringed at his touch. Obviously it hadn't been sensual, but still, she couldn't handle hugs from everyone. Maybe it was because she knew Brad meant her no harm. Curious.

"You look good, brat."

She groaned as he winked at her. He then checked on her dad before she could form a scathing response. She wanted to stamp her foot like a child and tell him to quit.

"Everything okay?" Matt asked her quietly.

Was it? She didn't know. Her mind was still in a jumble. The foundation? Her rapist's brother? Her ex-fiancé? Her father? No. Nothing was okay, but she'd get through it. She'd been tough—fearful but tough—all these years. She could do it again. This time, she had Matt and HIS by her side. This chapter in her life would end, and she would finally win.

"Sit down and let's talk," Adam directed.

Matt and Brad sat on each side of her on the couch, not giving her room to move. Ken positioned himself in the doorway. Were they that worried about Luke getting into the house? Good Lord, she hoped not.

"I have something to say," she started before anyone else could speak and decide her future without her input. "I can't let the thought of Travis Ripley ruin my life any longer. Even though he's in jail, I remained hidden and living in fear. I won't give him or his brother that power." She turned to Matt. "What do we need to do to catch Luke and make him pay for what he did to my daddy?"

Matt exploded. "We're catching him. You're"—he pointed a finger at her—"not catching him. We're keeping you safe until he's captured."

"And how long do you think that will take?" she asked.

"As long as it does." Matt's tone seemed more controlled than it had just been.

With a huff at that absurdity of an answer, she narrowed her eyes a fraction. She appreciated what they were doing—and would continue to do—for her, but she wanted to help capture the threat so her father and she would be safe again. "Not good enough."

Matt's face moved to mere inches from hers, and he ground out, "It'll have to be."

Breath hitching, she couldn't help but wonder why at that moment she hoped he'd kiss her.

Chapter Eight

"How could she even think that she could help us catch that fucker?" Matt railed to Brad as he settled on the floor in the living room while Brad, who had won the coin toss for the couch, settled into his comfy bed for the night lying on his side, facing Matt.

The home had three bedrooms, but Adam had turned the third one into an office, so they could either sleep on the furniture or floor, or travel to a hotel. The last was unacceptable to him. He needed to be where Caitlyn was, or he didn't think his heart could take it. She was in danger, and letting her out of his sight was damn difficult. Hell, he'd have crawled into bed with her if she'd have let him. Although, he doubted sleep would've been on his mind. She was still too hot of a package for his dick not to respond. Thank God he didn't allow that head to make the decisions.

"She's always been tough," Brad remarked. "She had to have been to survive what she did and come out so strong"

"Still."

"I can't get over the changes in her."

Matt's back stiffened and his ire went on red-hot alert. There was no telling what the hell would come out of Brad's mouth, but he had to know what his brother meant. "What do you mean?" he questioned slowly.

"You know. She's filled out more."

He could hear the laughter in his twin's voice, and he wanted to deck him right in his smartass mouth. "Fuck you."

Brad rolled onto his back and put his hands underneath his head, gazing at the ceiling. "You still love her, don't you?"

Sputtering, Matt didn't know what to say, but finally got out, "What do you mean?" There was nothing like sounding defensive to avoid answering a question.

With a sigh, Brad turned back to him. "You heard me."

He couldn't lie to his twin, and he didn't see a reason to even consider it. It would be the first time he'd admitted it out loud in eight years though. "I never stopped."

"Did she forgive you like you wanted?"

His heart pounded. His brother knew what he needed. Brad had been at the door of the hospital room when she'd yelled at Matt and told him it was his fault. "Yeah."

"And?"

Matt exhaled a long breath. "I don't know."

"I do. You can't forgive yourself."

How could Brad know him that well? Of course, he'd swear to know his twin the same, so that was a stupid question.

"If you want a future with her, you have to forgive yourself and move forward like she has."

"I don't know that she's moved forward. I mean, there's no us that she's considering."

Brad resettled himself on his back. "You won't

know unless you try, but, brother, I'm serious. It won't work unless you drop that heavy weight you carry. The shit happened, and you can't change it, so it's a waste to dredge it up."

Matt snorted. "When did you become the expert on relationships?"

"I'm not. I just know the two of you really well. Goodnight."

Brad hadn't told Matt anything he hadn't already known and considered. The questions were whether he could forgive himself and whether Caitlyn would ever consider a relationship with him again. Just because she forgave him didn't mean she wanted to rush back into his arms like nothing happened. No, she wanted to catch a fucking asshole who meant her harm.

That night, his dreams weren't filled with the SEAL mission where he'd lost friends. Instead, they were filled with Caitlyn running in fear and his inability to get to her.

The following day, he woke early and hurried to dress. "We're leaving today," he told Brad, who'd just stood to stretch. They'd been there longer than he wanted. Of course, he hadn't wanted to come here in the first place, but he couldn't have kept Caitlyn away.

Brad nodded. "The second team should be here by ten. Maybe we should just take that team instead of switching out teams."

"No, sir," Ken said, walking into the room with a cup of coffee. "Believe me, that was my plan, but Adam trusts these men, so he wants them on Caitlyn. I tried to explain the next set of men would be as good, but he wouldn't hear of it."

"Are you ready to transition and get on the road?"

Matt asked as he folded the blanket he'd used.

"We are. Besides your vehicle, we have two vehicles for the team, so we'll be able to see if anyone is following us. Brad said he's riding with you."

Matt narrowed his eyes at his twin, who just smirked. Since Devon had organized approval to drive through the three states and keep their weapons in open carry, he attached his nine-millimeter Glock to his hip. The subcompact Glock attached to his ankle was a no-brainer.

"Adam's sister should be here about the same time. He said she'd want to see Caitlyn."

"Hell." Matt wiped his hand over his face, his pulse racing. "It was bad enough coming down here. That fucker could be watching somewhere, waiting to know for sure she's here."

"We've got her covered," Brad stated, as if reading his mind.

"I want her out of here and back to the safety of her own home."

"It'll only be a short visit," Brad said, then clarified, "We'll make it a short visit."

Caitlyn came into the living room, helping her father as he struggled to walk the distance. All three men rushed to him, but Ken had somehow managed to put down his coffee and get there first.

"Catie said she'd cook breakfast this morning," Adam said, smiling.

Caitlyn, on the other hand, grimaced.

Seeing that, Matt piped up, "I'll help. Come on, Caitlyn." He touched her arm to lead her to the kitchen, and he felt the brief contact down to his groin. "Let's get cooking." In the background, he heard Brad chuckle at his comment.

Once they were in the kitchen, he turned to her and asked what they planned to cook.

Opening the refrigerator to look inside, she said, "Spend the time with my daddy is what I want to do."

Accepting the bacon she'd handed to him, making sure to brush their hands for the warm, electric touch, he smiled. "And he wants you to play hostess. We'll fix this up fast." He relieved her of the carton of eggs and placed them on the counter. Remembering where the pantry was, he searched it for pancake mix and syrup. Once he'd succeeded, he added them to the countertop. She went behind him and added grits. After they'd finished locating pantry items, they were ready to make breakfast. "I hope it's okay. I put pancakes in instead of biscuits because those boys will be hungry, and it'll be less work for you and more time with your dad." He didn't mention they were mostly northern boys and probably wouldn't eat the grits. Then again, with the manners that had been instilled in all of them by Kate, they'd probably eat them to be polite.

Their eyes met, and his heart did a flip-flop in her softened gaze. She was bravely dealing with her situation, and it fed his soul.

With the water on for the grits first—they took the longest since they weren't instant—Matt took the time to discuss their travel. "We'll give you a half hour to meet with your aunt before we get on the road."

"Thirty minutes. Are you nuts? I want an hour." Her emotions were pleading, her eyes asking for the time, and he fought not to wrap his arms around her for comfort.

"Do you realize it'll already be late when we get

there, and it'll be hard for the men to scope out the place their first time in the dark? You have a lot of woods nearby they'll want to check."

"One hour. And they shouldn't worry about it when we first get there. Luke doesn't know where I live."

But it wasn't impossible that he'd find out. He crossed his arms over his chest. "Good grief, you're stubborn."

A smile lifted her lips, and his breath caught at the action. "I remember you calling me that a time or two."

In that instant, he wanted to grab her and kiss her hard. Hell, it hadn't been the first time he'd wanted to do so since he'd seen her again, but her being playful jolted his dick to action. It made him crave her more than he already did.

He wondered what she'd do if he scooped her up into his arms. Nothing good. He remembered how she'd flinched when he'd tried to take her arm to come into the kitchen. And maybe it was automatic, but he didn't like it. Not one fucking bit.

How could he possibly attempt to win her love back, trapped in a situation where every tender touch, every subtle caress, was utterly forbidden? The weight of unspoken feelings hung heavily between them, like a fragile glass barrier that prevented even the simplest act of affection. He longed to convey the depth of his remorse and the intensity of his desire, but without the ability to bridge that emotional gap physically, he felt like a prisoner of his own heart.

"One hour," she repeated.

Roused back to the conversation, he sighed in resignation. "One hour. But that's it. We get on the road even if I must carry you kicking and screaming to the car."

She smiled sweetly. "Deal. Now, it's time to get this breakfast going."

In no time, Matt flipped the last pancake—his cooking chore—and served Adam and the first rotation of the men. As he'd predicted, the men ate small portions of the grits and gave a perfunctory smile. Kate would be proud of them. They'd taken to her mothering really well. They just enjoyed Kate's cooking so much that they'd do anything to get invited to her table. Even if it meant eating something they didn't like so they could have what they did like.

The second crew of men offered to clean the dishes before Kathy Fenton arrived. And when she did, Matt felt like he'd been through a whirlwind. The hour flew by, and he was exhausted when he, Caitlyn, and the men left in three vehicles. And he hadn't done anything but be in Kathy's presence. A great presence. Somehow he'd never met Kathy while he and Caitlyn had dated. It was intriguing to meet the woman Caitlyn had always raved about finally.

"What did you think of Aunt Kathy?" she asked as they buckled into their seats.

Matt noticed Brad, who sat in the back, kept his mouth shut, leaving the question to him. This would be a fun trip with his very own chaperone.

With that unfortunate thought, he started the car and tried to find the right words to answer the question. He didn't want to be in the doghouse before he'd had a chance with her.

Chapter Nine

They arrived in Kentucky without issue. Brad kept up the conversation by asking Caitlyn nonstop questions about her organization, the dogs, and the warriors who received them. She barely had an opening to ask about the Hamiltons. She wanted to know about Matt and his life since they'd been apart but couldn't bring herself to ask openly with Brad in the car. However, Brad did offer tidbits of what Matt had been doing since she'd left him. Of course, the incident that split them hadn't been brought up. Thank God. She had no idea if Brad knew what had transpired between her and Matt after the rape. Being that they were incredibly close twins, he probably knew, but Matt had always been private. She could only hope he hadn't spread that she'd been an irrational bitch.

When they'd been close to her home, Matt had sent one of the cars ahead to check things out. She'd already had to hand over her keys before they'd left Water Valley. Matt must've planned for it. His planning, taking over the trip, and protecting her relaxed her. Thankfully, Matt wasn't pushy about it. She might've had something to say had he been a big bully. But, as long as it kept those around her safe, she'd deal with it for as long as she could handle the intrusion.

She chuckled inwardly. Thank goodness it was Matt and not Brad. Matt had been right that Brad had changed. The twin had no filter and was dominating in almost any instance. No wonder he was still single. But she did concede that he was always gentle with her. How he discussed people outside the Hamilton fold made her notice his personality in full force.

Brad ended a call on his cell phone. "Ken says the house and facility are clear. They're still checking the woods. That could take a while."

Matt nodded, slowed, and took the next off-ramp from the interstate. "Hungry?" he asked.

She almost said no, but her stomach took that moment to rumble loudly. She laughed. "I guess I am."

"How about The Tower Treasure?" Matt offered.

"Oh, I love their shopping."

Brad grunted. "I think he meant to eat, not shop, brat."

Once again, she ignored the nickname. In truth, part of her liked that he felt close enough to her to give her a nickname. She only wished it was something else. "Oh, their food is good."

When they reached the restaurant door, she stopped when Brad pushed past her and entered first. *What the hell happened to gentlemanly manners?*

As if reading her mind, Matt leaned down and whispered, "He's checking the place out to make sure it's safe."

"Oh," she breathed. Of course. She'd felt so safe with them; how easily she'd forgotten. Yet, did they really think Luke had followed them, then driven ahead and stopped at The Tower Treasure on the off chance they stopped to eat? *The men might be taking this a bit overboard.*

"We don't expect him yet, but until we know

where he is…." Matt trailed off.

He'd placed his hand on the small of her back and slowly propelled her forward before she realized he'd said "yet." They didn't expect him *yet*. A shiver raced down her spine. They *expected* him even though they'd done what they needed to do to get her home safely.

Of course, they anticipated him at some unexpected point in time. Why else would they surround her here and at her home? She couldn't fret over it since there was nothing she could do about it, but she couldn't forget it either. The very thought of encountering any of the Ripley family sent a chill running through her, leaving her feeling hollow and unsettled. Caitlyn despised that unsettling sensation, knowing all too well the memories and emotions it stirred within her.

Realizing she hadn't shrunk back from Matt's hand on her back, she made herself stay the course. Allowing him to touch her—even so lightly and with purpose—it really was progress that she could accept Matt's touch, even as minuscule as it was, and even Brad's, but no one else's.

Sitting down to a carb-heavy dinner—they didn't have much else on the menu—she laughed as Brad told stories of the brothers.

"The night before Matt went into the Navy, me and some of the guys from college took him out. Boy was that a night to remember." Brad shook his head and took a big bite of his steak.

"Enough," Matt growled in response.

"Oh?" she quizzed, covering a french fry in ketchup. "What made it so memorable?" She bit into the fry and almost moaned with delight. There was something about the combination that just set her taste buds on fire.

"Tattoos," Brad stated while Matt said, "Nothing."

Glancing back and forth between the brothers, she smiled. "Tattoos, huh?"

"It's nothing," Matt reiterated.

"Don't listen to him," Brad advised with a mischievous smile. "We have matching tattoos, so we would always remember each other and the fun we had."

She couldn't help but laugh. Matt had never been a tattoo person; in fact, he'd always been a little opposed to them when they'd been in college. She guessed getting drunk must've fractured that thinking.

Not that she was opposed to them. She was indifferent since it wasn't her body. Men, and women, could have them or not, but she didn't want needles unnecessarily stuck in her skin. Only she didn't really care for them on the face. It could sometimes be a bit creepy.

"May I see?" she dared to ask, knowing Matt wasn't happy about the topic.

"Not in here," he directed at Brad, who'd grabbed his shirt as if ready to pull it up or off.

She stifled a chuckle. She wouldn't put it past Brad to rip his shirt off in public. That much hadn't seemed to change in him. "Ooh," she cooed. "I'm intrigued."

Brad winked at her. "I'll show you anytime, brat."

Again he called her that. But she wouldn't allow him to get a rise out of her, which she was sure he was doing. Or maybe he was trying to get a rise out of Matt since this tattoo thing seemed to bother him. She wondered why that was.

"You will not," Matt ordered.

The two stared each other down, and she burst out laughing again. As twins, they were identical, except she could tell them easily apart. Anyone who really knew them could. There was one slightly noticeable difference, and that was in their noses. They'd both been broken—by each other—but had healed a bit differently in how their bump rested on their noses. Matt's was to the left, while Brad's healed to the right.

The waitress arrived to check on them, halting the argument that seemed to bloom over the infamous tattoos. She definitely had to see them now. Or at least one, since they supposedly matched. In her thinking, it was odd to get a matching tattoo from guy to guy, but the two were really close when she hung out with them. And they were supposedly really drunk, so she should imagine anything. An image of pink unicorns flew through her mind, and she almost laughed. Wouldn't that be something?

Brad's phone vibrated, and he excused himself from the table to answer it.

Trying not to poke the bear too much, she asked lightly, "So, can I see it?"

Matt watched her a moment, then leaned close. "Anytime we're in private."

Goosebumps raced down her arms at the sensual tone of his voice. She didn't think she could handle Matt alone with his shirt off. Maybe even his pants, since he considered it so private. Sure, there'd been a time when that was just about all she wanted. They'd had a lusty relationship. They spent most of their time in bed or wherever they could find a bit of privacy. But now....

Returning to the table, Brad said, "They're ready."

Matt nodded and stood, leaving her with nothing to do but follow their lead. While Brad stood in line to pay, Matt kept her close. She wanted to shop, wanted normality, even in a shitty situation, but she knew enough that it was wise to stay by the man who had a weapon…the man who could protect her.

After they had returned to the car, they waited for the tail car to load up. Then they were back on the road.

Her work brain started kicking into gear as they got closer to her home. Despite everything going on, she had a job to do and people relying on her. She didn't get much work done at her daddy's with his health and well…Matt.

Taking the long gravel drive to her residence and the training facility made her wonder how they would handle the parking for the fundraiser. They'd have to hire professional valets to help coordinate proper parking if they planned to get thirty people in there. Thank goodness many would be couples and ride together

"Remember the rules," Matt told her, busting into her thoughts. "You do not leave the house without one of us. Even to go to the training facility. You do not leave the training facility without one of us."

"In other words, I don't go anywhere without one of you." Then to tease him, she smiled sweetly. "Who goes with me to the bathroom?"

"Smartass," he commented while Brad laughed.

"Where's everyone staying?" They'd never talked about that. Surely they weren't camping out.

"In your house," Brad answered. "They'll swap out sleeping in one of the spare rooms. Brad and I will swap out in the other one."

Thank goodness she had two extra rooms set up for guests, even though there was only one bed in each room. It would mean someone would have to sleep on the floor or couch unless they planned to share a bed. She'd allow them to figure that out. The fact that they were on-site meant that her employees and dogs would be safe at all times, and that mattered most to her.

"What about food?" She knew her pantry wasn't stocked enough to feed the group.

"They'll take care of that," Matt stated. "Someone will go grocery shopping, and everyone will cook for themselves unless you want to cook for them. As I recall, you are a mighty fine chef."

"I don't mind." It would be fun to cook for more than herself. She for her staff at lunchtime most of the time, but it would be nice to be able to jump back into her recipe box.

"You don't have to worry about beds or seating at the table," Brad said. "There will always be at least two on duty outside, and Matt and I will switch off."

"Have those on duty now eaten?"

Matt shook his head. "Probably not, but don't worry. Their other teammates will take care of it."

"No," she rushed to say. "I'll fix them something. If they're doing this for me, it's the least I can do."

When they entered her home, she went straight to the kitchen to prepare something for the men. She took a flank steak from the freezer and put it in the microwave to thaw it enough to work with without cooking it through. While that defrosted, she pulled out fresh vegetables that had to be cooked or would be tossed out soon and began chopping. When Matt came into the kitchen, after unloading their bags and conferring with the men, he asked, "What can I do?"

Without thinking, she ordered, "Cook some rice. I have some minute rice bags in the pantry instead of using the rice cooker. That will take longer, and I want to get them fed since it's well after dinner. After that, you can slice the beef."

A little stir-fry was the best way to get men to eat their vegetables, she'd always thought. At least that's what she'd done with her dad and Matt. Sure, he'd pushed some of them out of the way, but he ate more than if she'd put a steak out with a vegetable side. He'd all but ignore the side and wolf down the steak and potato. Caitlyn had given up making salads for him. He seemed allergic to lettuce, or at least he ate like he was. She smiled at the silly thought.

Her kitchen wasn't small, but it wasn't big by any means. Matt slid next to her to slice the beef, and she felt his warmth even over the short distance. This energy between them could not be happening. Couldn't. Could it?

"Is this good enough?" he asked after slicing two pieces entirely too large in her mind, but probably perfect for the big, brawny men who hadn't eaten dinner.

"They're fine."

"You're making an awful lot for just two men," he told her.

She almost snorted out loud. "It won't be long before one of you are hungry again. I remember how often you and Brad ate when we were in college."

They'd also been football players working out all the time, so it only went with the deal that they were always in need of refueling. That made her think about Matt and the NFL again. Why hadn't he told his family or pursued it? He could've been set for life financially if he'd been drafted. Was that it? Had he worried he wouldn't get picked up after all? Or had what happened to her ruined it for him? No, that couldn't be it. Sure he'd told her she'd make a great NFL player's wife, but…but what? She hoped she hadn't ruined a promising future for him. She dismissed the thought. The concept was too painful.

"Done." Matt dropped his knife and turned back to the stove. "The water's ready for the rice, so it's almost done."

She finished slicing the final carrot. "Okay, let me get this on the stove." Pushing around him—since he'd parked himself in the way—she pulled her wok from the lower cabinet and set about cooking a meal.

While she cooked, Matt leaned against the country sink and watched her. She knew because she glanced over her shoulder a couple of times, and each time he was staring at her. She didn't think she could handle this closeness if this was part of the protection. Her body reacted to him, and she wasn't sure she wanted it to feel that familiar again.

"Will the guys switch out so they can eat? I know you said they were going to rest since they'd be on tonight," she asked without looking back over her shoulder.

"We'll handle it," was all he said. Then she sensed him leave the room. There hadn't been any noise that told her he had; she'd just felt the heat drain from her. Wasn't that a bitch for her to get her head around?

Chapter Ten

Matt woke the following day to the wonderful smell of bacon. It'd taken him a moment to remember where he was, but the thought of Caitlyn alone kicked him into gear. He hadn't slept that soundly in a long time. Maybe it was the quiet out in the middle of nowhere as opposed to the city noise he was used to living in Baltimore. Plus, he'd booted Neftali to the floor so he could have a bed.

After his morning ritual to get ready for the day, he slipped into jeans and a black T-shirt then went in search of food. Actually, he went in search of Caitlyn, but he knew she'd be the one cooking so he'd get to fill his belly and watch her at work again. She was smokin' hot when she'd cooked the night before. The way her breasts were squeezed together when she chopped vegetables, and how she swayed her fine ass when she stirred the food. So much so that he'd had to leave the room to keep from coming up behind her, wrapping his arms around her, and grinding his erection against her.

When he arrived in the dining room that stood open to the kitchen, the table was nearly full with Brad, Ken, Neftali, Rick, and Caitlyn. They were laughing and scarfing down a breakfast of scrambled eggs, bacon, fried potatoes, biscuits, white sausage gravy, and grits. Most of the men had larger helpings of grits than they'd had before when being courteous, so he could only surmise the guys were growing accustomed to a southern breakfast, or they really wanted to please Caitlyn. He grimaced. They'd best not think anything romantic about *his* Caitlyn.

With only one seat empty between Caitlyn and Rick, he grabbed a plate from the kitchen island, which stood as the only separation between the two rooms, and slid into the seat. Caitlyn and Rick passed him platter after platter until his plate was heaping full. He noted there was still plenty for the men on duty. She'd definitely come through, but he didn't want her to feel she had to cater to them. They generally cooked their food on a mission or ate packaged foods like power bars and some MREs. Once upon a time, an MRE sucked, the meal tasting like cardboard. The newer ones weren't so bad. They still weren't even close to home cooking, but they were definitely edible.

Of course, they didn't always invade someone's home, but Caitlyn was a long way from the nearest hotel, and, well, it was Caitlyn. He wanted the entire team on site in case anything happened. He'd worry about the distance to the hotel if they needed a second team. God, he hoped they didn't. Plus, he wanted to always be on hand in case the sheriff got any leads or had any updates for them about Luke's location.

Ken and Neftali stood, and then Ken spoke. "Thank you for breakfast, ma'am. We'll relieve Danny and Steve now, and they'll be in shortly."

Christ, he'd almost slept through a shift change.

"Y'all are welcome. And thank you," Caitlyn said.

The men entered one of the guest bedrooms where they'd stored their weapons and prepared to relieve the men on duty. Loaded down with handguns, knives, and rifles, and who knew what else, they shuffled out the back door. Caitlyn watched them with a wary look that hit his heart like a sledgehammer. This had to be hard on her. What woman—or any person actually— wouldn't have some reservations and fear over having armed men protecting them from someone known to harm? The big question was, what were Ripley's plans for her? He'd said she wouldn't appear at the parole hearing, but Matt prayed that didn't mean what he thought it did.

A sliver of dread wove its merciless way up his spine. They needed to find Ripley, not wait until he came to them. God, he hoped Devon was enough. He'd been in the past, so there should be no reason to doubt him. But he didn't have boots on the ground. Jesse said they'd pull a man or two from Adam's detail, which pleased and worried him. Pleased because someone would be searching, but concerned because Adam needed full protection if Ripley came back for round two.

After everyone had eaten, the men who'd worked the night shift—except for Brad—offered to clean the kitchen. No, they really demanded and, after much back and forth, shooed Caitlyn away to the training compound and her office. She had put up a fight, but in the end, she acquiesced, and Matt had to chase behind her as she strode to the other building.

There waiting on them was a tall man in an expensive-looking suit. It appeared tailor-made for the lean man in his early thirties with clean-cut dark hair and bold blue eyes. Matt would admit that he was probably good-looking—*to some women*, he grumbled to himself. The green-eyed monster reared its ugly head and exploded in full force when the man looked Caitlyn covertly up and down and smiled. Yep, he could see ripping the head off this asshole in his future.

Matt stepped in front of Caitlyn, putting himself between the unexpected visitor and her.

The man's eyes widened briefly, and he looked down at the Glock on Matt's belt before he returned the gaze and smirked. "I'm here to see Miss Robinson."

The stranger's voice grated on Matt's nerves. Having seen a photo of Luke Ripley, Matt knew this wasn't him, plus he was too young, so he didn't interfere when her guest stepped aside and, ignoring Matt, looked at Caitlyn.

With a brief hesitation, her gaze caught on Matt's, and he could've sworn she sighed in relief. Looking back at the visitor, she introduced herself and boldly stepped forward, although Matt saw her trembling slightly. "I'm Caitlyn Robinson. And you are?"

The asshole thrust his hand out to her, still ignoring Matt, who was closer. "I'm Tate Hart. I called and spoke with one of your staff members the other day."

Matt's mind cycled through where he'd heard that name. Then it hit him—the potential donor. Why the fuck couldn't he have called and scheduled a convenient time to meet? Instead, he'd shown up uninvited. Very presumptuous of him. Of course, by the slick ooze flying off him, the guy did what he wanted when he wanted it. He was the acquiescent, spoiled rich kid, only he was a grown-ass adult. But if he were offering money for her service dog organization, Matt wouldn't stand in the way, even though he wanted to wipe the smug smile off his face. He also wouldn't leave her alone with the sleazebag—money or not.

"Mr. Hart, it's so good to meet you," Caitlyn said while shaking Hart's hand. The handshake lasted way too long. He'd been ready to reach out and break their contact, but her hand had been released.

Caitlyn turned to him. "Mr. Hart, this is Matt Hamilton."

Neither man had said a word in greeting, just a slight nod and a perfunctory handshake where each squeezed as hard as he could without Caitlyn noticing. When he removed his hand from the asshole's, he wanted to shake it out, and ease the pain the man had caused. He'd been surprised by the tightness of his grip. Satisfaction flushed through him when Hart shook his hand for what Matt could guess was the same reason. He liked seeing that and knowing he'd gotten the upper hand since he hadn't flinched.

Hart turned back to Caitlyn. "I'd like to discuss a possible donation with you." He tacked on "Alone" for Matt's benefit.

Caitlyn appeared rattled momentarily and looked at Matt, and his stomach dropped. Fear swam in her eyes. Did she have that bad vibe from this guy?

"Where Caitlyn goes, so do I," Matt announced. Knowing she didn't want anyone other than staff to know someone was chasing her, he tossed his arm over her shoulder, felt her stiffen, and lied his ass off. She'd probably get pissed, but it was his best thought at the time. "She's my fiancée, and we're going to be running Helping Paws together, so right now, I'm with her to find out everything I can to help run the place after we're married." He sharpened his gaze at Hart. "Which includes working with potential donors."

Redness crept up Hart's face and neck in what Matt

guessed was rage, making him dislike the man even more. After a moment, Hart turned back to Caitlyn and flashed a brilliant smile that didn't go with the looks he'd been giving Matt. They needed to get his money and get him out of there as quickly as possible.

It suddenly struck him. How did the man get past his men? Fuck. He looked around the break room in the training facility, wondering where the men were. "Who let you in?" he asked gruffly. He wanted to kick himself. His earpiece was in his pants pocket. He'd forgotten to insert it when he'd chased after Caitlyn to the facility. And he didn't want to set up his comm system with a stranger watching.

"I guess it was your security guard. Another man with a weapon, anyway." Hart shrugged like it was nothing. "He made me wait until someone could identify me." He turned back to Caitlyn. "Probably a bit of overkill, but you do live out in the middle of nowhere. Anyhow," he said, turning back to Matt, "one of the employees—Rick, I think his name was—vouched for me and had me wait here."

What the fuck? Did her staff know anything about security? Hart could've entered the office and destroyed things since she kept it unlocked. He could've been on her computer, hacking her accounts. In other words, he could've destroyed her, and no one would know unless they'd caught him in the act. Matt took a deep breath. Okay, he was being irrational, but it was Caitlyn's life, for Christ's sake.

Matt couldn't slam his employees if hers vouched for the person. Dammit. He'd have another talk with Tonya and Rick. He'd find a way to meet with the volunteers and visiting veterans also. The latter group would understand and be a bit of help.

"Miss Robinson, first, congratulations on your engagement."

She didn't respond. Matt guessed she was still seething that he'd taken that route. She might've preferred the truth to come out instead of a lie such as that, but he didn't believe she wanted anyone to know why he or she was there.

Hart's gaze flicked to her left hand, and that smirk returned when he noticed it was bare.

Goddamn motherfucker.

"Second"—his smirk changed back to a friendly smile—"I'm ready to learn about your organization. My accountant says I need to donate more money this year, and someone recommended you and your work. Know that I research every investment and donation I make, so I'll be close the next few days until I'm sure you're the one for my million-dollar donation."

Caitlyn went rigid at the mention of that amount of money. Matt didn't know her finances but knew, without a doubt, that a million dollars would greatly help her organization. That meant Matt couldn't screw up that big of a cash influx from Hart. But he'd also make Devon check the man out.

"Won't you come with me to my office?" Caitlyn smiled sweetly, as the tension he'd felt seemed to seep from her body at the mention of the large donation.

"I'd love to," Hart responded.

While Matt wanted to put himself behind Caitlyn, so Hart didn't get an unobstructed view of her ass, he brought up the rear, pulling his earpiece from his pocket and covertly inserting it. He couldn't do anything with the mic yet. But there wouldn't be any more surprises.

At least, he hoped.

Matt stood behind Caitlyn at the desk instead of sitting in a chair opposite it and beside Hart. The man still looked like he wanted to eat up Caitlyn. No way would he leave them alone. He didn't think the man meant her any harm, but he definitely wanted a taste. Then again, what red-blooded male wouldn't want one? She was a beautiful woman dressed in snug jeans and a Helping Paws T-shirt that, while it didn't mold to her form, fit well enough to show off her perfect figure. Perfect for him, anyway.

Settled in a chair, one leg crossed over the other, Hart began, "I want to know everything about what you do, and I want to see the operation. Those are my stipulations before I consider my donation."

"Well, Mr. Hart—"

"Please call me Tate. And I'll call you Caitlyn. It's much nicer that way."

Matt caught the stiffening of her body when he said he'd call her by her first name. He couldn't understand why she'd take offense to that, but he'd figure it out. He doubted it was just poor manners on Hart's side to tell instead of ask.

"As I was saying," Caitlyn continued, as if he hadn't spoken, "I would go to those lengths even with a nondonor. My employees and I are very proud of what we do here. We have nothing to hide."

"Then why do you have an armed guard?" he challenged.

"Oh, that…." She trailed off, obviously searching for an answer.

Coming to her rescue, Matt said, "They came with me." Which wasn't a lie.

"They? So there's more than one?"

Why did this weasel asking make him want to keep it all secret? He couldn't allow jealousy to cloud his judgment. He also didn't have to tell him everything. "One during the day and one at night." Okay, that time, he lied and hoped Caitlyn wouldn't think she needed to correct it.

"Is there danger here? Maybe I shouldn't be here," Hart challenged.

"You're safe, Mr. Hart," Matt said. "I own a security firm, and the boys didn't have anything to do, so I took them with me on this trip to see Caitlyn. They preferred to work, so I let them."

"You don't live here?"

Man, Hart was getting personal, and Matt didn't like that at all. "Not yet," he bit out, hoping that would end this inappropriate conversation. He wanted to tell him it was none of his fucking business, but he wouldn't upset Caitlyn's pain-in-the-ass donor.

"I'm sorry if I've been too personal. That was none of my business except to know the place is safe," he said smoothly and with that bright smile that Matt already hated.

Fucker, Matt thought.

Swiveling his gaze back to Caitlyn, Hart asked, "Now, tell me how you came to found this?"

Matt held his post and listened to Caitlyn explain how, at one point in her life, she'd been at a crossroads and had learned of this type of organization. She described her years as a trainer and how she started with nearly nothing and was now considering expanding to stop turning down deserving veterans. But they needed donations like his to make that happen.

She'd impressed the hell out of Matt. All that she'd done—alone. If he'd been by her side like he'd wanted, would she have discovered this was her dream, or would he have pushed her toward something like the fashion design she'd been going to college for? There had always been the chance of her being an NFL wife, but Matt had never really seen her happy in that role, and with that and Brad not getting noticed for the NFL, he'd squashed the idea long before the rape. After that, he'd tossed everything away and joined the Navy.

While his thoughts had drifted for a moment, Hart seemed entranced by her words. Maybe it was her beauty and her lovely voice. They'd be sure to snare anyone with a dick. She couldn't help how exquisite of a package she was, but he wished her jeans and T-shirt were looser. He didn't want another man, especially one who was flirting while asking questions, seeing her dressed like that.

Even though he imagined it to be tough, he'd keep his mouth shut until she received the money from this asshole. Internally, he grinned. He'd let Devon do all the talking, just as soon as he could get the man's name to his brother, a magician with information. Maybe even sic Emily on his financials to wreak havoc. Okay, they didn't do stuff like that for spite, but it felt good to toss the idea around in his mind.

First, he'd have to deal with a tirade that would surely come from Caitlyn when Hart left. Yep, he'd done it big time by saying she was his fiancée. Hell, at one time she was. And even though he'd been around her for a short time, he knew in his heart that if he could make it happen, she would be again.

Chapter Eleven

After she waved goodbye to Tate Hart, Caitlyn went inside and seethed so badly she should have had steam streaming from her ears. She tightened her hands into fists. How dare Matt tell Tate he was her fiancé? She wondered if he still saw things that way. But he hadn't said anything about their broken engagement before meeting her potential donor.

The other part of her knew he'd made it up to explain his presence in the meeting. But, engaged? Couldn't he have thought up something better? Of course, she'd gone blank trying to explain him and the men. As had always been the case when they'd been younger, he rode his white stallion to her rescue. Still, couldn't he have thought of something else? And, why hadn't she argued it? To keep from looking the fool in Tate's eyes. Or so she told herself.

Since she'd got a vibe from Tate she didn't like, Matt's lie worked in that sense. Mostly. Tate still had flirted with her, and she couldn't figure out if that was his style or whether he was hitting on her. She didn't care for either reason. Nothing in the rules said she had to like every donor.

She opened the door and walked into the building in the direction of her office with Matt hot on her heels.

"Look, Caitlyn," he began, seeming to know the direction of her thoughts. "It was the first thing that came to my mind. I'm sorry. I should've prepared a credible story for any visitors."

She rounded on him. "That was the first thing that came to your mind? How about something like being another donor, an employee, or even a friend? Any of those come to your mind?" She exhaled loudly, knowing she had to move on.

"You didn't want to be alone with him. Did you?"

She laughed. "With a handsome man?" Laughing again, when his shoulders straightened tight and heard his muttered curse, she answered his question, "I just don't like being alone with someone I don't know." She shrugged. "It's a trust thing."

Fortunately, when she was alone with Matt, things were different. The ability to let down her shield existed. She still craved him despite fearing she'd never desire another man. While she wasn't ready to jump into his arms and scream, "Make love to me," something was still there between them. Something solid and loving.

Could she muster the courage to willingly step into his arms, embracing the warmth and safety they promised? The thought sent a shiver down her spine. If she made that leap of faith, would she be able to maintain her composure, or would her anxiety resurface, as it had on two previous dates? She had been overwhelmed in those moments of panic, fleeing from the intimacy offered. But if she faltered again this time, would Matt, with his gentle demeanor and understanding eyes, decide that she was simply too much trouble? Would he ultimately give up on her, leaving her alone in her self-imposed isolation, shattered and questioning her worth? He wasn't physically forcing her. Still, every lingering gaze exchanged between them, along with each gentle touch, was laden with an overwhelming sense of longing and desire that was almost palpable. It was as if each glance and caress spoke volumes of unspoken feelings, creating a charged atmosphere that neither of them could ignore. She longed to reciprocate his deep affections, feeling an intense pull towards him that made her heart flutter. However, a cloud of uncertainty loomed over her thoughts, creating a barrier to her own emotions. She questioned whether she would ever reach a point of readiness to embrace his love fully. That uncertainty weighed heavily on her, casting a shadow of disheartenment over her spirit.

She'd forgiven him and apologized for what she'd said after the incident, and she held no ill will against him for it. He'd confided in her, his voice heavy with regret, that he would never be able to forgive himself for not being there for her. Perhaps, she thought, she could show him the true essence of forgiveness—the profound release it could bring, an opportunity to unburden oneself from the chains of regret. She believed that through understanding and compassion, he might learn to embrace the idea of letting go, discovering the newfound freedom that comes from releasing the past.

He didn't seem surprised by her answer about trust. Maybe he'd figured her all out again. That brought her up straight. Could he tell she had thoroughly enjoyed his touch and missed it when it had been absent? She hoped not. The embarrassment would be too much.

"Well, I'm your shadow now, so you won't have to worry about being alone with scumbags like that."

"He wasn't a scumbag." She had no idea why she needed to come to Tate's rescue even though she really didn't like him. "He was a very nice man who will give Helping Paws money. Money that the organization needs."

"Why didn't he give it to you now?"

Midway through their discussion, Tate's phone had rung, and he told them he needed to get back to— He never said where, and she didn't ask where or why. She'd thought Matt had been about to do it, but she'd turned and implored with him in her gaze to let it go. Instead, they'd scheduled the tour for another day. That seemed just as crucial to Tate as did the company info. She'd come to find that some—a small portion of—rich people were funny about how they spent their money with a charity. But when shopping, they didn't seem to have a discerning bone in their bodies.

Caitlyn turned back toward her office. "He wants a full tour."

"That shouldn't take long. If he really wanted to do it, he'd have stayed."

She whirled on him again and thrust her finger in his face. "Don't you screw this up for me with your male macho bullshit. He isn't the first donor who wants to talk with me and tour the facility first. I'm not one of the big charities where everyone knows everything about them. I'm small potatoes, so we grab onto anything—and anyone—that might share our love for the program and shake out some cash for us."

Seeming to understand, he sighed and gave her an apologetic smile. "I'm sorry. I won't stand in the way again. When he comes back, I'll keep quiet."

Caitlyn dropped her finger and turned back to the

office. *Keep quiet, my ass.*. At least maybe he wouldn't be so hostile. She couldn't afford to lose this donor. One million dollars could go a long way for them. She'd finally be able to expand and hire more trainers and acquire more dogs, resulting in more potential clients getting the help they needed.

Following behind her, his question stopped her in her tracks. "Are you sure he's got a million dollars to give you?"

No, she was never sure of a donation until the check cleared. She couldn't be sure since she didn't have any charitable donation information he might've given or someone to acquire and check them. Her heart nearly sank. What if Tate didn't have the money? Then why would he pull their chain like that? There were plenty of people who donated, and she had no idea if they had that kind of free cash. People surprised her every day. Tate dressed and acted the part. He'd have no reason to be something he wasn't. Still, she'd Google him when she had a free moment. She wouldn't do it in front of Matt because she didn't want him to see that she'd been rattled by Tate and by Matt's big lie.

"I can have Devon check him out."

She whirled on him. "No," she said sharply. "You're here because of Luke. You aren't here to intrude upon my business." That was a stupid thing to say. Based on their bragging about Devon's skills, she could use his help. No. She'd try first, and if she wasn't satisfied, she'd ask for help.

Holding his hands up in a surrender pose, he cracked a smile. "You'd best tell your staff that you're off the market so when he returns, they won't say something wrong to deter his trust in you."

Dammit if he wasn't right. If Matt were still around, she couldn't think of a good way to explain his presence or the lie. "We'll only pretend to be engaged when he's here." She looked deep into his eyes and couldn't understand the emotion flowing through his gaze. It warmed her though.

He closed the short distance between them and pulled her close. She stiffened like a board but wasn't afraid of what he would do to her. Her pulse raced at the contact.

"You're mine," he growled before his lips landed on hers, soft and teasing.

When her lips began to move—against her better judgment—she melted into his embrace. His tongue pushed past her lips and entered her mouth, sending a bolt of lust flashing through her body. Good God. What the hell was wrong with her kissing him like this? She didn't want something between them. Yet, she couldn't stop her own body from responding.

And with their bodies melded into each other, she felt his growing erection and jumped back as if she'd been burned. "No," was all she could force out. She trembled at what could've happened.

Matt uttered an apology, then turned on his heel and left her.

Her eyes watered, and she wiped at them with the back of her hand. She had no reason to cry but felt the overwhelming need to do so. Staunching it, she entered her office and sat down behind the desk. She picked up the select list that Tonya recommended they invite to the small fundraiser and reviewed the names and their past donations to make sure they might be willing to donate again.

The million dollars from Tate would go a long way, but she wouldn't refuse money where she could get it.

Still reeling from Matt's kiss, she hopped from her chair and strode down the hallway and into the training area. Some time with one of the young dogs would be good for her soul. Because Lord knew Matt Hamilton was once right for her soul, and she feared he might be again.

Chapter Twelve

The shower revived him. He hated the heat and humidity of the south and had struggled with it while in college. It didn't seem as bad as his memory though, but still, he just preferred cold and snow. Something they got very little of down here.

He slipped into jeans and then put the earpiece in so he wouldn't be taken by surprise again. Before he could put on his shirt, he stiffened when he heard, "We've got a problem."

Neftali, their strongest sharpshooter—well, second to Jesse—spoke softly as if his voice would carry across any distance outside and give away his location.

"To the east, we've got someone who thinks himself a sniper. That's a decent distance he'd made it to without us seeing him. I'd say he's close to three hundred yards out and just briefly poked his head out of the edge of the woods." He paused. "He's trouble, because I've got trees in the way and can't get a shot off. Give me a minute to move, and get Caitlyn the hell away from that damn window."

Heart pounding, Matt rushed from the bathroom, not sure which window Neftali meant. He found her in the living room and launched himself over the couch, heard the rifle fire and the subsequent sound of glass breaking as he dragged her to the floor, not very gently.

Frantic, he lifted himself as best he could and ran

his hands over her body, checking everywhere for an injury. "Are you hit? Are you hit?" he repeated.

"Was that what I thought it was?" Her breathing was erratic, and her eyes were wide with fear.

"Yes."

She shook, so he leaned back and pulled her into his arms. He'd love to sit up and pull her into his lap, but there was still a shooter out there.

"How did he find me?" she whispered shakily.

"I don't know, but he wants us to take him seriously." In his mind, he couldn't see Ripley as a sniper wannabe. Something didn't feel right.

"Status," he called out but realized he'd come out of the bathroom *sans* microphone and *sans* shirt. "Shit."

When he didn't hear another shot fired—Neftali's shot—concern crept into his bloodstream. Son of a bitch. The shooter would've hit her had he not put his earpiece in when he had and acted. There was just too much area out there for two men to cover. Usually two could work it fine, but not when woods on three sides was a barrier.

"Ken's got him," Neftali stated.

The rapid staccato of his pulse settled until Neftali added, "It's not Ripley."

Fuck! Had Ripley hired someone to kill her? He couldn't think about this threat to her life without wanting to choke someone.

Matt and Caitlyn moved away from the window. Sitting awkwardly, he double-checked her for injuries. He'd figure out how to get up without her noticing his difficulty moving to a standing position.

"Oh my God. Matt, you've been shot!" She pointed to his lower leg.

Seeing the bullet hole in his jeans but knowing it went straight through the material, he said, "I'm fine. It missed me."

But Caitlyn wasn't having any of it. Despite his fighting her off, she groped at the hem of his jeans and pulled the pant leg up a little then stopped and gasped. Her eyes searched his. "Matt?"

He sighed. He'd hoped they'd have this conversation much later after she became more comfortable with him. Wanting to cover himself, he reached for his pants leg and removed it from her hands before sliding it back down. "There's nothing to it. I lost part of my leg while on active duty."

Wide-eyed, she asked, "What happened?"

After almost being shot, she worried about him. Him—not the fact someone just tried to kill her. Maybe it hadn't sunk in yet, and she was diverting the conversation so she didn't have to deal with reality. Yet his life as a leg amputee was about as big a fucking reality as it got.

"Let's talk about it another time. We have a situation here that needs our focus." He stood, no longer caring how awkward he'd looked standing up, and held a hand down to her to aid her in standing. She swayed a second, and his arms shot out to her waist to steady her.

A knock sounded on the door, and he told her to stay back while he checked the peephole. Seeing it was Ken with a pissed-off man decked out in camouflage, he opened the door.

Ken shoved the man into the room toward Matt and away from Caitlyn. Their unwelcome visitor had his hands secured behind his back. "Does he look familiar?" Ken asked Caitlyn.

Please, God, don't let it be tied to Ripley. He wanted to eradicate the man but didn't want her suffering in the meantime.

She gasped and put her hands on her mouth. "Neil Holbrook."

Neil narrowed his eyes at her but didn't speak.

"Do you want to call 911 or take care of him ourselves?" Ken asked Matt, probably to put fear into Neil what "take care of him ourselves" actually meant.

What he wanted to do was rip the asshole to shreds, but he wouldn't be any good to Caitlyn if he were in jail. He needed to know more before they progressed. "Who is Neil Holbrook?"

Seeming to gather her courage, she stood confident, not fearful like when she'd first seen the man. She almost appeared…angry. He'd prefer that emotion to fear, but now he really had to know what this asshole had done.

"He applied to the program, but I denied his application."

"You had no right, bitch," spewed from Neil's mouth.

Matt's automatic reflex was to deck the man, and it felt good watching Neil's head snap back. He wouldn't even give the man the satisfaction of watching him shake off the pain in his knuckles. Caitlyn opened her mouth to speak, her face red, but Matt was faster. "Don't talk to her like that."

"Fuck you," Neil spat at Matt.

Unperturbed by the statement, Matt turned to Ken and nodded. The team leader, toting his firearms and Neil's, walked away and put the phone to his ear to speak with an operator at 911. Since this had nothing to do with Ripley, they'd turn it over to local law enforcement. But they would keep an ear to the ground on what happened with Holbrook. The man proved himself resourceful enough to sneak through their net. The net he'd decided earlier wasn't large enough—case in point. However, the only extra men available were protecting Adam in case Ripley returned for more. He couldn't pull them from her father, not after what Ripley had done to Adam already.

Thank God Neftali had spotted him through his scope. All decked out in camo in the late evening, he'd have been hard to find. Pity that Neftali hadn't had a clean shot, then the events wouldn't have unfolded as they had. And while insignificant to everything happening around them, he hadn't wanted her to discover his injury. Oh, she'd probably want to talk about it, but that was the last thing he wanted to do. He hoped she didn't think him weak because of it. He'd worked hard in physical therapy when he'd gotten his prosthetic. It was a part of him now, and that would be hard to explain since many people throw out the term disabled right off the bat. Somehow, he doubted she would, but he didn't have practice discussing his injury.

Ken turned back to them. "They're on their way." He raised his eyebrows at Matt as if just noticing something. "You might want to put on a shirt or something."

He'd forgotten that he'd rushed from the bathroom without a shirt. With the way Caitlyn looked him up and down, she seemed to realize it also. Her gaze also stopped on his tattoo.

Matt guided Neil to the couch and shoved him

down. "Ken, I'm going to finish dressing. You've got him." He grabbed Caitlyn's arm. "You're coming with me."

She huffed. "No, I'm not." Jerking her arm, she tried to wrench it free from his grasp.

"Yes, you are. I'm not leaving you out here with our unwelcome guest."

"I am not going to the bathroom with you while you dress."

"Good grief. It's just a shirt. Quit protesting and come on." Why the hell was she fighting him? It wasn't like he was dragging her to her doom.

When Neil expelled some expletives her way, she changed her mind and followed him. Entering the small bathroom, she handed him his shirt off the commode and scooted as far away as possible.

Her fragrance drifted to him, and he smiled to know she still wore the same fragrance. One day, in college, they'd laughingly gone down the perfume aisle at a department store where she'd allowed the women who worked there to test different fragrances on her. When she came to this one, she fell in love with it. And when he'd got a whiff, so had he. He'd purchased a large bottle of it on the spot. Over the years, he'd sometimes go to the perfume counter and smell the fragrance to remember her. It was sad, but it'd make him smile at their good memories.

After donning a shirt and his comm system, he turned to her and wondered what was going through her head. She almost looked frightened again, and his gut lurched.

Then she surprised him with a question out of the blue. "I want to hear about that tattoo on your belly. Is that the one you and Brad got?"

Automatically, he looked down, but his stomach was covered with his navy blue T-shirt. He knew what she meant. He just hadn't expected that to be her question. Maybe she'd missed seeing his shower prosthetic leg in the corner. He hadn't had an opportunity to return it to the guest room.

"There's not much to say."

She cocked her head to the left. "I know you didn't have it when I knew you. You were with Brad. There's always a story. He said it was before you went into the Navy."

He didn't want to correct her that she still knew him, so he just pulled up his shirt to show her the tattoo again.

Matt chuckled at the memory of when he'd decided to get the tattoo. "What good tattoo story doesn't start with 'booze was involved?' As Brad said, the night before I shipped out to boot camp, Brad and I went on a bender with friends. I knew it wasn't wise considering I had to be ready to process all day, but when have my twin and I ever done what is wise?" He narrowed his eyes, and his lip quirked. "Don't answer that. Anyhow, I'm not sure how we ended up at the tattoo parlor, but come morning, I woke with a pounding head, my stomach a nauseous ball, and this damn tattoo." He gestured to his stomach.

She'd moved closer to him and reached out to trace the outline of the flaming sun around his belly button. He wasn't pulling down his pants so she could trace what fell below the belt. He'd never survive the touch.

His dick twitched at the tender fingertip outlining his tattoo, and he willed it to halt so it didn't scare her.

"And that's the same one Brad got?"

He forced his focus on her words and not what her hand could do to pleasure him. "Yes. Even in our inebriated state, we remained twins."

Then, as if realizing what she'd been doing, she jumped back and removed her finger from his skin. "I'm not surprised Brad lured you into doing something you wouldn't have done by yourself. He was always a bit wilder than you."

His back stiffened. His twin might be a major pain in the ass, but he never pushed Matt out of his comfort zone. Even drunk Brad knew the boundaries. "It was mutual," he said before leaving the bathroom so she didn't see she'd been right and Brad had led the charge. In reality, they'd allowed one of the chicks with Brad to choose the tattoo. The worst thing was it hadn't been the stupidest thing they'd ever done together. Although Caitlyn knew most of their adventures. "I heard sirens, so the cavalry should be here in a minute or two. Please stick with me and always keep me between you and Neil. Got that?"

She nodded but didn't speak. Had he offended her with his comment about Brad? Sure it'd been Brad's idea, but he'd wanted something to remember his twin by, which seemed appropriate at the time.

Brad took that moment to knock on the bathroom door. "Are you two okay in there?"

Okay, how? Okay with the evening events that left a hole in his pants? No. Okay with Caitlyn needing protection? No. Okay with each other in a confined space? Not really. They were only okay with the fact that the men apprehended the shooter so he couldn't harm Caitlyn.

After a nod to Caitlyn, they exited the bathroom to an angry Brad.

"Why the fuck didn't you wake me?"

With Matt close to Caitlyn during the day, Brad remained close to the house during the evening to allow Matt to sleep peacefully about as peacefully as he could.

"We were just about to do that," Matt told him.

"Were either of you hurt?"

"No, we're fine," Caitlyn stated, forgetting or ignoring the shot near his calf.

Something warned him she hadn't forgotten. He prepared himself for the explanation he'd have to give her.

Brad looked back and forth between them and drew in his brow. "The sheriff is here."

Good. It was time to get rid of this unexpected threat to his woman. Yeah, he said she was his. Let her fight it all she wanted. Even though they'd come together under unfortunate circumstances, he knew in his heart that she was his woman. Time hadn't changed how he felt. She'd learn that soon enough.

Chapter Thirteen

With the sheriff gone with Holbrook in custody, and Brad positioned outside to help cover the blind spot that Holbrook had snuck through, Matt sat on the couch sipping iced tea, a little calmer than he'd been earlier. Caitlyn sat as far away from him as possible. It made him want to laugh after thinking about the kiss they'd shared.

"Thank you for saving me from being shot by Neil," she said quietly.

A soothing warmth enveloped him, spreading gently through his chest as he absorbed her words. "How's your head and your shoulder?" Although he had made a conscious effort to be as gentle as possible during the chaotic moments, there simply hadn't been enough time to thoroughly shield her head from the unforgiving impact with the floor. The very thought of inflicting any harm upon her caused a deep ache in his heart, sending it plummeting to his gut like a heavy lead ball. Fortunately, despite the close call, the bullet had miraculously missed her entirely, allowing a glimmer of relief to push aside his overwhelming concern over her minor injury.

She touched the back of her head and winced. "I'll be okay."

They sat in an uncomfortable, stilted silence, a tension hanging between them that hadn't been there before. The air felt thick and heavy, each second stretching painfully, amplifying the unease that settled between them. He shifted slightly in his chair, glancing at her with unease, disliking the awkwardness that now filled the space. He didn't like it one bit; it gnawed at him, making his stomach twist in a way he couldn't ignore. "What's going on in your head?"

Shrugging, she said, "Nothing."

Sure, and he'd love to buy swampland in Louisiana. Yet, he couldn't tell if she was bothered by Holbrook...him being there...or the lack of his lower leg. Something told him the latter was on her mind, even though it should be the last thing.

Would she treat him differently now? Some people did—treated him like a disabled person or someone incapable of doing regular things—and he didn't want that from her. He didn't want anything that might allow her to pull back on their relationship.

He decided to grab the reins and get it over with. This would be the only person he'd share the story with outside his immediate family and HIS team. Not so much because most of it was classified, but for how he knew they'd see him...treat him. He had been in charge, after all.

"I lost my leg below the knee when I was in Pakistan."

Caitlyn appeared relieved he'd brought up the topic, but her relief turned to confusion. "I didn't know we had men in Pakistan."

Stoically, Matt told her, "We have small contingents of men almost everywhere. It's just not advertised." The mission was shrouded in secrecy and classified at the highest levels of government. A small team had been assigned to aid a pivotal figure whom the United States was keen to interrogate. Their goal was to ensure his safe departure from the country, but the operation was fraught with complications. Simply landing a helicopter in the area where the man lived to extract him was not a workable option. It would draw too much attention and risk compromise. This individual, however, was not just any informant; intelligence reports showed he possessed critical information that could lead to significant breakthroughs in their operations. Matt couldn't tell her that, though. Not only was it part of why the mission was classified, but so was the man's identity. She'd never let it go if he became vague on the reason, so he tried to skim over it without her seeing through him.

"I can't tell you what we were doing. In fact, I'm pretty sure I wasn't supposed to tell you Pakistan."

Her eyes were earnest and imploring. "I can keep the secret."

It wasn't that he didn't trust her. He just believed in OPSEC—Operations Security. That meant he couldn't give her much, but he had to give her something. *Like you fucking blew it and gave her Pakistan, asshole?* Thinking before he said each word, he gave her an overview. "Well, my team and I were trying to leave the country, and our vehicle broke down. It's not like there was a repair shop at hand, so we started walking and felt good about our egress when someone traveling with the team stepped on a land mine."

The images of what had happened haunted him day and night.

From the beginning, their informant had displayed a stubborn resistance, a particularly revealing attitude considering the circumstances—they had come with the explicit intention of rescuing him. Instead of accepting their help, he insisted on moving beyond their reach, pushing ahead with reckless abandon that put him in even greater danger. Recognizing the potential for disaster, the team instinctively formed a tighter circle around him, aiming to detain him for his safety. It was widely known that he had reluctantly yielded to the pressure from the Americans, which further complicated the situation.

Yet, instead of successfully reining him in, the attempted intervention had unforeseen consequences. Their world would be irrevocably altered as a result of this pivotal moment. The dynamics of their mission shifted dramatically, leaving the team grappling with the aftereffects of a choice they never expected having to make. It was clear that the attempt to secure him had spiraled beyond their control, setting into motion a chain of events that would change everything for them in ways they couldn't yet comprehend.

He swallowed hard against the memory of not only his loss but also the loss the team sustained. "Two of my teammates lost their lives." So did the idiot who'd stepped on the mine, but she didn't need to know that. "Another team member and I, who'd been close to the blast, lost limbs." Matt had never felt so much pain before. The long wait for evac had been agonizing. Thank the fuck they'd had morphine in a medic pack because it wasn't an easy feat for the bird to get there and evacuate them from that hellhole when they'd been trying to be stealthy. He hadn't wanted to be dosed at first. He'd wanted to retain his senses to take care of his team, but it had hurt so fucking bad, and looking down and not seeing a foot had put his emotions in a blender. His second in command told him that he had the team and that Matt needed to take the damn shot. After the morphine had kicked in, he'd been glad for the forcefulness of his second in command.

During his retelling of that fateful mission, Caitlyn slid down the couch toward him and then put her slender hand on his thigh in a supportive gesture. The heat seared through his skin and settled him somewhat.

"Oh, Matt."

He removed her hand and surged up from the couch at the tone of her voice. "I don't want your pity, Caitlyn." Anger laced his veins. Anger at believing she'd be different. Maybe she once had been, but apparently not today.

Breathing heavily, he stood with his back to her as if that would erase how she'd reacted, how *he'd* reacted.

He heard her quietly standing a moment before her hand touched his shoulder. He wanted to be mean and shrug her touch off, but in truth, he liked her touch…craved it because it grounded him. It always had. "You misunderstood. That wasn't pity, Matt. I was just heartbroken to hear what happened to you and your team."

"They were good men," he croaked through heavy emotion. He wondered if the team had blamed him for the loss. He'd been the officer in charge—like always. But he hadn't controlled the man they'd been sent to retrieve. Something about how the man acted had bothered Matt, but he'd never find out what it was.

She wrapped her arms around his waist with loving care and squeezed tightly.

Her touch was a balm to his tormented soul. For a few moments, he did nothing, not wanting to scare her off. Then he covered her arms around his waist with his own and relaxed. Her body next to his helped him combat the horrendous scenes that played in his mind.

Brad entering the room startled them both, and they jumped apart like teenage sweethearts who'd been caught doing something they shouldn't. Brad shook his head at them. "Hey, brat, what do you want to do about the window? It's not in danger of shattering tonight, so we can leave it until you can call someone to fix it tomorrow, or if you have some wood, we can cover it. We could run to town to get some, but I think everything's probably closed by now."

Caitlyn stared at the small hole in her window for a good minute before she responded to Brad. "I don't have wood to cover it, so we'll have to leave it uncovered. Are you sure it won't shatter?"

Matt shook his head. "No, it won't break tonight. You're in trouble when it starts spider webbing out." He looked directly at her. "But you need to have it replaced tomorrow."

"I wonder how much bulletproof glass costs?" she murmured.

"It's pricey and doubtful you'd get it tomorrow," Brad told her, playing along with a smile. He turned to Matt. "Neftali is beating himself up for not spotting Holbrook until it was too late."

Usually, he'd say good and let him stew in it. But not in this instance. They gave him too much area to cover. "Make sure to tell him it wasn't his fault. We gave him a lot of indiscernible ground to cover."

With a shrug, Brad said, "Won't matter."

"I'll talk with him tonight. Is everything else okay?"

"Yeah, the men are changing out now."

Matt looked at his watch. "Why so late?"

"They overlapped and walked the woods closest to the house to see if anyone else might be hiding out."

"It's dark outside," Caitlyn said incredulously.

Both men chuckled. Matt gave her a wink. "They still need to do their job in the dark."

"You're right," she murmured as if she didn't really want to tell him that he was right and she was wrong.

Had this been an argument between them and she'd said that, he'd have reacted differently. Yes, he'd be smug about it. But this wasn't, and her defeated voice made an impression in his heart that he couldn't hide.

In one swift movement, he was in front of her, so close he could smell her perfume. He opened his arms, and she fell into them. When wetness hit his T-shirt, he nodded toward the door. Understanding, Brad quietly left them alone.

Holding her tightly, he rubbed his hand up and down her back soothingly.

Among sniffles and hiccups, she asked, "Why? Why me?"

Was there a proper way to answer that question? She was good and wholesome but had the unfortunate luck of two men after her who were bent on revenge. Thank the fuck they'd captured the one they hadn't been aware existed. If they'd have left her alone, she'd been seriously injured or dead at the hands of Neil Holbrook. He hoped no more surprises lay in wait for them. "I don't know. All I know is that evil exists, and it can impact good people."

"If you hadn't been here…," she started, changing her flow. "Thank you for saving my life." That brought fresh tears, and he wondered how soaked his shirt would be. He also considered if she noticed how tightly she clung to him.

When she looked up, he gazed into her blue-green eyes and fell in love again with her compassion, warmth, and heart for the man he was. It brought back vivid memories of the first time he saw her on the bustling Ole Miss campus. During her freshman orientation, it was a day filled with excitement and nerves. Yet, she appeared utterly lost amidst the throngs of new students and the confusing layout of the university. As he caught her gaze, something magical happened. It was as if time stood still, and he found himself irresistibly drawn in by her warmth and vulnerability. Without hesitation, he stepped forward, offering his assistance. He guided her toward her classroom, completely disregarding the fact that he would be late to his class. The mere thought of being near her, of helping her navigate those uncertain moments, filled him with a sense of purpose that he had never known before.

Unable to resist the magnetic pull of her presence, he leaned down slowly, feeling a rush of anticipation in his chest. As he drew closer, the warmth of her breath enveloped him, igniting a spark within. With a tenderness that mirrored the moment's significance, he brushed his lips softly against hers, savoring the sweetness of their connection as the world around them faded away.

Chapter Fourteen

Starting at where their lips met, pleasure exploded throughout Caitlyn's body. Gently, Matt's warm, damp lips covered hers. His kiss—hesitant and cautious, almost too careful—seared its way to her soul. And when his tongue entered her mouth, she forgot her fear of a man's touch...of a man's nearness...and of being alone with a man in general.

As their lips and tongues tangled, she slid her arms up his body and around his neck, eagerly tugging him closer. She couldn't get close enough, and that was so unlike the woman she'd become. Did she enjoy his touch and kiss because they'd once been lovers? One thing was for sure, she'd never allowed a date to kiss her with the heat of the kiss she found herself locked into now.

Her heart raced furiously, the adrenaline coursing through her veins igniting a thrilling sense of excitement. Every nerve in her body tingled in anticipation. Without a moment's pause, she surrendered herself to him, allowing the weight of her inhibitions to lift, embracing the moment completely. It felt as though time stood still, enveloping them in an intoxicating atmosphere of shared desire. Their tongues battled, and she felt almost limp with desire. She'd thought she had lost it and would never find it again..

His mouth left hers and then blazed a path down

her chin and under her jawbone to the sensitive spot below her ear. She shivered under the assault on her senses. She'd forgotten how intense his kisses could be and the effect on her body and soul.

A moan slipped from her lips, and she wished she could call it back. She shouldn't be loving him like she was. She'd pushed Matt from her life when she hadn't even wanted to live. She'd blamed him when it wasn't his fault. After all that, he'd shown up to protect her when she needed it the most. Christ, her mind was so screwed up, and his passion-filled lips were the reason.

Her need for him tingled in her most private place, and she wanted to jump for joy at the feeling only Matt invoked. When he pulled her closer, his hands on her backside, she stiffened, but he took her lips with his and coaxed her relaxation into his touch.

Breaking the kiss that left them both breathing heavily, Matt leaned his forehead to her. "Oh, Caitlyn, I want to make love to you."

Before she could think, she whispered, "I want it too." And she did. Her body yearned for the familiarity of his touch. She hadn't been saving herself after the rape. She'd just been waiting for the right man to come along. *Matt.* It was always Matt. He'd been her first…her only outside of that bastard who'd touched her under threat of her life. But she wouldn't allow that memory to resurface while she was with Matt like this.

Cautiously, as if he thought she might break, he clasped her hand and turned toward the hallway.

Her heart throbbed inside her chest, the sound reverberating in her ears, blocking out all noise and common sense. If he spoke to her as he led the way to her bedroom, she couldn't make out what he said.

After pulling her into her bedroom, he closed the door, hesitated for a moment, and then locked it, keeping everyone out. She appreciated that action because she didn't want an unwanted intruder, even by accident.

Almost nervously, he returned to her, and before reaching out, he asked softly, "Are you sure?"

Was she? She surely wanted to feel the love she knew he could give. That had to mean yes. Didn't it? Her mind lighted on the fact that men filled her home. That didn't make it feel very private, even with the door secured. With a worried look clouding his face, she decided she'd best answer with what she wanted, not her fears. Fears only made her weak and she was not weak any longer. "Yes."

"Thank God," he said on an exhale while relaxing his shoulders as if the world's weight had been on them.

She smiled at that. It endeared him even more to her.

Next, Matt placed both of his hands on her face, cradling it, before he moved in, tilted her head, and kissed her until her toes curled. Almost literally curled.

He gently broke the kiss, just long enough to tug their shirts off, revealing his tattoo. As he did so, a wicked grin spread across his face, a teasing spark in his eyes that seemed to touch something deep within her. He leaned in again before she could catch her breath, capturing her lips with a fervent kiss that ignited a fire between them, drawing her closer as they lost themselves in the moment.

As he reached for her jeans, an unwanted flash entered her mind. That bastard had ripped her jeans down when he'd.... *No!* She closed her eyes tight to ward off the images. She had to forget it. She would not allow the memories to ruin what she had, or used to have, with Matt. She still loved him as much as she had when she'd first met him at Ole Miss.

Noticing her stiffening, Matt stopped his exploring hand and broke the kiss. "Are you sure you're ready for this?"

It almost sounded like he knew she hadn't been able to live with another man's touch. But how could he know?

"I'm fine." To prove it, she removed her shoes, stripped the rest of her clothes, and dropped them in a pile beside her, where her shirt had landed after Matt had discarded it.

Before undressing, he took a long moment to search her eyes. When Matt dropped his pants, she looked at his prosthetic leg. Her heart broke for his losing part of a limb. Then her breath hitched as he dropped his underwear and his huge erection popped forward.

She took a deep breath and swallowed hard, feeling the weight of her own determination settle in her chest. This moment was pivotal. She knew she could do this, not just because it was a yearning deep within her heart but also as a testament to her strength and resilience. She wanted to show the world—and herself—that despite her hardships, triumph was still within her grasp, and she could rise above the shadows of her past.

A very naked Matt closed the short distance between them and reached a hand out to gently touch her breast.

Even though the amazing sensation increased the burning need between her thighs, she unconsciously stiffened.

Matt halted and frowned. "Maybe this wasn't a good idea."

Her heart plummeted to her stomach. It was a damn good idea. "I'm sorry. I'm fine. That felt incredible."

Believing her, or just pretending to, he raised both hands and placed them on her breasts. He also leaned down and kissed her like there was no tomorrow, pulling her mind away from his touch to the gloriousness of his mouth.

The movement of his lips relaxed her, keeping her from freaking out at his sensual touch. He slowly backed her to the bed, and she obligingly crawled to the center, a little self-conscious of her naked body on display. It had been a long time since they'd been naked together, and she'd changed some. Had he noticed? If so, it didn't seem to stop his desire for her.

Instead of crawling up on top of her, he kissed the top of her foot and then moved to her calves. When he hit her thighs, she fought the urge to stop him. She won in keeping her body relaxed, wanting him.

Moving up her body, he kissed the top of her mound before moving to her stomach. Then, his body was covering her.

Oh my God. No! In a panic, she shoved him away, her lower body squirming as she tried to escape the weight on her. His actions triggered painful memories of her attack, evoking a primal instinct to flee. She needed to break free from him.

Immediately, Matt hopped off the bed without a word.

With erratic breathing, she curled into a ball and

tried apologizing, but no words came forth. Terror ran through her veins, turning her into a useless piece of mush.

Matt ran his fingers through his short-cropped hair. "Hell, I'm sorry, Caitlyn."

Why the hell was he apologizing? He'd done nothing wrong except make her desire him.

To recover from her embarrassment, she alighted from the bed and began to dress while Matt stood still as if a physical barrier separated them. "I'm sorry. I want this, but while I know it's your hands, the feeling of that monster touching me comes back."

"I think it's incredibly brave of you to admit that, Caitlyn. Believe me, I'd never want you to feel that way again."

"I fear—" She swallowed. "I fear it'll be worse if you try to enter me."

He softly swore. "I have an idea," he said while she twisted her bra around after clasping it. The same bra her shaking hands could barely fasten.

"What?" She pulled the straps over her shoulders and settled her breasts in the cups. Couldn't he put something on? Against her better judgment, her eyes sought out his erection.

"Now, don't get mad," he said and raised his hands to ward off her response.

That only made people defensive when someone mentioned it. She tensed up at his potential response.

"I spoke to a psychiatrist a few months back."

Did he have PTSD or something else he hid well? Why else would he seek out a mental health professional? He was damn near perfect, as far as she could tell. Granted, they hadn't been together—this time—for long. He could've changed and had deep, dark secrets she didn't want to know.

"It's okay, Matt. You don't need to share what you spoke with someone about."

His spellbinding gaze held her hostage. Standing there in her jeans and bra, she felt exposed, which she found odd because moments before, she reveled in the idea of their getting naked together.

"No. I think I should share because it was about you."

What the hell? That threw her for a loop.

"I blew off everything the doc advised me about when I started kissing you." He walked to her and pulled her hand into his, intertwining their fingers. "Come here." He tugged her toward the bed, but she remained frozen to the spot. He was still naked, and while she wanted him, she obviously couldn't handle it.

"Trust me," he beseeched her.

She shook her head. "I can't. I just can't do it." It had already been humiliating enough the first time; now he wanted to try it again. What the hell was wrong with him?

He sighed and dropped her hand before walking the short distance to the bed and sprawling across it. Reaching for her brass headboard, he grabbed a post with both hands and spoke. "My understanding was there might be a control issue and that you needed to be the one to dictate the levels we enjoy."

Startled, something just occurred to her and it gnawed at her insides. "You said you did this months ago. How did you know we'd be seeing each other?"

He flashed a grin that made her want to get naked and join him. "I didn't know, but I always like to be prepared." He shrugged as best he could with his arms above his head.

So he'd planned to find her no matter what. That must've been why he'd started spending time with her dad. Her heart expanded at the thought. Yet her fear of a man's touch—even Matt's intimate touch—warred with her determination to defeat it, and at this moment, she wasn't sure which emotion would win. She prayed she'd win the battle, but after what had just happened, it was too soon to say if her body would sway in her favor.

"So the doc suggested allowing you full control over how far we go or don't go together. She gave more advice, but I gathered it all meant I need to be submissive until you're comfortable." He smiled. "Of course, I could've misunderstood her completely. I never asked for clarification on that specific issue."

Mildly shocked, she asked, "You? Submissive? I don't see it." In all the years of their lovemaking, he'd been the typical alpha male. Oh, he'd let her have some control now and again, but he'd never relaxed enough to be labeled "Submissive."

"For you, Caitlyn, I'd be damn near anything." He quickly went on to say, "You get to do the touching and decide what we will and won't do. It'll be damn hard not to touch you, but I'll keep my hands to myself. This time," he slyly added.

"So what I'm hearing is that you expected me to have trouble doing this?" She obviously had, but she didn't like the idea that he planned for it. Although he did plan for it turned her into a puddle at his feet.

"I planned for several contingencies." He winked at her. Winked, for Christ's sake. "How about you join me on the bed now?"

She worried her lower lip with her teeth. How could she still allow what happened to her to dictate her life? Her love life? If she found she couldn't do the act, would he leave her after she was safe? Whoa. When did she want him to stay after his job was completed?

The thing was, Caitlyn was still a little turned on with want for him. Maybe since him crawling on her brought her meltdown, her being on top of him, without his moving, she could do the act. Maybe. Of course, she wouldn't know until she positioned herself near him on the bed. She had to trust he'd keep his hands wrapped around her headboard posts, because she didn't have kinky things like rope and handcuffs. Those things always appeared in Brad's bragging. She guessed she could make use of a bandana, but she doubted her tying skills. Either the knot would fly open if he moved his wrists or it'd have to be cut off his person.

Hesitantly she stepped to the bed and sat on the edge ever so gently as if it would explode if she sat wrong. She kept one foot grounded on the carpeted floor, just in case she needed to bolt.

"I promise I won't touch, so you can come closer to me."

The heat in his gaze almost mesmerized her, and thankfully it drew her to him. She took that step of lifting her foot from the floor, and power flooded her veins. It was a heady feeling that moved her forward.

Caitlyn scanned his naked body and gulped when she saw he still held an erection standing at attention. She couldn't help but appreciate his finely shaped body. He'd expanded his chest and arms since she had last seen him naked in college. And, his leg, or lack thereof a whole leg, still brought tears to her eyes at his loss.

"Caitlyn, if my leg bothers you, we can pull a sheet over it. But, know this, you're going to have to get used to how I am."

She turned and captured his gaze, the emotion there shooting an arrow into her heart. It sounded like he meant long-term. But that couldn't be, because she wasn't leaving Helping Paws and he had a business back in Baltimore. Their lives were so different, and she didn't imagine he'd give up his job, just like she wouldn't hers. It was a hopeless, silly daydream that he'd bring all the joy and love back into her life and be with her forever.

She tried to smile but felt it failed to convince him she was okay. With her eyes still watery, she responded, "There's nothing wrong with what I see. My heart just aches for what you endured."

To forestall any conversation on that topic, she tentatively reached her hand out and lightly touched his muscular chest. Matt stiffened for a moment when her fingers traced the outline of a round scar. A bullet wound? What had this man suffered during his time in the military?

When no feelings of the need to flee turned up, she slid her index finger across his upper torso, circling around his nipples. Matt had always been a bit sensitive there, and she'd always teased him during foreplay.

Normal. So far, things felt normal, as they had been before the rape. Except Matt never laid this still. That might take some getting used to, but in the interim, she'd take advantage.

Gliding her finger down, she circled the blazing sun around his belly button tattoo. She'd never been big on tattoos, but she loved this one on him. She was also surprised he didn't have any from his days in the Navy. Didn't SEALs get big tattoos to show off? Then again, Matt never was a show-off. Brad took those honors.

She turned to his face and almost wanted to laugh. His eyes were closed tightly, and he had a near death-grip on the bars. Matt had always spoiled her when they'd been a couple, but he'd never gone to this extent to help her overcome her fears. She still couldn't believe he'd gone so far as to ask for professional assistance so that he could help her. Love filled her heart at the thought.

It was little things like that that made her glad she'd chosen Matt when both he and Brad had asked her out. Behavior like this showed she'd chosen the perfect twin for her.

It took her a moment to realize Matt had opened his eyes and looked straight at her, and her hand slid to his hard-on. Some things just felt so natural to her, and she didn't want to run while touching him. She held his gaze and rubbed her hand up and down his erection. She gauged the length and speed of her movements to the tightening of his jaw and the fire burning in his eyes.

Connecting with him, she reveled in knowing she was enjoying a sexual act more than she had in eight years. And she didn't feel panicked or afraid. Maybe it was because he wasn't on top of her. But she wanted him on top of her, driving his erection to her core, but not yet. It was too much too soon.

When he groaned, she grinned in delight, pride encouraging her to keep going. She was doing that to him, making him enjoy the sensations instead of him being the one to do the pleasing. Since it was her turn to pleasure, she turned from his sizzling gaze to look at his erection in her hand. She slid down the bed and bent over his crotch, her hair whispering over his body. She could do this. She would do this. She'd give her best and fight any demons that tried to ruin it for them.

Another groan sounded, and she thought he might have a tough time living up to the rules in a minute or two.

To tease and please, she slowly licked his length underneath, making sure she circled her tongue on the tip, licking up his precum.

"Dammit, Caitlyn," he rasped through heavy breaths.

She ignored him and took his erection in her mouth to the back of her throat.

His pelvis lifted to bring him deeper. She adjusted to accept more of him. For the next few minutes, she moved her mouth and hand in a steady rhythm that seemed to agree with Matt. He groaned and cursed many times, so she knew she'd retained the knowledge of how to make love to him this way.

"Caitlyn, if you don't stop, I'm going to come."

Was he an idiot? That was her purpose. Maybe he worried it would frighten her. Besides, she didn't desire to try anything else sexual. Not today anyway.

Reaching out to clasp his tight balls in her hand, she massaged the tender flesh and watched his breathing become erratic and his white knuckles grasp the headboard. It only took one more minute for her effort to pay off. When he came, she swallowed everything he gave and then licked the head clean.

What she didn't do was bring up him calling out how much he loved her when he came.

Chapter Fifteen

Thoroughly embarrassed and ready to bury her head in the sand, Caitlyn couldn't believe what she'd done the day before. She'd freaked when Matt's body covered hers—really freaked, as in thinking she would be raped again—and then she'd given him a blow job. Thoroughly confused about her behavior, afterward she'd declined his offer to spend the night together—only to hold each other, as he'd promised. Even with the power that had infused her when she was in charge of the situation, it wasn't enough to sleep with a man. Although she wanted to with every fiber of her being, she feared she wasn't ready for the intimacy he offered.

She agonized about what he'd said when he'd orgasmed. She didn't think he realized the words had slipped from his lips. Had it just been a habit for him to cry out that he loved her? He had in the past when they'd been together. Maybe he'd changed and said that to any woman who pleasured him. She mentally shrugged, doubting the latter was accurate, but she couldn't discount it either. She didn't know this Matt well, even though he seemed the same to her. It was a well-known fact that appearances could be deceiving. Yet Matt had never had a deceiving bone in his body. From all she'd discovered so far, that hadn't changed.

Caitlyn knew she still loved him, but they were virtual strangers to the persons they were today. When they'd dated, he'd been barely an adult, but today he was a full-grown man. She suspected he was still an alpha, which made what he did for her last night even more intriguing and unnerving.

In need of soothing her frayed nerves, she decided to work with the dogs. While she didn't have a service dog—or truly need one—the dogs kept her going when fear and doubt crowded her mind. And today she was fearful that she'd fallen into a hopeless situation. Had Matt's attempt to help rehabilitate her meant more than just rehabilitation?

"I'm going to work with the dogs for a bit," she told her ever-present shadow over her shoulder.

"I'm right behind you," Matt informed her unnecessarily. "But first, let me make sure it's clear. We don't need another Holbrook situation."

No, they didn't need one. She'd never have thought Neil would go that far. He may have threatened her when she rejected his application, but while she'd worried, she'd felt it was simply him reacting and blowing off steam. No matter the result of her declining him, she was glad she hadn't approved him in the first place. A dog was not what the veteran needed. He needed psychiatric counseling and probably even medicine. Quite possibly lots of medicine. And, of course, a prison cell. One of her dogs would have never thrived with him.

Matt stopped her from exiting her home. "Are you wearing that?" he asked incredulously as he eyed her critically from head to toe.

She glanced down at the cutoff jeans and a plaid shirt that she had tied at the waist. Her white Converse tennis shoes topped off the outfit. What was wrong with it? "Of course I am. We don't get visitors on Sunday, so I like to be comfortable."

He grumbled, "Those shorts are too short."

Laughing at his audacity, she shot back, "For whom? I'm quite fine with them and I'm the one who's wearing them."

Matt narrowed his eyes at her. "Someone's just full of sass this morning."

Caitlyn laughed at him, harder than she'd already laughed at the situation. Something inside her changed in a positive way. What he'd said didn't bother her. She rather enjoyed getting to the calm, level-headed man he'd become. Turning to the door, she gave an exaggerated wiggle of her behind in the shorts he obviously wasn't a fan of. She'd have to put this pair on the top of her pile of shorts, so in the future, she'd always grab them first. She smiled. Maybe she was full of sass this morning. And she liked it.

To bother him even more, she looked over her shoulder as she strutted to the front door and smiled brightly, noticing his eyes glued to her rear. "Are you coming?"

Matt swore under his breath, but she heard every word and felt his presence close to her back. Shocking her, he grabbed her forearm and spun her toward him. "Me first," he ground out through a clenched jaw.

Since she'd promised to always listen to him about protection, she didn't balk at his going out first, except that he could draw a bullet. That thought nearly panicked her. She didn't want anyone hurt because of her, and especially not Matt. She wanted to push past him, but she kept her promise. She'd just silently pray he didn't get hurt.

Given the all-clear, they walked to the training area, and she asked, "Do you think this is still necessary? It's obvious Luke hasn't figured out where I live. A team on Daddy is a must, but here"—she spread her arm to encompass the area around them—"is clear."

"If he really wants to find you, he will. And he could already know and just be working on how to get to you since he'll see me with you. Plus, one of the men tries to remain visible for everyone to see."

A chill spread over her, leaving goosebumps in its wake. She rubbed her arms to stave off the feeling of being hunted. Part of her wanted to cuddle up in a corner and rock until Luke Ripley was no longer a threat. The other part of her had her stiffening her spine because she wouldn't let that asshole ruin her life any more than his family already had. That part of her won out, and she trudged forward with purpose—to survive and show the Ripley men that she was in charge of her life.

They entered the converted barn and bypassed the office and break area. Caitlyn informed Tonya and Rick, who'd come in to work this Sunday since they were close to releasing four dogs, that she'd be testing the dogs. They smiled and nodded, as her showing up and administering surprise tests wasn't unusual. Only today, she did it to clear her mind from her actions of the previous evening, not just for the new handlers' sake.

When Matt stayed attached to her hip, she whirled to him. "You can wait in the break room if you'd like."

"It's okay. I'd like to watch and learn what you do."

She considered it for a moment. Since she wasn't

training, his being there could help. The dogs had to work with a distraction. "Okay."

"What are you going to do?" he asked as she released Cooper from his large kennel.

The dog obediently followed her to a spot where she'd have enough room to work. On her way to the kennel, she'd picked up some items with which to train.

"We train them depending upon the owner's needs. Any dog could be paired with a new handler—owner—who is wheelchair bound or has difficulty bending, so a simple command of 'Get it' means a great deal." Cooper's owner fell into the latter category with a back injury.

"Get it?"

"Watch." She let a money clip fall from her hand. "Cooper, get it."

Matt watched in amazement as the dog picked up the item and placed it in her hand.

Caitlyn tossed a cup on the ground. "Cooper, get it." Again, the dog performed flawlessly.

Beaming a proud smile at him, she said, "See?"

"That's amazing." He grinned in what appeared to be excitement. "He'll do that for anything?"

"Pretty much. It has to fit in his mouth, of course."

"May I try?"

"Sure. Take out your wallet and try."

He did and laughed out loud when the dog performed the simple task that can be so important to a handler. The deepness and obvious heartiness of it wove around her in a soft cocoon of warmth.

She'd missed his laughing, although his voice seemed to have deepened since she'd seen him last. She liked it—a lot.

"Why don't you use fetch as the command? Isn't that what most people use?" he asked curiously.

"Fetch usually involves them leaving the owner's side to get something. That's more like when a ball is thrown at a distance. Besides, we're reserving the fetch command for hunting."

"Hunting? You teach them to hunt?" he asked with unveiled surprise.

Caitlyn shook her head. "Not at the moment, but we've had a couple of requests to do that. If it keeps the veteran living as close to a normal life as they had in the past, we take it seriously. The dogs are quite capable, but it's not an easy undertaking, as the training is extensive since we still must take in the veteran's limitations."

Matt shook his head. "Amazing."

His praise made her heart beat faster, and her body welcomed the joy that rippled through her. That brought her back to where she'd begun the morning. Did she feel embarrassed or empowered? She felt both, but Matt's presence this morning had flipped most of that embarrassment away. He hadn't treated her differently, which she appreciated. It also told her he wanted to be the man to help her back into the world of sex. She mentally shook her head. Maybe she was imagining it because the fanciful thought balanced her.

Over the next few hours, they laughed while she worked with Cooper, Bella, Sadie, and Gabe, who were almost ready for their new handlers. Matt dove in to learn commands and how to train a dog to answer to one. His genuine interest surprised her. It also pleased her.

She would miss him when he returned to

Baltimore. He would leave no matter how much she wished it wasn't so. To salvage their hearts, she'd make sure he did. She was hopeless at a relationship if she couldn't abide a man's touch while making love. Matt, or any man, wouldn't live with just a blow job while he couldn't touch for long.

If she felt deep within her heart that she could never provide him with anything more than what she had already given, then it was clear that he needed to leave her life. The weight of unfulfilled promises and the emptiness of potential would only create a chasm between them that neither could bridge. Realizing this truth, she understood that holding on would only cause further pain.

Why did that thought feel so torturous this time?

Chapter Sixteen

Matt had truly enjoyed himself with Caitlyn and the canines. He'd seen service dogs in passing but had no clue they could be of such value to their handler. If taught the task, they could even interrupt nightmares their new handler might experience. He just kept repeating "amazing" because he couldn't think of a better word for all he'd learned in that short time.

When they put Sadie in her kennel, Rick interrupted them to let them know they had a guest. Both he and Caitlyn stiffened. His radar went up, and his stomach clenched. Didn't she say no one visited on Sunday? She certainly wasn't dressed to accept visitors. Hell, when she'd bent over a time or two, he saw part of her bare butt cheek, which had him wondering if she'd gone commando. He imagined that wasn't the image she wanted to be portrayed of her as the head of Helping Paws.

She locked the kennel and turned to Rick. "Who is it?"

"Tate Hart."

For some reason, red-hot rage seized him and almost tossed his common sense into a blender. He didn't like the guy, but, against his better judgment, he'd promised to be nice. After he'd settled his rage, the green-eyed monster immediately took its place. "You're going to change first, aren't you?" He said it as a question but meant it more like a demand. Tate didn't need to see her bare legs or her belly when she lifted her arms, and the shirt followed.

She looked again at her outfit, just like she'd done before they left her house. "It's not what I'd normally greet a potential donor in, but I don't see anything wrong with it."

He snorted. She had to be joking. "There's a lot wrong with it," he declared. "Did you know I saw your bare ass cheeks more than once? And they barely covered your…" He felt the heat seer his face in embarrassment at having this conversation. "…your private parts when you bent over."

Her face flushed flaming red. He hadn't meant to embarrass her, only to tell her why she shouldn't wear that outfit around another man. He'd been upset about Rick seeing her like that, but she'd explained that she wasn't on Rick's sexual radar. Matt didn't care about the man's sexuality but doubted—gay or straight—any red-blooded male wouldn't appreciate her assets in that outfit. In fact, he'd have to abscond with the outfit after she undressed and keep it for a fantasy roleplay or something just for the two of them. He liked the country girl getup on her—way too much.

Not for the first time that morning, he covertly shifted his thickening erection. Damn, that woman drove him nuts without even trying. Just seeing her toned legs, looking a mile long with those shorts, did it to him. The thought of them wrapped around him when he thrust into her…. *Shit. Think football stats*, he directed his brain so he could pay attention to the current problem facing them. He did not want Hart to see her like this.

As if finally realizing what he'd meant by his awkward wording, Caitlyn decided it would be best to change after all. Although she reminded him there was still nothing wrong with the outfit. She only wanted to look more professional for a potential donor.

He didn't care about her reasoning, as long as she covered more of her sleek, sexy body so her clothing left it open to an imagination instead of touting her figure. If he could pick an outfit she'd wear to see Hart, he'd have her covered from head to toe in something like a nun's habit.

Before they made it to the exit, Hart, dressed in jeans and a blue button-down shirt unbuttoned a bit too far for Matt's liking, slipped in from the break room, as if he'd been waiting to corner them—or her. How long had he been watching? Matt felt the overwhelming urge to walk up and punch the guy in the face for peeking in on Caitlyn.

Trailing Hart was a flustered Tonya who must've been trying to keep him occupied until Caitlyn was available. Hart didn't make any secret of checking out Caitlyn's attire, or lack thereof. Matt thought the man might've licked his lips. Son of a bitch. It took everything he had not to launch himself at the asshole.

"Hello, Caitlyn," he said slickly. "I'm sorry to drop in unannounced, but I was in the area and thought about that tour you promised."

They approached, and Hart didn't drop Caitlyn's hand after shaking it. He grinned broadly, a wide, almost mocking smile that seemed to stretch from ear to ear.

Not for the first time, Matt envisioned the satisfying moment of his fist connecting with that smug face, that arrogant expression eclipsing any sense of humility. After all, Matt had promised himself to play nice, but the way Tate flaunted his confidence made it increasingly difficult to maintain composure. Damn, he was jealous and stupidly so since Caitlyn didn't appear to care for Hart in any sense except as a money bag, but he couldn't help it. That was how he felt with Caitlyn. He'd finally gotten her back into his life. He didn't want anything or anyone interfering with his second chance with her.

"Say, Caitlyn, I've got an idea. How about I treat you to lunch, and we can chat then?" Hart asked, deliberately excluding Matt.

Bewildered, she sputtered and turned to Matt with pleading eyes.

Matt stepped forward and stuck out his hand over where Hart held hers captive, so he had to release hers in order to grab his or snub him, which Matt doubted he'd do in front of Caitlyn since he seemed to be showing her his best side. "Sorry, but she's not available for lunch." Not dressed like that or with you, he wanted to add snidely but knew that would piss Caitlyn off. "Why don't we go to the office?" he offered as if he'd been invited to this meeting. When she sat behind the desk in the office, her assets were mostly hidden from view.

Hart looked a bit pissed, but he quickly covered the expression. Oh, he was a cool fucker, all right. Matt had his eye on the asshole. He needed to donate his money and leave Caitlyn the fuck alone.

"Sure," he said smoothly, proving Matt's point. "That sounds like a great idea, but my offer to Caitlyn stands." He turned on a thousand-watt smile at her.

"How about dinner then?"

"She's not available for that either." Angrily, Matt plowed his way between them, pushing Hart back and grabbing Caitlyn's hand to all but drag her to the office. When he realized that left Hart the opportunity to ogle her ass, he shifted her in front of him and nudged her forward. Oh, he'd seen her jaw tighten at him but knew she'd wait to vent her frustration until they were alone.

"Please get behind your desk and stay there." He'd decided pleading with her would be the best course of action, and he hadn't been wrong. It'd thrown her thought process, which had probably been her upcoming tirade to him, and all she did was nod and drop in her seat.

When Hart entered and sat, Matt remained to the left of her desk as if standing sentinel beside her. He wasn't about to let this man be alone with her. Something about him bothered Matt. Maybe he just hadn't rubbed noses with enough rich playboys who got what they wanted—at any cost.

With his arms folded across his chest and his stance broad, Matt listened to Hart stammer through questions. His frown deepened. The man hadn't come here for the tour or to learn more about where he could donate his million dollars. He came here for Caitlyn. Now, how to convince her of that? The man may never give funds until he had Caitlyn. How far would the asshole go to achieve his goal? That was it. Matt was staying long after they'd caught Ripley if this fucker was still in the picture.

When Hart pushed again to take her out for a meal—alone, he added with a glare at Matt—she appeared to get it finally.

"I'm sorry, Mr. Hart—" she started.

"I've already asked you to call me Tate."

She hesitated before replying, "Okay, I'm sorry, *Tate*, while you seem like a nice gentleman, I wouldn't dare go to dinner with another man without my fiancé."

Thank the fuck she reminded the prick of that little white lie. Now, he was glad he'd come up with it in the first place. Although Hart just put on that damn slick smile of his and asked, "Even if it's only a business dinner?"

Matt wanted to jump forward in his face and say, "Look, fucker, are you giving her the money or not?" but he wasn't stupid enough to believe Caitlyn would appreciate that, even if she might be thinking the same thing.

Hart surged to his feet. "How about this? Save me a dance at your fundraiser?"

Her hand went to her throat. "How—how did you know about the fundraiser?"

With Matt's keen observation, he saw panic entering her eyes when she briefly passed her gaze over him. He shifted closer to make her feel safer.

Continuing to the door, Hart said as he passed the desk, "Tonya told me. I'll see you there."

Matt didn't like leaving anything to chance, so he shadowed Hart down the hallway, through the break room, to the door, and then watched him drive away in a shiny, new pickup truck.

He didn't care what Caitlyn wanted or how much she trusted potential donors. Matt was having Devon check Hart out as deeply as he could get—none of the glossed-over basic stats and background bullshit. The man had to have dirt, and Matt wanted every bit of it.

Nodding to Ken who'd been patrolling outside, Matt returned to the facility and steeled himself for what was to come. Maybe she felt she had a right to get angry at his high-handedness, but she didn't. He was only trying to protect her, and that also meant from lechers like Tate Hart.

Sure, part of it was possessiveness, but that didn't matter. She'd made a breakthrough by making love to him with her mouth. It only confirmed his knowledge that they should be together. Somehow.

As he walked into her office, one sight of her made him freeze. Caitlyn had her head in her hands, and her shoulders shook. Holy crap, had his actions made her cry? She'd always told him he could be a bit over the top, but he'd worked on that after she dumped him. That word—dumped—tasted like cardboard on his tongue that he couldn't spit out.

Hesitantly, he stepped closer to her, and whispered, "Caitlyn, are you all right?"

When he reached the desk, she looked at him, and her expression shocked him. She'd been laughing. Here, his heart had worried that he'd done something wrong and she'd been enjoying a private joke. Well, hell.

"Is it just me, or is it pretty obvious that he wants to take me out, even though we've identified you as my fiancé?"

Wondering where she was going with this, he said slowly, "I got that feeling."

"I'm beginning to wonder if he'll give me the money without a date."

Anger at that fucker dropped like a stone in his gut. "If that's his condition, what will you do?"

Caitlyn twirled a lock of hair around her finger as she seemed to consider her response. "I'll give him a dance at the fundraiser, but that's it. I would've considered a business dinner with him if he'd allowed someone to accompany me. But it would've had to be business, not what I think he wants."

He placed his hands on her desk and leaned his upper body forward. "But you said you need that money."

"No amount of money is worth my self-respect," she all but growled at him.

Fuck. He hadn't meant to upset her, but her answer pleased him.

Surprising him after her tone of voice, she smiled broadly, so much it reached her sparkling eyes. "I'm glad you're here, Matt. Before, I wouldn't have been able to handle someone like Tate Hart. Heck, I still might not have been if you hadn't been right here. I can't fathom being alone with a man." She cleared her throat. "A man other than you, that is."

His heart did a somersault. They might not be truly engaged any longer, but he considered it only a matter of time.

Chapter Seventeen

The initial excitement of Tate's potential donation had glided off a slippery slope after the way the man had behaved. She'd have to decline his offer if he expected something for his million dollars besides a tax write-off. Her gut clenched at losing what could be a bigger and better Helping Paws. But she had standards, and they didn't include whoring herself out for donations.

With her hard efforts, she'd achieved a lot and wasn't disappointed they hadn't grown more at this point. Things were comfortable. It wasn't wrong to want to help every veteran who needed a service dog. Initially, she'd even considered training dogs for children with autism but decided to stick with one group of clients since the need was abundant.

While considering this, she flipped back through Rick's packet of the not-so-recent donors. She'd had Tonya add them to the fundraiser. Someone who'd donated at least once was a prime candidate to donate again. If they saw where their money went, including the final product, they'd surely pull out their checkbooks again.

As she studied the numbers, she became perplexed. With her finger, she followed along the line of Vivian Blanche who had donated $9,000. Hadn't Vivian promised $10,000? That's what she'd donated previously, albeit once every year or so. Caitlyn clearly remembered the conversation that led to that last donation. In fact, she knew she could probably get more out of Vivian as the widow had nothing to spend her money on, and she loved dogs and veterans. Her late husband had been in the army, though Vivian had mentioned training dogs for people with epilepsy. It'd be something to consider for the future.

Mrs. Blanche—Vivian as she preferred to be addressed—was bigger than life, growing up with old family money and no children to inherit when she finally passed on. In fact, Caitlyn was surprised when Vivian talked about her considering the foundation in her will. Vivian didn't strike her as a woman not to keep her word, so the donation difference bothered her more than she'd like to admit.

She flipped to a couple of names who she distinctly remembered the promised donation amount. Upset, Caitlyn flopped back in the chair. Except in the beginning, she'd never checked what someone committed and what they actually delivered before today. It frustrated her they didn't live up to their commitment, but she was relieved they at least sent something.

It also told her why her mental calculations of where they should be were wrong. The differences would be why they ran lower on funds than she expected. She'd never followed back up with the donor after their check had been received. A thank-you was sent, but she never mentioned the monetary amount itself. People didn't always remember what they promised when they wrote the check.

While she was making a note to Rick to confirm

specific donations were correct, Tonya interrupted her, and the distress in the woman's eyes had her stomach knotting.

"Caitlyn, Cooper's missing," Tonya cried frantically. Wringing her hands, she continued, "He was there earlier. I just thought of saying goodbye, which is why I stopped by to see him. He's not there." She fretted with her hands.

Icy dread slid down her spine. It took her a moment to clear her mind of the fear of what could happen to a loose dog outside the fenced barrier. Wild animals, including foxes and venomous snakes were in the woods surrounding her property.

"Matt." He immediately came to her mind in a crisis, and she didn't question it. Time to do that later. "We need Matt. Let me get him and see if Rick is still here."

Tonya pivoted and hustled off.

"Meet us out front," she called after her employee before hustling from behind her desk to the break room where Matt was whispering with Ken, Clifford Ewing, and Marshall Hollister—two of the veterans due to receive dogs. Clifford was matched with Bella and Marshall was matched with Gabe. They must've arrived early to work with their soon-to-be service dogs. She loved how devoted the men were to the process and how well they understood the need to be involved while the dog learned and matured. She knew Mac Thuhoiska, who would receive Sadie, would be here soon. Hadn't Melvin Holden come in today to work with Cooper? Maybe he didn't close the kennel all the way.

Seeing the look on her face, Matt surged to his feet

and came to her, putting his hands on her biceps, comforting and supportive. "What's wrong?"

"Cooper's not in his kennel. It's getting dark, so we need to find him."

"Melvin was working with him earlier," Clifford offered.

"Good. Maybe he just has him out practicing," she said hopefully, knowing that wouldn't be true because he'd have remained in sight of the training facility as per her rules.

Marshall wiped his hand across his jaw. "I haven't seen him in hours. I just figured he'd gone on home for the day."

The men had arrived early for their ten-day final training with the dogs. They'd worked with them so much during the past year that she expected things to go smoothly. Yet, this was not efficient by any means.

Matt and Ken exchanged a look before Ken excused himself and rushed out the door. Maybe he was getting more help. She could only hope. Thank goodness they'd have extras with Clifford and Marshall. Marshall may be a double amputee below the knees, but by the way he used his prosthetic legs, you'd rarely know. Wistfully, she thought on a side note, just like Matt losing part of his leg.

"Tonya is getting Rick, if he's still here, to help," she said, a bit weaker than she wanted.

In a soothing motion, Matt rubbed his hands up and down her arms. "Do the dogs get out often?"

Caitlyn shook her head. "No. But someone must not have closed his kennel all the way. He's probably checking out the woods. He's as curious as a cat." She pulled from him and turned to the door, but he grabbed her forearm.

"Wait," he requested.

She tried to shake off his hold, but it was ironclad. Okay, so not a request. How dare he halt her from searching for her dog? "We're meeting out front," she informed him.

"I'd rather you weren't searching, but since I know you won't sit back while someone else does, you stay beside me, Caitlyn Marie." The use of her middle name and his tone brooked no argument. He'd only used her middle name when it was serious.

"Fine. Whatever," she said flippantly, then immediately regretted her tone, but she was impatient to get started. "Let's just get to searching."

Before they stepped outside, he reminded her, "Remember."

She nodded sharply. There were potential threats to her canines out in the woods. He needed to understand that time was of the essence.

The first thing she did when she went outside was call Cooper. Tonya came up beside her. "I've been trying, too. Nothing."

Fear clenched her gut. If the dog wasn't responding to their commands, something was definitely wrong.

Now, she wished she'd taught the dogs to hunt. It would've come in quite handy.

"Rick's already gone for the day," Tonya informed her.

Although she wished she had him here to help, it was well past time for him and Tonya to take off for the day. With Clifford and Marshall here, it was no wonder Tonya had stayed. She was just as fanatical as Caitlyn about ensuring the dogs were locked in correctly.

Ken approached with Brad and the other two HIS men who'd been sleeping since they worked the night shift. They were armed to the teeth. What the hell did they expect to face in the woods? A shiver overtook her, and she rubbed her arms to warm herself.

The fact that neither Marshall nor Clifford commented or acted surprised by the weaponry told her Matt had informed them of the potential danger from Travis. Had he told them why? No. She couldn't believe Matt would explain that unless absolutely necessary. Without question, he had been right to warn them there was a potential for trouble while they were there.

Caitlyn found herself unable to quiet her relentless stream of thoughts. They surged through her mind like a tempest, each one jostling for space and vying for her attention. Instead of permitting her to concentrate on the moment unfolding around her, these errant musings collided and intertwined, distracting her from the present reality. Memories, worries, and fleeting desires danced in a chaotic whirlpool, swirling endlessly while her focus remained elusive, slipping further away with each passing second.

What if someone on the board decided she was endangering the employees and dogs and asked her to step aside? As much as she liked to believe she owned Helping Paws, she didn't. She may have used her blood, sweat, and tears to get it started, but to follow the rules for a reputable charity, she had to include the board of directors who'd hired her to run Helping Paws. Although she never liked to think about it, they could ask for her resignation at any time. She gulped. Or they could fire her. No, she'd step down before it came to that drastic of a measure.

Pushing her mind to think of the here and now and not what could happen, she shouted to Cooper once again, hoping to see the dog trotting toward her. But that didn't happen, and her anxiety grew.

"Neftali says Melvin and a dog entered the woods about an hour ago." Ken pointed to a spot on the tree line.

"Did you hear that?" Brad asked.

Everyone stood stock still, and with the quiet, they could've heard a pin drop through the light wind that breezed through the air. Eventually, the group's disappointment showed.

"I swore I heard a dog. It was faint, but it was there," Brad assured them. "It came from that direction"—he pointed to the woods on the east—"but I can't be sure exactly where. I can probably get in the general direction, though."

"Let's split up and see what we can find," Matt said, taking the lead. He assigned areas for individuals to search, having Brad lead him and Caitlyn to where he thought he heard the sound.

They walked across the yard and entered the woods with the snakes, foxes, and who knew what else could be deadly to the dog. Cooper might win a war with a fox, but he could end up hurt or worse, with rabies. Clearing the rest of the land needed to be added to her wish list of improvements. Especially if they decided to add hunting, they'd need a more extensive clearing to train the dogs.

Training idea aside, being included in the search meant so much to her, and by allowing her to go— albeit with rules—Matt continued to endear himself to her heart more than she thought possible. She'd follow his orders, and he'd keep her safe. Finding a dog that wandered should be harmless for them, although not easy if the dog is injured and can't bark or whine loud enough for them to hear.

Caitlyn's thoughts drifted to Neil Holbrook in the woods, and she shifted closer to her fake fiancé. Sure Neil was in jail, but it brought to her mind that she might have made a lousy choice joining this hunt. Not only did she have Matt, but she also had Brad to protect her should the situation warrant such an action. She relaxed, but only a fraction.

As she called to Cooper, Brad cautiously held up branches that would've hit her in the face while Matt followed behind and took the brunt of his brother's snapping the branch back. Shaking her head, she held back an untimely laugh. Men.

After an indeterminable amount of time of watching her white shoes become dirty after stepping over tree roots and marching through the foliage, Caitlyn finally heard what she thought might be the whimper of a dog. Her heart soared, and she rushed her steps, tripping over a dead log. However, she was caught by Matt's strong arms before she face-planted in the path they were creating. "I hear him," she said excitedly.

She'd find out how this happened and ensure it didn't happen again. Her facility could not be lax in protecting its dogs, nor could she allow a new trainer to take care of their animal unsafely. If Melvin couldn't protect Cooper, then she'd have to reevaluate his application.

They'd pushed under a particularly thorny bush

when she saw Cooper. Matt grabbed her arm to keep her from racing to him. Relief gushed forth that Cooper was okay, but she wasn't fool enough to believe he'd tied himself to a tree with his leash. Wait. Where was Melvin?

Caitlyn's breath hitched when she took in the full scene before her. Lying on the ground near where the dog whimpered was Melvin. Fear and anxiety crept into her body. "That's Melvin," she breathed out unsteadily. "He's going to be Cooper's new handler," she informed Brad and Matt, unsure if they had met him with the other vet.

Pulling her tighter to him, Matt scoped out the area. "On me," Matt said quietly but urgently.

Caitlyn turned to question that bizarre command when his team came rushing toward them, somehow being quiet while crashing through the woods, and formed a box around the two of them. Nice and tight. If she moved her arms, she'd elbow someone.

As the net around her tightened, she noticed Brad lean over Melvin and check for a pulse. He gingerly felt around the man's head, being careful not actually to turn it. "Based on the goose egg, it looks like he's been hit from behind."

"Ken, the house and grounds need to be swept before we head back," Matt ordered. "Leave Brad behind. He and I will protect Caitlyn until it's clear. Then you can come back for Melvin if he's not awake yet."

Marshall and Clifford strode to them, looking out of place without weapons at the ready. "We can carry Melvin back," Marshall offered.

"What's the problem? Why can't we grab Cooper,

let the guys carry Melvin, and head back?" She wanted to kneel and check on Melvin and then soothe Cooper, who was a whining bag of bones, but she stayed as she'd promised she'd do. Not that she thought they'd actually allow her out of her protective box of hulking men.

Matt gave her a look that made her feel like she'd just asked a stupid question. "I don't know why the two of them were out here, but while they were, obviously, someone hit him over the head and tied up Cooper. My guess is they expected everyone to search, leaving your property clear or you to search on your own and be vulnerable. Until my guys say it's okay, we don't return, and you stay tight with us."

Her fear warred with her anger. Someone had messed with one of her vets and one of her dogs, which meant they'd been on her property. How dare they! Then, her other side told her this had occurred without them knowing it. Was she really as safe as she'd thought with Matt's team?

Chapter Eighteen

"Jesse, we can't cover this vast wooded area with the few men we have," Matt told his brother on the phone.

"I can't help you, Matt. Christ knows that I wish I could, but we're already stretched. To give you a team for Adam, I cut down the size of the teams for our planned job. If you can wait a few more days, I might be able to swing something, but not today. What about the safe house? It's available and much easier to guard than you've got there."

Although his brother couldn't see it, he shook his head in answer. "Caitlyn worries that if Ripley finds out where she lives and she's gone, he might torture the employees to find out where she went. Like he did her dad. Because of the dogs, they can't leave the place unattended."

"Shit. Could we move them all? People and dogs?"

"It'd be such a big production to pack up the stuff for the staff, the dogs, and the veterans that just arrived, and Ripley would only have to perch in a tree out in the woods where we can't see him and watch through binoculars. Besides, we don't have a setup to house that many dogs at the safe house."

"You're right. Does the sheriff have anything?"

Matt pinched the bridge of his nose between his thumb and forefinger and heaved a heavily burdened sigh. "Nothing. There's no trail to follow. Ripley disappeared from Water Valley after he attacked Adam, but hasn't been seen in Winchester." He paused to collect his frustration. "It had to be Ripley."

"Are you sure that Melvin guy didn't tie up the dog

so he could take a piss and fell, hitting his head? Your men found no evidence of foul play at the house and training facility. Did they?"

"No, I don't know, but it doesn't feel right." With Melvin still unconscious, they'd had him rushed to the hospital. Although what Jesse said could be a viable option for what had occurred, Matt knew it to be wrong. Somehow, Melvin had been lured into the woods and attacked from behind. He still held that the attacker had hoped to catch Caitlyn when she rushed to the rescue, or to quite possibly set a trap of some sort at the house or facility. But nothing had been there. No one had been in hiding, nothing had been disturbed as far as they could tell, and the other animals were okay. Regardless, it still didn't feel right to Matt.

They'd been in the emergency room waiting area since Melvin had been brought to the hospital. Protecting Caitlyn at this location stretched their resources while keeping her home site clear, but he had to be there when Melvin woke up. He had to know the truth and didn't want to wait for the answers.

"Look," Jesse said, "I'll get you extra help there as soon as possible. Devon still hasn't located Ripley, but we'll assume he's in your area. Tighten up what you can until we're there."

"He's here. I'm just not sure what he's planning, and that pisses me the fuck off." The blood flowing in Matt's veins picked up as he ended the sentence. He couldn't help the emotional response to what might happen to Caitlyn. Anyone really, but definitely Caitlyn.

Jesse grunted. "If it's anything like what I felt when Kate was a target, I understand. I also understand

I'll never be able to send you enough men to protect her in your mind, but continue to trust your team. You might want to speak with Ken. He's bound to be kicking himself for this incident, especially after Holbrook."

"How? He was with me when Melvin wandered off. The team didn't know he wasn't allowed to go into the woods with the dog. As for Holbrook, he was way the fuck out in deep woods as cover. Ken couldn't have caught that. Hell, it took Neftali and his sniper scope to see him and that was pure luck considering the expanse he searches."

"Doesn't matter. You know how close to the vest he takes it all."

Ken would definitely take this as a personal affront to his ability to do his job. He'd try to work harder—if that were possible. Matt made a mental note to speak with him when they returned.

"Listen, talk to everyone, whether she wants you to or not. Make up a bullshit threat if you must, but get everyone on the same page. Especially since she's about to start that class with the four you mentioned. Speaking of the vets, Devon says all four all check out. He's sending you their workups. Even though the men pass muster, are you sure you can't get her to cancel that class?"

"No. I'd rather she didn't do it, but I know she must. The vets have been promised these service dogs for a long time and the canines are ready. The good thing is she can leave some of the training to her employees. They're quite competent. And they've been watching out for anything out of the ordinary since we returned." He had to hand it to Rick and Tonya. They

172

hadn't freaked out when they'd heard about the potential threat. In fact, Tonya had seemed to recognize the Ripley name, so maybe Caitlyn had shared it with her. But the two had been smart, observant workers, and he couldn't ask for more from them.

Knowing his options were limited, he thanked his brother for his support and told him that while they'd make do for the time being, the benefit bothered him. If HIS couldn't be there in force, then he'd hire security to fill in the gaps. No matter what Caitlyn said about that decision.

After signing off with his brother, he placed his cell phone in his pocket and returned to Caitlyn's side, sliding down into a thoroughly small and uncomfortable chair in the waiting room. Without asking, he reached over and laced his fingers with hers and squeezed, trying to comfort her. He just needed to touch her. When he noticed her body relax, he inwardly smiled. Baby steps in their relationship.

"Is everything okay?" she asked quietly.

"Of course," he offered, even though it would not be okay until Ripley was behind bars or six feet under. At this point, he didn't care which. The man had abused Adam and now terrorized Caitlyn. If that motherfucker ever laid a hand on her, Matt couldn't guarantee his response would be acceptable to most. To make his answer seem more sincere, he picked up their joined hands and placed his lips on her skin in a soft kiss.

She shivered at the touch, which shot a stream of exhilaration through him, setting his heart to flip.

"Holden family?" a hospital employee dressed in scrubs and a white lab coat said at the entrance to the room he, Brad, Caitlyn, her veterans, and half of his

173

men had commandeered.

They all stood, but Matt spoke for the group. "We're here for Mr. Holden."

"He's awake, and we're admitting him and moving him to a room. We'll keep him overnight for observation, but he seems no worse for the wear. The nurse will give you the room number once we get him settled, and you can visit him." She looked around the large group waiting. "Maybe a few at a time," she suggested.

"Thank you, Doctor," Matt said, sticking out his hand to shake hers. She did and turned back to where she'd entered.

The mood in the waiting room was less depressing after they'd received that news. Melvin not waking had worried them greatly. Clifford and Marshall had their heads together, whispering. He figured they had questions for him. When he'd spoken to them for the first time earlier, he'd alluded to possible trouble and that his men would be armed and watching the place but hadn't come out and said exactly what or who or why to expect trouble. Jesse was right. It was time he did. The men would be significant assets, even if the military had given up on them due to their limitations. Some skills never went away. And from what he'd begun to learn about the two men, he had a feeling they had continued to hone those vital survival skills in any manner they could.

Only in the beginning, when he'd first lost his leg, had he allowed loathing and self-pity to settle into his mind. It hadn't taken long for his father to be all over him, pushing him and pissing him off regularly before he began to realize he wasn't worthless—that he could live an everyday life.

He'd had to learn to get around on one leg, and not all tasks were easy. Some were still impossible, but he didn't stop until he was sure he physically—not mentally—couldn't do something. And that list was very short.

The day he'd received his prosthetic leg had changed his life. It'd taken a lot of getting used to, but he didn't allow any minor failures to set back his entire outlook and attitude. Then he'd learned of an outfit in Memphis, Tennessee, that made custom socket liners and suspension sleeves for his prosthetic leg. That had made all the difference in comfort and control. Sure, his leg would need rubbing out after a day on the prosthetic, but it was worth any pain or discomfort he felt while being as close to whole as he could be. The prosthetic was part of him. He'd accepted that, and it wouldn't change.

The only thing that worried him was how Caitlyn would react looking at his stump. So far, she hadn't balked at his prosthetic leg, but it was much easier to look at than the leg without it. If they continued the path he wanted, they'd eventually spend the entire night together. That would mean taking off his prosthetic for the evening and putting it on when they woke. He could do it all after she fell asleep and before she woke up the following day, but he needed her to accept him as he was.

Would she turn away from him then? She had enough to deal with in the lovemaking department to not worry about what her man looked like with half a leg.

Before he could, he'd been shown in to see Melvin.

He, Brad, and Caitlyn entered first. She grasped the man's hand and lightly squeezed. "How are you?"

"Feeling pretty stupid. Is Cooper okay?"

"He's fine. Melvin, these are Matt and Brad Hamilton, and they're in charge of the security at the facility. I don't think you met either of them earlier." She grinned, and her eyes twinkled. "Brad's the oldest and wearing the red T-shirt."

Brad was older by two fucking minutes. Not even two full minutes. It meant nothing more than his twin got his butt spanked first. Although she was cute when mischievous, Matt couldn't deal with any fun now. They had a problem to tackle, but he had to admit he was happy to see her have a laugh and bring a chuckle to the wounded man, even if it had been at his expense.

Since Caitlyn held Melvin's hand, Matt stuck with a head nod in greeting. "We're glad you're going to be okay," Matt said.

"Thanks." Melvin closed his eyes. "I bet you have some questions."

He nodded when Melvin opened his eyes and held Matt's gaze. "Tell me what happened."

"I was working Cooper, and I heard something. It sounded like a wounded dog. I was far from everyone, including the man patrolling the area, so I thought I'd check it out. I'd hate for one of Caitlyn's dogs to be injured or lost."

The sentiment resonated deeply within the whole group gathered around Caitlyn, creating a palpable connection among them. Their expressions and murmurs revealed their collective concern, as none wanted to see her hurt or distressed. Despite their shared support, they also grappled with the understanding of vulnerabilities that life often presents, underlining their desire to protect her well-being at all costs.

"I thought I saw something, so we went in that direction. Cooper started barking, and before I knew it, I felt a sharp pain in my head, and then I woke up here." He squeezed Caitlyn's hand and looked at her. "I'm sorry. The security guy I met when I went outside told me to be careful and stay in sight, but I thought it was one of your dogs loose."

"It's okay, Melvin. You just rest now." Caitlyn let go of his hand and fussed with his blanket, her hands shaking.

After speaking with Melvin, Matt ushered Caitlyn home and quickly ensconced her in the safety of the HIS team.

Sitting on the couch in her living room, he turned to her. "Caitlyn—" He cleared his throat somewhat nervously. "I'm in no way trying to scare you, but we need to tighten things up and share with your veterans the danger that potentially surrounds us."

Her mild expression crumbled and it nearly gutted him. "It's Luke. Isn't it?"

He thought for a minute about the best way to respond, then nodded. "I think so. We can't be sure, but it's probable him since Holbrook is still in jail."

"Are you sure he is?" she asked hopefully as if she could have her choice of maniacs after her.

Matt nodded his confirmation. "Yes, I checked."

A tear silently slid down her cheek, and without thinking, he reached out and picked her up, depositing her on his lap. Instead of freezing up, which was what he expected to have to deal with, she ducked her head onto his shoulder. "I'm so scared," she whispered.

Matt never would've guessed, considering how brave she was when he was near. She did what he told her without hesitation and never acted fearfully. Granted, they hadn't actually faced Ripley yet, but still, she'd had Holbrook shoot at her, and this incident where she could've been injured or killed had she not called him and his men first.

To soothe her, he rubbed a hand up and down her back while the other held her, anchoring her in place to keep her from bolting but not feeling like a captive. "I'd be surprised if you weren't."

Because it appeared she needed it, he remained steady while she cried into his shirt, leaving it wet with the remnants of her tears. He'd wanted to pull her closer but didn't want to destroy the breakthrough she'd made by being so close to him, even if she hadn't realized she'd done it.

As she eventually dozed in his arms, his mind played through memories of previous times when they'd been so carefree. Could those days really exist for them again? God, he hoped so because his love hadn't changed.

Standing, he toted her to her bedroom and deposited her on her bed. After removing her shoes and socks, he used a throw blanket to cover her. If she were like he'd remembered, she'd have her feet kicked out of it in no time.

Although he wanted to stay with her, Matt found himself tired but watching her. In sleep, her face was peaceful...relaxed...and beautiful. She shifted and poked a foot out from under the covers. He smiled as he leaned down and kissed her forehead. "I'll protect you,

Caitlyn. You can count on that."

He removed his communications system and placed it on the dresser in his and Brad's room. With a yawn, he moved to the bed. After stripping off his clothing, he sat on the side of the bed and began removing his prosthesis, first with the suspension sleeve. Next, he unlocked the artificial leg, then removed the socket liner and the thin sock he wore underneath, placing it all within easy reach before massaging in lotion on his stump to help with the discomfort.

He scratched his chest as he lay on the bed. Why the hell was he so damn tired? The day hadn't been that demanding and stressful. Nothing to make him so drowsy.

As he dozed fitfully, his head began to hurt. He fought for coherence so that he could get an aspirin from the bathroom. But he had to fight harder than he should. Then nausea hit his gut and he wanted to scream as he noticed the faint smell of rotten eggs.

"Fuck! A gas leak." They had to leave the house, which meant he had to wake Caitlyn and the team off-duty. He took a shallow breath and coughed. His blood raged in anger and fear. That bastard must've come in the house when they'd been looking for Cooper and Melvin. Matt would get that asshole, but first they had to get to safety.

Where the fuck was his comm set? He needed to raise the red flag and get help from the outside team. Where was Brad? He should've been close to the house but may not be inside it. Or, had he fallen asleep too, unaware of the deadly consequence of that action?

With a fumbling swipe, he grasped his socket liner

and quickly worked to pull it on. Sitting awkwardly, he reached for his prosthetic leg and locked the mechanism in. The bed-to-bath mode, which bypasses the other sock and sleeve, was the setup he'd be using to save the woman he loved.

Matt stood and immediately collapsed on the floor. His limbs weren't strong enough to hold his poisoned body. With a pounding heart and not allowing himself to be defeated, he shook his head hoping to clear it and pull himself to the dresser where he'd left the comms. Grabbing handfuls of the carpet reminded him of the times before he'd had his prosthetic leg. It had been a dangerous time. Now didn't seem any different since his life was on the line.

He prayed it was weighted down enough at the dresser as he pulled himself up by the drawer handles until he could run his hand over what he needed. Releasing the dresser, he slid back down to the floor and said, "Gas leak. Get Caitlyn clear."

He had no idea what happened after that, but he woke outside, lying on the ground beside Caitlyn, who was still asleep. Ken and Neftali, who must've been sleeping like he had been, were sitting up with their heads in their hands. Matt understood completely, his head hurt like a fucking bitch, but all his worry was on Caitlyn. He awkwardly made his way to her side.

The fire department, an ambulance, and a sheriff's deputy arrived in short order, and Caitlyn was given oxygen and monitored until she woke. Her beautiful eyes latched onto his, and the sight set his stomach on tumbling. With a weary sigh, he thought of how he could've lost her. Flat out, he'd failed her.

Brad came up beside him and slapped him on the

shoulder. From what he understood, Brad had roused Matt enough to get him to stand, albeit weakly, and half carried him outside before he collapsed, but only after crying out for Caitlyn who Steve had carried out.

"Matt?" Caitlyn asked in a scratchy voice as she removed the oxygen mask.

He smiled at her and pushed the mask back into place. The EMTs recommended he and the other house occupants take some oxygen. They'd do it only because they knew their bodies needed it, but not before the men were certain the EMTs had taken care of Caitlyn.

With his hand, he gently brushed her cheek. "Hey. We're going to be okay." He could tell she wanted to ask more, and justifiably so, but he halted that communication and added, "Just rest for now." He almost said that she was safe, but Christ, that wasn't the case at all. Was it?

His headache raged, and his nausea continued, but Matt wasn't leaving any of this to someone else. He had to know.

The fire department told them they'd located the leak and had stopped it. It'd been in the line to the water heater. Matt knew it'd been no accident the line had been loose, but he couldn't prove it. He couldn't fault his team for not catching that when they'd cleared the house after returning from the woods.

According to the fire department, after turning off the gas and airing the home out, having the gas company come out and double-check, they could return to her house. He'd prefer to take Caitlyn away but knew she needed to be here to conduct her business. No matter that she said she was scared, he didn't believe she'd allow this to scare her away from doing her good work for veterans. And he'd hate to ask her to halt it, even for a short period.

But he knew she'd listen to him and take her safety seriously. Hell, she'd listened to everything he'd said so far and never tried to run off by herself without protection. He couldn't ask for more from her. Except to love him again.

Would she blame him for tonight? She could have died. Fuck, they all could have. She hadn't looked at him accusingly but had been confused by what had happened. A cold chill raced up his spine at the possibility of her no longer trusting him.

First things first. It took some convincing, but they transported Caitlyn to the hospital to be checked out. She requested to ride with him and Brad instead of the paramedics, and Matt wouldn't deny her that feeling of security if that were what she wanted. She tried to say she was all right, but when she vomited, she lost all credibility. He didn't expect them to admit her for the night, but it would give them time to make things safe again.

Because he would keep her safe.

Chapter Nineteen

While waiting for the final all-clear to enter her home, Caitlyn rapidly paced back and forth in her office. They'd had to wait for the gas company until this morning, so she, Brad, and Matt had stayed in town for the night. Thankfully their men stayed behind to protect the property and watch over her dogs.

With a sharp turn to walk back in the opposite direction, she admitted that she was officially freaked out. It must've been Luke. He'd been in her home and had almost killed them. Not just her but Matt and some of his men. Her mind kept screaming, *He got into my house!* Granted, they hadn't been in it when that asshole had created the leak, but still, it gave her the willies.

Worse yet, Matt kicked himself for not leaving a man behind when they searched for Cooper and Melvin. He'd been so sure she needed protection during the search that he'd kept the men near them while they'd found the missing dog and vet—a man who'd been hospitalized because of Luke's brutishness.

She stopped and curled her hands into fists at her sides, not noticing the crescents her nails were creating in her palms. She'd never be safe until they found Luke and put him in jail with his brother, getting him out of her life.

Stalking to her chair, she plopped down hard, sending the chair spinning in a circle before she stopped its movement. She placed her elbows on her desk and dropped her head into her hands. She wanted to appear strong for all those around her so they didn't worry, but inside, she shivered with fright. When would this nightmare be over?

At least Luke hadn't gone after her father again, which went to prove that he'd found her…and Matt. Matt could've died, and that made this all the worse for her to consider. She hadn't really thought out what could happen to him protecting her. His injury or death would be unacceptable.

She was just learning to love again—physically and emotionally—and had Matt to thank for it. Yet she'd paid him back by him almost dying in his sleep? Thankfully, he'd been the one to recognize and save them all. Her heart expanded with love for him.

The memories of her making love to him were strong. She wanted more with him. She wanted to be the woman she used to be with him.

A knock interrupted her thoughts. She didn't usually keep her office door closed, but she hadn't wanted anyone to see her fretting.

She lifted her head and assumed a more businesslike persona. "Come in."

Sticking his head through the now open doorway, Rick smiled. "I thought you might want to know that Mac has arrived, which makes all four vets since Melvin will be released from the hospital this morning. He still wants to participate. If it's okay, we can start their camp tomorrow as scheduled."

Of course. The final stage of the veterans getting their service dogs was needed. She wouldn't do anything to stop that. She would not take part in the transition to keep danger from spreading to others. It would be disappointing, but she'd keep them safe.

With a weary heart, she smiled. "Yes, I'd like you and Tonya to continue as planned. I—" She took a fortifying breath. "—I'll not participate this time." Just saying it wrenched her heart more than she thought possible.

Rick nodded, now informed of the entire situation. "We'll take care of it." He looked like he wanted to say something else but nodded again and left, closing the door behind him.

Her first urge was to grab something and throw it as hard as she could to see it shatter into a million pieces like her life was becoming, but she tamped it down. She'd work on other aspects of the business, fundraising, and finding a grant writer, she'd been thinking about to help with some large grants she saw they could acquire. She'd get the advertisement ready, but before she printed it, she'd research some grant writers and see if she thought she could convince anyone to help her so she didn't have to dive through hundreds of resumes.

Deep in research mode, her focus was on her computer. She didn't hear the office door open, but she felt the presence in the room. She stiffened, and her hand on the computer mouse stopped moving. Taking a breath, she slowly turned her head to the door to find out what threat had intruded now. Although she didn't feel anger or bad vibes, for a split second, she considered it could be Luke and everything would be all over. Matt wouldn't be able to save her like he had last night.

Seeing the incredibly handsome man standing just

inside the door, she relaxed. "Matt, you scared the crap out of me."

He moved forward and smiled. Was he swaggering and smiling seductively? Her mind must be playing tricks. This was not the same man who'd been terrified for her and also take charge last night. "You've been locked up in here for far too long. It's time you take a break. How about some lunch?"

Lunch? She looked at the clock and was surprised to see it was after one. Rolling her neck and shoulders, she released the tension and sighed at the welcome relief.

Hands lightly touched her shoulders, and she started. She knew it was Matt's hands, but being unable to see them bothered her. He leaned down and whispered in her ear, "Relax."

Easy for him to say. But she focused and thought only of Matt's hands on her as they'd been so many times before. He'd always been a gentle lover, treating her like a precious queen while always ensuring she enjoyed their lovemaking. It took a couple of minutes until she finally relaxed, and his hands became a welcome pleasure on her body.

"That's better," he murmured.

"I didn't realize it was so late in the day." Oh, his fingers were magic on her tense shoulders.

"Are you getting some work done?" He removed his hands, and she almost reached out to make them return to work.

"Yes."

Matt turned and leaned his magnificent butt on her desk. "You'd rather be with the dogs, though?"

She smiled sheepishly. "Yes."

"It's only until we catch Ripley. I talked to Jesse today, and more men are on their way. They'll help search for him."

"I thought the rest of the men were working other jobs."

"They were. A few men are on their way home and will do a quick turnaround to get here."

"Oh, Matt. I don't want to take away the break these men probably thought they had after returning home."

Reaching down, he clasped her hand, looking at it as he wove his fingers into hers. She wondered what he thought in moments like that. He always looked so engrossed in watching their hands join. "They want to help," he told her.

Not fighting, she allowed him to pull her up from the chair and rest close to him. Her heart pounded, and her stomach rolled with nervousness.

"Look at me, Caitlyn," Matt said softly.

She did and fell into the depths of his smoldering golden-brown eyes that contained tiny gold flecks floating around in a ring when he desired her. Her pulse ratcheted up at their intimacy.

Matt's arms wove around her back and pulled her close while her hands held hostage between them at his chest. Beneath her palm, she felt his heart beating as fast as hers. His breathing hitched, and he whispered, "Caitlyn."

With her erratic breathing, she couldn't find a way to respond to his calling her name. When his head leaned down to her, she welcomed the touch of his lips on hers, tentative but soft and loving. Her body went afire, but not in fear and fright, but in a wanting, needing Matt's touch. Surprise flittered through the recesses of her mind at the change he pulled from her. But this was Matt. She would never feel the same with someone else.

Ecstatic that she'd relaxed enough to kiss him, she wound her arms around his neck and moved her lips hungrily.

Taken aback, Matt stopped moving for a second, before he tightened his hold on her and deepened the kiss, moving his lips as hungrily as hers and sending a tingling to her core. Shocked at the sensation, she wondered if she could be ready for more.

When Matt slipped his tongue past her parted lips, an explosion of pleasure flitted through every nerve ending in her body, making her hyperaware of every inch of him. Their tongues danced and dueled, loving the other one's taste.

Her nipples pebbled against his rock-hard chest. Since she could tell he was waiting for her next move, using her hand on the back of his neck, she angled his head to take the kiss deeper as their lips moved against each other.

Heat nearly singed her when his tongue stroked the roof of her mouth, and she moved even closer to his body.

With a groan, Matt pulled back. "We'd best stop now," he rasped. "Otherwise, I'm bending you over this desk." He used a hand to act as if he were testing the denseness of the desk's surface.

God, that sounded so good, but she didn't want to ruin what had just been blissful happiness by her possibly freaking out. How much could she take? She knew Matt would allow it to be as one-way as before.

He'd want to please her, to love her, to be inside her, but he'd do only what she felt comfortable doing. A delicious shiver slid up her spine at the thought. "You did say lunch, didn't you?"

He removed her hands from around his neck. "Yeah, lunch." Then he leaned down with a wicked grin. "Soon, you'll be my lunch." He stood, winked, and walked out the office door, leaving her with her mouth wide open at his audacity and secretly loving it.

Chapter Twenty

With several fist bumps, Matt welcomed two of his brothers—two because Jake was still a brother to them even though he was technically a brother-in-law—and the two HIS brethren on the front porch of Caitlyn's home. AJ, Jake, Mike, and Rob arrived with little fanfare and looking eager while a bit tired from going without rest between jobs. Even though he felt grateful and knew the extra help was helpful, the heavy weight of responsibility for Caitlyn's life didn't ease. At least now, maybe he wouldn't almost allow her to die.

Only two of the men would be helping at her home. The other two would be working on finding Ripley, although they'd all stay in a hotel in town. At least that kept more men from being underfoot in the house, albeit not on the property. No matter how gracious she'd been, he doubted Caitlyn would appreciate more men to trip over. It was the best he could do. Thankfully, the men tried to stay out of the way as much as possible.

"Guys," he said, "thanks for doing this."

AJ slapped him on the shoulder. "It's nothing. We're family." He shrugged. "That's what we do. Besides, I haven't seen Caitlyn since my freshman year."

"Ditto," Jake said as he scoped out the property. "No wonder you needed extra help," he added after spying the woods on three sides.

"Yeah. More importantly, I need someone chasing that son of a bitch down."

AJ grinned, his boyish grin always getting him whatever he wanted as the youngest Hamilton brother. "That's why we're here. Jake and I have taken up that challenge." Two former FBI agents. Perfect.

Even though he knew half of this team would be investigating, actually hearing the words shot relief through him, almost making his limbs weak. Firming his limbs, he nodded and spoke around the lump lodged in his throat, "Thanks, man." He never thought he'd have to count on his baby brother to keep the woman of his heart safe. It's not that AJ couldn't do it, but because he was the older brother, he should be saving.

"Ken is headed this way. We'll go meet with him," Mike said, waving to Rob. The two men stepped off the porch toward their team leader.

"Well, let's go see Caitlyn," AJ suggested.

"Let's go then." Matt led them off the porch toward the training facility, explaining the area, blind spots, optimal spots, and everything else he could think of to ensure they understood what they had to work with on this end so they could keep their eyes open when they were around and not chasing that asshole Ripley.

Stepping into the break room, Matt stopped them. It occurred to him that having so many men crowding into her office might frighten her. No way would he do anything that might trigger something unpleasant. "Hang right here. I'll get her and bring her in. Have some coffee, or there's water in the fridge." He pointed to it like they couldn't figure it out.

At her door, which was closed again, Matt knocked softly. "Caitlyn, AJ and the team are here."

The door swung open. "AJ?" she asked with wide, hopeful eyes.

A smile swam across his face. "Yes, AJ. He's in the break room."

Surprisingly, she pushed past him and hustled down the hallway to where AJ waited. Matt hurried to keep up, hoping AJ didn't do anything stupid, like grab her up like he used to. Why didn't he think to warn his brother not to do that?

As she entered the break room, AJ opened his arms, and she jumped into them, laughing.

Matt stopped and muttered, "Son of a bitch." She could rush into AJ's arms and not his. What. The. Fuck? He had to remind himself that he had been able to hold her more than once, but still…AJ?

Still laughing, AJ released her, and she slid to her feet. "AJ, it's so good to see you."

"You too, Catie." As far as Matt knew, AJ had never heard Caitlyn's father call her that, yet he'd adopted it from the first time he'd met her. While with most people who tried to shorten her name, she'd corrected them and told them it was Caitlyn, she'd never done that with AJ. *It had to be that damn grin,* Matt thought.

"You remember Jake?" He turned to his foster brother and now brother-in-law with a smile. "Emily's husband," he added with an eyebrow lift.

"Husband?" she asked in surprise, even though he thought he was sure he'd told her that information. "Wow. Jake, that's so great." She reached up and gave him a quick hug. It was nothing like AJ's, but she'd still touched him. Was it because she knew nothing sexual existed? That she knew from experience that they were no threat? It was something to think about.

"Okay, enough of the love fest," he groused. So what if he sounded like a jealous old man? He didn't give a damn. They'd received easy liberties he'd been fighting for. He was pissed.

His younger brother scrutinized Matt's face before a grin broke out on AJ's. "Right. We need to get busy. Want to sit down here?" he asked Caitlyn. "Jake and I are going to find this bastard for you, Catie."

She looked at Matt before answering, and his chest swelled with pride that she'd checked with him first. It shouldn't, as he wanted her to be self-sufficient, and he knew she was, but with this whole matter, she deferred to him, which made everything else better.

"Yeah." He pulled out a blue plastic chair for her. "Let's sit here and chat."

After nearly an hour of discussing what they knew and what AJ had found out from the local sheriff, they realized they still had nothing. If Luke was in the area—and they were betting odds he was—he was a ghost.

"Here's what we're going to do," AJ said, focusing on Caitlyn. "We're leaving Rob and Mike here to help cover the area. Like before, you go nowhere without someone. Preferably Matt." He nodded to his brother. "Jake and I will see what we can do to find him. I won't lie; it will be tough, so just because we're out there hunting doesn't mean you can let down your guard. Got it?" he asked pointedly.

With wide, disappointed eyes, she nodded. Matt figured she'd hoped they'd say they could catch him lickety-split and be done with it all. His men never gave false hope to a client, and as much as he didn't count her as one, she was a client. Her safety was paramount to anything else, including his feelings for her.

Bullshit. He couldn't discount his feelings for her or set them aside because she was in danger. In fact, the feelings seemed to increase, and deepen due to the danger surrounding her. No, he couldn't stop loving her or wanting to make love to her, just because some bastard was after her. He'd just have to use his head and not lose sight of potential danger.

"I don't know," AJ said, and Matt realized he'd missed whatever question Caitlyn had asked.

"I'm sorry. What?"

They looked at him strangely, as if he'd suddenly grown two heads.

She cleared her throat. "I asked if he knew how long before they caught him."

"And I said—"

He cut AJ off with a growl. "I heard you."

The corners of AJ's lips tilted up.

Matt glanced at Jake and saw his had also. Fuckers. "About time you two get on it," Matt groused. He stood, not caring what the others thought.

AJ and Jake stood. "Yeah," Jake said, "we'd best get on it." His repeating Matt's words was intentional. They were definitely making fun of him.

Caitlyn stood also. "Well, thank you." She appeared at a loss for words. Truly what did one say? Good hunting? He'd say that if she hadn't been standing there, but it sounded too crass with her close by.

They all exited the building, and his brothers left in

their rented SUV. Matt turned to Caitlyn. "What's on your agenda now?"

She looked at the training facility wistfully and sighed. "I'd be watching the training with the new handlers, but I'm going to stay away since I don't want anything to happen to them."

His stomach twisted painfully, overwhelmed by the profound sadness that radiated from her words. Even though they hadn't physically removed her from the familiar comforts of her home and the responsibilities of her job, they had stolen away a vital piece of her profession. This element had been her lifeline, providing meaning and fulfillment throughout all these years. "How about we make some lunch?" he offered. Being with her in close confines of the kitchen appealed to him. Maybe he'd find something they had to cook or prep together so he could touch her.

"That sounds good." Without looking at him, she turned to her home.

Now, he had to figure out how he got as exuberant a hug as she'd given AJ, whom she'd always thought of as a kid, even though he was only one year younger than her.

Chapter Twenty-One

Nothing changed around her home with the new arrivals staying at the hotel. Caitlyn still didn't see the security team except at mealtimes. In the evenings, like this one, they went straight to the room they shared after the kitchen had been cleaned so as not to intrude upon her life. They'd insisted on taking on the task of doing the dishes. She'd never seen more polite men, and Ken ma'amed the hell out of her. Granted, growing up in the South, she'd seen plenty of polite men, but these guys took it to a whole new level of gentlemanly.

Sitting comfortably on the worn, familiar couch with Matt, she leaned back and tried to immerse herself in the movie—a light-hearted comedy that played on the screen. The colorful characters and laugh-out-loud moments flickered before her, but her mind felt distant, barely registering the plot. She forced a laugh with each quip and punchline, hoping it landed at the right moment, even if her heart wasn't in it. The laughter from Matt beside her filled the air, a reminder of the joy she wished she could share wholeheartedly.

At some point, Matt executed a high school move where his arm made it to the back of the sofa behind her head. Only, he didn't stop there or try to cop a feel. His warm hand massaged her neck, relaxing her muscles, but the contact tingled her spine and lit her nerve endings.

She wasn't afraid of his embrace any longer, but she still feared an increased level of intimacy. What if she froze when he tried to…to penetrate her? God, that word sounded so clinical. When he tried to push inside her? She had no idea whether she'd be able to have sex ever again, even though she wanted it…with Matt.

"Come here." Matt's hand on her neck nudged her closer, removing the small space between them.

The movie obviously ended when the news was on television. Still feeling the loving effects of his touch, she slid closer, and a sliver of elation slipped through her veins when she didn't tense when their bodies touched.

Matt slid his hand on her neck down the couch behind her until it was under her butt and placed his other hand under her legs. He hefted her in the air and deposited her onto his lap. "I want you, Caitlyn." One hand slipped around to her hip and pulled her against his erection.

Desire blossomed within her, causing her heartbeat to race like a wild stallion. A thrill surged through her, whispering that she had reached a significant breakthrough in her feelings. The night was still young, and she could sense more passionate moments on the horizon. She reminded herself consistently that this was Matt, the man who had always cherished her, fully aware he would never intentionally inflict pain upon her. Her longing for Matt was profound, enveloping her entire being in a warm embrace of yearning. It had been far too long — an eternity, it seemed — since they had shared the intimacy of their bodies, a connection that filled her with both excitement and desperation. Too damn long since their souls had intertwined in the mesmerizing dance of love. "I want you, too." She wrapped her arms around him and placed her head on his chest, listening to his rapid heartbeat until it seemed their hearts beat as one, even as fast as they moved.

"Caitlyn." He cleared his throat, and the rumble from his chest eased her last shred of nerves. "I love you. I've always loved you. I never stopped."

Her vision blurred, and her heart swelled in delight. When he'd said the words when he'd orgasmed, she hadn't been sure he meant it, but now…. Could it be true he'd never stopped, even after he had been run off? In no way did she deserve this wonderful man.

Love filled her for him with every fiber of her being, a profound emotion that enveloped her heart and soul. Caitlyn felt an overwhelming desire to hold onto him tightly, refusing to let him go. With a hopeful heart and a wish that everything would unfold positively from that moment onward, honesty was the only path forward. Disappointment and despair were not new acquaintances. She had encountered them before. Although resilient and able to face such emotions again, she genuinely hoped to avoid the displeasure that went with them.

Pushing aside that they lived in different states and had jobs that tied them there, she looked up at him and blinked her vision clear. "Matt, I love you, too. I never stopped. But you have to know, I may not be able to"— she audibly gulped—"to be with you." When his jaw tightened, she rushed to add, "But I want to. I want to right now, but I'm scared."

She could feel her nerves creeping back, fluttering like restless butterflies in her stomach. With his gentle encouragement, she believed she could push those anxious feelings aside and regain her composure. Yet, a nagging thought lingered in her mind: shouldn't a touch of nervousness be expected? After all, it had been a considerable time since she last faced this situation. The memory of her past encounter loomed over her, a shadow that had long overshadowed her desire and enthusiasm. Those feelings had been tainted, dimmed by the events that happened last time, leaving her hesitant and uncertain. But now, there was a flicker of hope within her, a spark that suggested this time might be different.

She took a deep breath, reminding herself that she wasn't alone. With his steadfast support, perhaps she could finally confront her fears and embrace the opportunity that lay ahead. The prospect of moving forward filled her with a mix of trepidation and excitement, revealing a path toward reclaiming what she had once lost.

With a slow smile, Matt raised a hand to her cheek and rubbed her jawbone with his thumb. "We'll work it out. I promise."

How could he promise such a thing? He wasn't in control of her body and mind. "But what if I—"

His finger on her lip silenced her. "Shh. We'll worry about it later. Now"—he raised an eyebrow— "did you say you wanted to be with me right now?"

She nodded slowly since his finger still lay on her lips. Then the finger began tracing them and her pulse shot out of control. His touch ignited an exquisite symphony of sensations deep within her body, each gentle caress sending ripples of warmth and pleasure coursing through her veins. It was as if every nerve ending had come alive, responding eagerly, creating a dance of passion that left her breathless and yearning for more. Did he realize he turned her to mush so easily? Maybe he'd just learned her body.

"If I do this, you have to look at me and tell me if you can't handle it." Once her eyes landed on him, he asked, "Promise?"

Caitlyn took a deep breath, knowing she had reached a pinnacle in her life, released it, and nodded. "Promise."

"Good." He leaned down and touched his lips to hers lightly, softly, and sweetly.

A tingling left her mouth and rode down her body like it was chased by the devil, leaving an urgent need behind. When it reached her core, she wanted to cheer. She also wanted more. Burying her fingers in his short, unruly dark hair, she clutched his head, trying to get him to deepen the kiss, but he kept his lips gentle on hers. Without considering the consequences, Caitlyn nipped his lower lip to gain his attention. When he opened his mouth and eyes in surprise, she took control and moaned in pleasure. With an intense need, she took charge and surged her tongue forward, devouring his mouth in a searing lock of their lips.

After his clear shock had worn off, he tried to regain control over the kiss, but she wouldn't allow it, and he must've realized she had to be in control because he followed the movements of her tongue as they explored each other's mouths and tangled like wildfire. At his submission, she shivered with a surge of power and control. The power to bring a man as big as Matt to his knees. To be able to explore and taste this sexy male on her terms.

Oh, how she loved his taste. Like a scent he

carried, it was masculine. Not like the sickening taste of—

Abruptly, she pulled back from the kiss and looked at Matt to clear her mind. So she didn't look as frazzled as she felt, she tried to play off her breaking the kiss. She would not allow thoughts of that night to intrude and ruin what she'd decided would be the best night of her life. "Do you want to go to my bedroom?" she offered.

He searched her eyes for what seemed like forever before he smiled and nodded.

Butterflies bounced around in her tummy. His smile was one of the most attractive things about him. It brightened up his face, and his eyes glittered with something that made one feel like that smile was special—just for them.

Scooting off his lap, she grabbed the TV remote and turned off the television before going to her bedroom with Matt hot on her heels. An eager excitement built inside her bones. They were going to make love.

Matt's presence inside her bedroom made the room seem much smaller. He had a bigger-than-life feel about him. When he locked the door, a slight tremor of unwelcome fear slid through her.

I can do this, she reassured herself. Purging the fear, she called upon her fortitude and moved to Matt. Reaching for his shirt and pulling it from his jeans, she didn't look at him—only focused on her task. When he stood stock still, she finally looked up into his eyes. Those eyes burned with desire. It pushed her almost recklessly to be near him…be a part of him…be with him.

She tossed her arms around his neck and pulled herself on her tiptoes. "Kiss me," she whispered her demand.

That was all it took. His arms wound around her and pulled her snugly against him. His mouth crashed down on hers in a hungry, demanding kiss. One that reset the fires that burned deep inside her. The fire flashed to her core. A place only Matt had ever brought to life.

Before Matt, she'd never been with a man. Of course, since it had only been her father and her growing up, she'd not understood exactly what to expect during sex. It hadn't been like she could check out instructional books at the school library. Before she went into college, Aunt Kathy had explained the birds and the bees in depth to her. Matt had been her first lover after that, and he'd far exceeded her aunt's explanation of the pleasure that could be had with an inexperienced college boy.

Matt broke the kiss. "Are you sure?"

How did she get so lucky to have Matt back in her life? He cared about her. He loved her. She didn't know how it could get better. Sex excluded. "Yes," she breathed.

"Remember that you can call a stop at any time."

"I remember. Now, make love to me."

With a lopsided grin, he slowly reached to slide Caitlyn's shirt over her head. Without hesitating, she raised her arms, allowing him to pull off her top.

He reached for her bra and stopped. "Are you still okay? Still ready for this?"

"Yes, now quit stalling." She laughed.

"This won't be the last time I check. It's important

I don't take over and move too fast. I love and respect you too much."

"I love you." When he didn't move, she reassured him, "Yes, I want more."

With uncanny skill, he easily unclasped her bra and slid it down her shoulders. When the cool air hit her bare breasts, her immediate reaction was to cover them—hide them with her hands. It was that small voice that screamed at her to throw her arms around herself and hide her body from him, but she squashed it and stood proudly. She wouldn't hide from Matt. So she stood before him bare-chested, and a driving need to be with him flooded out the noise of that screaming voice. As for her figure, granted, she could be bigger up top, but Matt had never seemed to be displeased before. A sudden wariness crept into her thoughts. Had he changed what he liked? It had been a long time since they'd been intimate.

"God, you're beautiful." The rasp in his voice beat the wariness away. When his hands touched her aching breasts, she arched her back in pleasure.

"So are you," she replied in a hushed whisper. She couldn't get anything else out because he'd begun to massage her breasts, as if weighing them for something important or…remembering them in his hands. When his thumbs touched her puckered nipples, she whimpered. Her nipples had always been sensitive and his teasing both at the same time had her core flaming hot, the flames being fanned until that old erotic feeling she'd thought she'd lost had ignited deep within her.

"I want to taste you, Caitlyn."

"Okay," she breathed.

"Do you want to undress the rest of the way, or

may I?"

A pang of nervousness hit her again, and she swatted it away, tired of allowing it to interfere. She knew it'd never go away—her past couldn't as much as she'd like it to do so—but she could allow herself this pleasure. "How about we undress ourselves the rest of the way? That way, you can get your pants over...." She didn't want to imply he had a problem, but she didn't want to catch his pants on his artificial leg.

When she'd half expected him to dispute her comment, he just nodded and went for the button on his jeans. Shrugging, she did the same, and that pang of anxiety returned as nervous excitement this time. She liked that feeling much better.

They scrambled out of the rest of their clothing and rushed to unfasten buttons and zippers before disposing of underwear. By the time they were both nude, Caitlyn's need for him rocketed to desperation. She burned hot and needed his touch.

Naked, they stared at each other as if one touch would bring an end to the fiery passion they shared. Matt crawled onto the bed and moved to one side, breaking the tension. He patted the space next to him. "Come here. I need to lick and kiss every inch of your luscious body. Be ready for pleasure, but know I still remember your ticklish spots."

With a chuckle and a smile, she hurried up next to him. He didn't even kiss her. He did exactly what he said, and his mouth went straight to a breast. She sucked in all the air around her in bliss. As he suckled her nipple, goosebumps spread over her body. When his tongue flicked her stiff bud, she nearly came off the bed in ecstasy. The man was trying to kill her, and they'd only just begun.

To turn the tables, she moved so her breast was free from his sensual ministrations, and scooted down until she could kiss him on a level field. He was faster than she was and took her mouth, devouring it with his lips and tongue, showing her how much he wanted her to be his.

Breaking the kiss, she fought to catch her breath. Both panted as they gazed into each other's eyes.

"I've missed you, Caitlyn. I need to taste *all* of you," Matt rasped. "Like you got to taste me."

She wasn't stopping this. She wanted him to taste her. Braving it, she rolled to her back in open invitation.

Maybe a bit of her tensed, and Matt didn't cover her body fully as he moved down her torso. Instead, he loved her body from the side, which felt incredible. Each kiss along her chest and belly ignited a match to her burning desire. Lost in his red-hot kisses trailing her skin, Caitlyn hadn't realized Matt had moved his entire body between her thighs, his head level with her mound. She took a deep breath. Oh, the anticipation. Sweet Jesus.

"If you can't do this, we won't," Matt told her gently.

A small part of her wanted to scream, "No. Leave me alone," but she didn't feel the need to do it. She just had to remember that it was Matt and that he wasn't trying to overpower her. She could do this—with Matt. "No, I'm okay," she said honestly.

And after the first flick of his tongue on her, she was okay. More than okay. His tongue ran the seam of her wet folds, and when his fingers split them so he could taste the core of her, she moaned so loudly she was sure the entire house heard her.

She grabbed the covers on the bed tightly when he flicked her stiff, throbbing nub. Her body arched in invitation when he sucked on it. His mouth and tongue were magical.

Imitating what he planned to do with her in a few minutes with his erection, it was all she could do not to come right then and there. She wanted to come with him inside her.

As his thumb rubbed her clit in unison with the work his tongue did, the erotic sensations climbed inside her, fighting to get out with each movement he made.

"Matt."

He didn't respond except to double his efforts in pleasing her. And he was doing that. His fingers joined the mix, and two of them slid inside her, curling to find that magic spot while he sucked and licked on her clit.

She hadn't felt this much desire, lust, and pleasure in a long time, since Matt. It was mind-boggling that she'd finally feel it again—something she'd been sure would have been absent for the rest of her life—with Matt.

Her flesh felt afire, and her core was the epicenter, ready to erupt. Her muscles tightened, and she bowed from the bed as her orgasm exploded, shooting rays of euphoria rapidly through her veins to leave her in a state of extreme, sated paradise.

As she lay there, limp as a pleasured woman, Matt slipped back up her side, not on top of her. She looked over and saw him stroke himself, and her lustfulness returned to full force. "I want you now," she said. Every nerve ending flared red-hot, making her frantic for more.

"You're in control. I'm yours to command."

Although what he'd said hadn't been the entire case so far, ripples of anticipation built inside her. She didn't want the chance to freeze, so, like he'd done, she wasn't about to take the chance their position would do that. With a hand on his chest, she pushed him on his back. "I'm on top."

A devilish grin spread across his handsome face, and she knew how much he loved this position. Although she didn't do it to please him, she was glad it did. Besides, he'd just given her a monster orgasm. She wanted to do the same to him.

Seeing him lying on his back with his rigid cock ready for her, she steeled herself, gathering her courage to continue. Reaching for him, she wrapped her hand around his hard length and stroked him briefly. The man was more than ready for her, so she climbed up his body and positioned herself above his cock.

He stopped her movement. "Condom," he growled. Then he pulled a packet from his wallet that he'd set on a bedside table and ripped it open, grasping the condom inside. He slid it down his erection, then motioned her to continue before lying flat for her pleasure.

With her hand on him, she took a deep breath and slowly slid him inside her. She didn't freak out with him inside. Granted, he wasn't fully sheathed inside her yet.

It took a bit of movement, even though she was wet because she was so tight. But when he was inside her, they both froze and stared at each other as if the mysteries of the universe were held in the other's eyes. Realizing she'd stilled on purpose and not frozen up in fear, Caitlyn discovered how perfect lovemaking had been. How perfect he felt inside her. How perfect he made her life.

She met his heavy-lidded, passion-filled eyes that smoldered with desire. "God, you feel so right for me," he told her, mirroring her thoughts.

With his hands on her hips, he raised his eyebrows. "I'm ready when you are."

Oh, she was ready. Nodding, she said, "I'm more than ready."

She moved her hips, and he helped her achieve a rhythm that drove them to near ecstasy.

True to Matt's old habit, he reached out and played with her breasts, and a blissful smile broke out on his face. She'd told Matt he was right for her, and that was the truth. The touches, the loving feelings, their strong connection all played into the rightness not only of them together but of the moment.

Without prompting, she leaned down and shifted her breast near his lips while she moved her pelvis in a teasing, circular motion. He growled and took her nipple in his mouth and shards of pleasure rocketed through her body.

"Oh, God, Matt. I think I'm going to come again."

"Then do," he said as he changed nipples, feeding her sensual need. The one that had come alive at his kiss…his touch…his love. He drove her cravings…her desires…her want of him, and the lovemaking they were sharing.

Caitlyn changed the movement of her hips, and she felt that prelude to erotic bliss. The one she'd already made once. Could she really do it twice after so long of not having an orgasm? As the ecstasy in her system began to climb, she knew it would happen, so she didn't even fight it before she cried out and fell into another cloud of immeasurable joy.

With a fog of realization, as soon as she climaxed, he flipped her onto her back. She didn't freak. She didn't stiffen. She enjoyed Matt as her lover and felt his shudder as he came.

He immediately rolled off of her but left his head resting on her chest. Rubbing her hands through his damp hair, she smiled. Being in his arms, security and contentment flowed through her, followed swiftly by love. He rose from the bed, telling her that he had to dispose of the condom. She also knew he'd need to remove his leg to sleep.

She may not be healed entirely, but she'd made another major breakthrough tonight and wanted to jump up and do a fist pump at the beauty of it. Luke Ripley may be after her now, but his brother's time for ruining her life was over.

Chapter Twenty-Two

They woke entwined in each other's arms, and Matt smiled in pleasure. Even when he'd removed his prosthetic and shown Caitlyn his stub of a leg, things had gone well. She hadn't cringed or looked away in disgust. She'd even helped him rub the soreness from it.

Of course, nothing could've gone as well as their sexual encounter had. He'd worried the entire time and had kicked himself when he'd realized he'd taken over and positioned himself on top of her. The last thing she'd wanted.

But it'd worked out fine. Thank the fuck. He hoped it meant it'd always be okay. Although, he'd probably never stop worrying because he wouldn't want to hurt or scare her. Having her back in his bed was too important, yet being able to keep her there wasn't in the cards they held right now.

"Good morning," he said, kissing her lightly on the neck and catching a whiff of the lotion she always wore. Sweet Pea. Wasn't it? He remembered the odd name from buying a large gift basket with it for her birthday one year. She'd been crazy about the gift. He couldn't take credit for the creativity of the products in the metal washtub-looking base, but he had picked the scent, and she'd worn only it after that. Of course, she said he'd given her enough shower gel, body spray, and lotion to last a lifetime.

She smiled and snuggled closer into his arms. Her words, "Good morning," tickled over his chest, and a slight shiver of exhilaration rushed over him. Just watching her sleep had brought his dick to life, but he wouldn't keep her in bed all morning. Or would he? He'd probably do it if they hadn't had men around and her employees. But with all of them, she'd surely be embarrassed that the others would know what the two of them had been doing. Plus, he felt she might be a bit sore since it'd been so long for her, and he knew she wouldn't tell him if that was the case.

"How about some breakfast?" he asked, stroking her back. He was still in awe of her breakthrough. He wouldn't lie to himself and say he hadn't been worried it might not happen, but he'd been hopeful. Truthfully, it happened faster than he anticipated. He sent a silent prayer that there would be no flashbacks later that intruded upon her sex life.

"That's a good idea." But she didn't move from her position cuddled up to his side.

Maybe she wouldn't mind another tumble. As soon as that thought flitted through his mind, she moved to get out of bed. He just lay there watching her in all her glory. That pert body always turned him on and now was no exception. He groaned, and she looked at him and smiled at his growing erection, tenting the covers.

"I—" She broke off.

"It's okay." He swung his legs over the side of the bed and reached for the thin sock to put on. Putting on his prosthetic leg had become such a habit he didn't even think about it until he realized she stood watching him. A shadow of nervousness at her reaction bothered him. She had to be okay with this because he couldn't change it. He'd come too far to allow himself to regress to that man who felt less than whole and unwanted by the woman he loved.

"Are you—" He cleared his throat. "—okay with this?"

He hadn't expected her to smile, and the gesture warmed him inside and out. "Yes. I was just fascinated. You took it off so fast last night that I didn't see what you did. Does it hurt?"

It hurt like fucking hell when the lower part of his leg had been blown off. Now? Somewhat. Phantom pains now and then, and the changes in his muscles needed to use the prosthetic leg properly. But nothing he couldn't handle since it was that or his life. Besides, even if it did, he wouldn't tell her because she'd worry or fret over him. "Just the little aches like I told you about last night." He returned to putting on the thin sock, custom socket liner, prosthetic leg, and suspension sleeve on top. He didn't move as quickly as he usually would since she watched. Finishing, he looked up at her.

Awe washed on her face. "You make that look so simple and easy."

He stood. "Well, I've been doing it for a while now. How about we dress before I take you back to bed?" His dick was screaming for him to do that, and the longer he stared at her naked body, the better chance that head would take control.

Matt's clothes were in one of the guest rooms, so he held the clothes he'd worn to his crotch and slipped from her room. She'd protested, and her face flamed when he said no one would see him. Obviously, she didn't believe that. Who cared if they knew the two of them were sleeping together? His brothers probably already figured that. They knew how the two of them had been and how much he'd always been in love with her.

Once dressed, he went to the kitchen, where Brad sat at the table with a raised brow. "Running late, brother?" he mocked.

Instead of the "fuck you" he wanted to hurl, he asked, "All quiet?"

Brad choked back a laugh. "Good. Now that you're up, I'm off to bed."

"Aren't you going to eat first?" Caitlyn asked with a carton of eggs in her hands.

"No. The boys and I already ate. You two are up a little later than normal."

After looking over and seeing Caitlyn's flaming face, Matt thought a right hook to Brad's smirking mug would feel awfully good.

"Goodnight," Matt said forcefully. "Don't let the door hit you in the ass on your way out." Granted, Brad wasn't leaving the house, but it felt good to say since Matt wouldn't get physical with his brother.

After his twin left, Matt went to Caitlyn and put his arms around her from behind. "Don't let him get to you."

"Do you think he knows?" she asked quietly.

Reaching out, he removed the eggs from her hand and placed them on the counter. Then he spun her around and placed his hands on her shoulders. "Caitlyn, you and I used to be together, so it goes to his thinking that we'd be together again. I imagine he's thought it for a while."

She covered her mouth with her hand. "Oh God."

In concentration, he drew in his brow. "What's the matter? Is there a problem with Brad thinking we're together?" He didn't add the men probably thought it also. That might be too much for her to process after Brad's snarkiness about them being absent.

She released a sigh and dropped her hand. "It's just…I mean…it's just temporary. I don't know that I like Brad or anyone else thinking I just sleep around like that. Temporarily, I mean."

Fighting the urge to shake her, he tried to keep his voice calm. "Look at me, Caitlyn." When she did, he continued, "What do you mean temporary?" He knew, but he didn't like that he'd thought that also.

"Well," she visibly swallowed, "my life is here, and yours is in Baltimore. We each have a business to run in those cities. And it's not economical to travel back and forth between the two."

He scoffed at the idea of "economical" as if that would ever be a good enough reason for them not to give their relationship a second chance. *Dammit.* There had to be a way for them to be together. He couldn't ask her to give up Helping Paws. She'd been working on this since her life turned upside down. It grounded her back to the person she'd been to become the person she was today. A survivor. With her heart and soul, she'd built Helping Paws from the ground up, and working with the dogs helped her relax. She wouldn't want to do anything else.

And he couldn't give up HIS. He'd also built it from the ground up. As each had joined, he and his brothers had worked hard to make it the thriving business it is today. He enjoyed what he did. *Dammit*, he thought again.

"How about we eat breakfast," he said since he didn't have an answer to their problem.

She nodded. "Breakfast."

Neither moved. He pulled her close to him and into a bear hug. Her arms wrapped around him, and she buried her head against his chest. At that moment, he promised himself he'd finally find his way back to her. With everything he had, he'd find a way for them to remain together again.

****

Sitting at her desk, Caitlyn realized she'd done so much hiding in her office lately that it'd made her notice the room needed painting. Maybe a soft green would work. Or she could go crazy and do an orange accent wall. Wasn't orange an inspirational color? With Matt's arrival, her life had turned into a chaotic mess. She liked organization and control, yet she was slowly losing both. It'd always been that way around him. Desire had driven them both in the past.

She wouldn't complain too much about him arriving. Thank God he'd come to help her with Luke, who, unfortunately, no one could find, but the emotional side of Matt being there was almost too much to handle.

He'd helped her open back up, and that sucked because when he left—and he would—she'd close right back up again. But this time, it wouldn't be from fear. It'd be from heartache. Heck, she'd told him she still loved him, and she'd actually *made* love to him. She sighed in remembrance of the pleasure he'd given her, and her body tingled.

Placing her elbows on the desk and dropping her head in her hands, she groaned at how she'd almost had unprotected sex with him. Thank goodness he'd been prepared.

Yes, he'd released her from freaking out at the touch of another man. His touch had always been magic. She'd be forever grateful for him helping her. But just like when she'd tried to date after moving here, even though Travis's face came to mind and frightened her away from any chance of a relationship, the thought of Matt had always made her feel like she was cheating. She knew it was a stupid feeling, but it'd been there nonetheless. Her love for him had never stopped. She'd been an idiot to turn him away when she'd needed him the most.

They had lost eight years. She was damn lucky he forgave her and came looking for her. Otherwise, she'd never have seen him again, and she didn't know if her heart could've taken that. But it was about to go through a heartbreak again.

What did she do now? Her love for him obviously would never stop. She guessed she could resign and follow him. Another groan and a mental head shake followed that thought. No, she couldn't leave Helping Paws. This was her baby. She wouldn't release it to anyone else. These dogs and the men and women they helped were her life now. Besides, the board of directors probably wouldn't accept a resignation unless it was for a drastic reason. Heartache might not qualify.

She couldn't move Helping Paws to Maryland, and he couldn't move HIS to Kentucky. And his traveling back and forth each week would slowly suck them financially dry, so they were at an impasse. No, there was only one answer. She groaned again. Being an adult sometimes sucked.

The phone rang, pulling her from her little pity party. Checking the readout, she smiled and answered. "Hi, Daddy."

"Hi, Catie. How are things going there?"

Besides almost dying? she wanted to scream, but didn't want her dad to worry more than he already did. Plus, there was the whole sleeping with Matt again thing she definitely didn't want to be brought up in conversation.

"It's fine. How about you? Is Aunt Kathy taking good care of you?"

She should be keeping her dad in the loop. But he'd want her to give up and come home. She was safer here with the extra men.

"She treats me like an invalid," he groused, and Caitlyn smiled. She figured that would happen. Her aunt had walked all over her dad as long as she could remember. Probably their entire life. A pang of sadness at being an only child hit her. She immediately swatted it away. Being an only child gave her all her dad's attention. She wouldn't trade that for the world.

"What about the men? Are they behaving?" Not that she really could do anything if they weren't except tattle to Matt like a four-year-old little girl. But she needed those men to protect her dad even though the thought was—and the gas leak pretty much confirmed—Luke was in Kentucky, not Mississippi.

"Don't even know they're here. Kathy is spoiling them though with her home cooking. They'd planned to go to a hotel since the only space available was the floor, but she convinced them to stay." She could imagine him shaking his head at that. "She could convince a card shark that gambling was evil and he needed to quit and become a deacon or something. She really missed her calling. She should've been a counselor."

Laughing, she remembered all the times her aunt had convinced her dad to do something for her and her aunt. Heck, she'd convince businesses to allow Caitlyn in, even though the age limit excluded her. Not bars, mostly gambling places. She probably would've convinced carnival ride lackeys to allow her on something she wasn't tall enough for, but Aunt Kathy drew the line at safety. "Or a lawyer," she added jokingly. She had no doubt her aunt would have excelled at that profession.

"Do you forgive me for sending Matt? I know you hadn't wanted to see him. But I thought…."

When her dad trailed off, she knew he needed her reassurance that all was well between the two of them. "It's okay. I needed to see him. To tell him…how sorry I am about how I treated him." She'd also needed to tell him she loved him still. Why had she done that? Just because he'd said it didn't mean she had to throw that out there also.

"Do you think there's a chance you two might get back together?"

The hopefulness in his voice was almost her undoing. She'd just figured out they couldn't work. She didn't need it tossed back in her face, even unintentionally. "No, Daddy. It won't work."

"Oh." Disappointment laced his words. He'd always loved Matt, almost like the son he'd never had. Teasing him by saying maybe when she knew better would've been cruel. "I had just hoped."

"I know you love him"—*and I do too*—"but we

live two different lives, too far apart. It can't work."

"Ah, hell. Kathy just poked her head in the room and gave me the evil eye."

Caitlyn remembered her aunt's look all too well. It happened when Caitlyn had messed up something—on accident—or had gotten into something she wasn't supposed to touch—like the pretty doll collection any young girl would want to play with, but they held a "look only" status. "Uh-oh. Were you supposed to be resting?" she teased, secretly grateful for the change in subject.

"Yeah, well. I rest enough." His tone turned serious. "Are you really okay?"

She gulped at the lie she was about to tell. She had a man trying to kill her and a man destined to break her heart. "Yes, Daddy, I'm fine. We've even got a team looking for Luke. It'll be over soon, and I couldn't be safer." Realizing she'd crossed her fingers like an adolescent, she untwined them. "Promise."

Adam sighed loudly. "Okay. I love you, my Catie-bug."

"I love you, too, Daddy." She ended the call before he could ask for more information.

Setting the phone down on her desk, she saw the donation list she'd been perusing before. Her dad was safe, and so was she, with enough men to trip over at her disposal, willing to give their lives for her. Her stomach turned over at the thought. She couldn't control the problem of Luke Ripley being after her, so she would work on something she could control.

She'd help make this fundraiser one of her best, even if it killed her. Immediately, she realized how crass her thoughts were. She didn't want to die, no matter the reason.

Chapter Twenty-Three

After the training had been completed for the day, and the staff members had departed, Caitlyn led Matt to the training room. "I want to see the dogs. They'll be gone in no time."

The sadness in his gut burned for her upcoming loss. With how she was with the animals, he couldn't imagine it was easy for her to say goodbye. He knew it killed her not to be mingling with the dogs—and the humans—during the final training sessions. Her closest concession to staying away had been to work in her office, which she still had to consider her choice since it was in the same building. With ease, she'd skirted out through the break room, didn't stop to chat, and had asked the staff not to come to the office or her house until this thing with Luke was settled.

She'd been floored that they'd still wanted to come to work, considering the potential danger surrounding them. Matt hadn't been surprised. He'd seen the devotion Rick and Tonya had to the animals...and to Caitlyn. She probably didn't see how they nearly worshipped her. Besides, the veterans were angry over the situation and told Matt that no matter their disabilities, they were there for Caitlyn. With his health improved, Melvin joined them in this cause. Matt wouldn't turn away extra eyes as long as they worked with his team instead of trying to be heroes.

As for visiting the dogs this evening, he was eager to see them do some of their tasks. Even though it was a simple task, he enjoyed "Get it" and could do that all day with different items, in awe of the dog's astuteness. It amazed him how the dog stopped what he was doing, picked up what had been dropped, and ensured it was returned to the owner's hand or lap if wheelchair-bound. These dogs were so damn smart. Caitlyn and her team had done an excellent job with them. And considering she'd done it with them for a year and a half or so, she'd definitely have bonded with the dogs. Anyone would.

This wasn't the first time she'd sent dogs off with a veteran, and it wouldn't be the last time. She'd been at it for years. She had pictures of some recipients and their dogs in the hallway for the employees and anyone else to see. Their success stories even made his heart swell with love and pride for the job they did. Caitlyn had a gift with the animals, and this was her place. Nothing would change that. Even their burning love for each other. She'd needed this place when she'd opened it for her rehabilitation, but now, she needed it because it was a part of her—like HIS was part of him.

His mood sank through his gut and churned like curdled butter.

Entering to see the dogs, he'd expected her to run to Cooper or one of the dogs. Instead, she went to the kennel of a younger dog, probably less than a year old. She allowed him out and laughed while he smothered her with doggie kisses. Obviously, the puppy was a little tyke.

He loved her laugh. It always made him stand up and notice the beauty in that melodious voice. Plus, it did his heart and soul good.

When they'd stopped their game, Caitlyn sat on the ground, and the dog curled himself in her lap.

"Come and meet Chip," she said, petting a much calmer dog now that he'd bulldozed Caitlyn with his ball of energy. At least his entire butt wasn't wagging with his tail any longer.

Bending over, since squatting wasn't something he could do comfortably with his prosthetic leg, he gave the dog affection. The pup, a yellow lab, soaked up the petting, nudging his head tighter into Matt's hand and affecting his balance. He laughed. "Whoa there, Chip."

With a sharp "Sit" command from Caitlyn, the dog plopped his butt down and didn't move a muscle.

Amazing. The dog went from ninety to nothing in zero seconds. The results were disastrous when he and his brothers tried that with the two dogs they had growing up. "Wow. I'd figured he hadn't been trained yet since he was so…crazy. I've never seen a dog change behavior so quickly. What else can he do?"

"Not much more than basic commands. Although I'd prefer that veterans learn to handle their fears on their own, we'll train Chip with "Block" and "Cover" commands.

Having no idea what those commands meant, he felt like an idiot, but she just smiled and explained as if she'd planned to do that all along.

"With the 'Block' command, the dog will position himself or herself in between the handler and the threat to his or her personal space, giving a much-needed bubble to the vet. The issue is more of a common problem than you'd expect. The dog will know how to perform the task, but as I said, we hope the veteran is learning to overcome that obstacle in their life. It won't always happen, but that's why we teach it. A veteran, after serving our country and being injured—in any manner—shouldn't have to feel threatened when they go outside and into public.

"With 'Cover,'"—she changed commands so quickly his head almost swiveled to keep up—"the dog moves behind the handler, again creating a space buffer and that feeling of security." She petted Chip softly on the head. "The dogs can do so much to help the veterans face issues that therapy can't help eradicate."

Matt could fully understand that. It'd taken nearly six months before he could talk about his SEAL team and the incident that cost them so much. Even then, it all became too much to handle, and he'd hit the gym and worked out his anger and frustration at the unfairness of it all.

He remembered something she'd told him before, which still bewildered him. "You can really teach them up to eighty-five or so tasks?"

"We typically don't give that many to a single dog. Based on their new handler, we give them what we know they'll need. Chip here just met his future handler the week before you arrived, so we've been planning the rest of his training."

She smiled and stood, then gave a command to Chip who followed her back to his kennel. "I just let him play. I'm sorry he's in the early stages of training so he couldn't do any tricks for you." She winked, and his mouth fell open. Damn, if she didn't get playful after being with the animals. He loved seeing her so carefree.

After she'd closed the gate on Chip's kennel—

palace really with the size of it both inside and outside—she turned right into him. He'd moved behind her to catch his little minx in his arms. Leaning down, Matt kissed her hard, demanding the same fire in return. When she opened her mouth to him, he took advantage of her parted lips, stroking her mouth with a swipe of his tongue and a possession that told her that no matter the barriers, she belonged to him.

Her hands reached around him, gripping his shirt tightly as if to tug him closer. When that didn't work, her arms moved between them and crept around his neck before she ran her fingers through his hair. Whether she knew it or not, he loved her hands in his hair, especially when he was dominating her with his mouth.

With a groan, he broke the kiss to catch his breath. Gulping the air to bring in large quantities, he steadied himself to remember where they were. Throwing caution to the wind, he managed to say between much-needed breaths of air, "I want you."

"Not here."

He loved how she sounded as winded as he did.

"Yeah. Not here," AJ said, startling them and pissing Matt off that he hadn't known of his brother's approach. That type of protection would get them both killed. He had to do better.

They jumped apart as if on fire. A blush crept up her cheeks until it bloomed bright red. She looked so cute, but damn his brother and his timing. Not that he'd have caught them doing anything more. Or would he have? That ship had sailed, so it didn't matter, except his time with Caitlyn had been interrupted.

"What do you want?" Matt asked gruffly, wanting

to pull Caitlyn close to him, but she was putting distance between them as if AJ hadn't just caught them making out.

With a wickedly devilish grin, AJ responded, "I thought you might want an update."

His heart nearly stopped. Could it be almost over? Then he took in AJ's grin again. "Did you catch him?" Matt shot back.

"Not yet," Jake answered, stepping up next to AJ.

Matt wanted to tell them to get their asses out of there until they had caught the bastard, but he knew that wasn't the right thing to do. They might have information that would be helpful. Hopefully.

"Let's go to the break room since it's closer," Caitlyn offered.

With his hand on her lower back, Matt nudged Caitlyn's stiff form forward, with AJ and Jake bringing up the rear. Warmth flowed through her back to his hand. He couldn't get enough of touching her, and now that he could do so without her panicking, he was a very happy man.

Settled at the break room table with Matt and Caitlyn on one side and AJ and Jake sitting on the other, Matt scrutinized his brother's face, and then his foster brother turned brother-in-law's face. Nothing. Damn them and their cool reserve. Of course, it definitely came in handy in their line of work, but they didn't need to be that way around him. Then he glanced to the side at Caitlyn. Okay, maybe they did need that stoic resolve with her pale face and worried features.

"Well?" Matt prodded, ready to get it over with so he could return to kissing Caitlyn. Or better yet—if anything could be better—catching the asshole after her so they could finish kissing.

AJ and Jake looked at each other, and Jake nodded toward Matt and Caitlyn, apparently giving AJ the lead on spilling the information.

His baby brother turned back to them. "First, J.T. Ripley met with his parole officer as scheduled. What he's done outside of that is anyone's guess, but as far as we know, he's obeying the law. He told his P.O. that all his prison talk was bluster and he wants to do whatever it takes to stay out of jail."

"J.T.?" she asked, panicky before turning to him. "Who's that?"

Shit. Matt forgot to tell her. "That's Ripley's son."

"I didn't know he had a son."

AJ spoke up, "He was in jail during…."

She took a deep breath and released it. "Is he—Is he after me also?"

His heart broke for her with all she'd dealt with…all she was dealing with…and what might be on the horizon. He offered her a smile in reassurance. "No. We just wanted to check on him. As far as we know, he's never said a word about you." That wasn't a lie. He'd only said he wanted his father out of jail. His uncle decided he didn't care if it was at Caitlyn's expense.

Hoping to avoid discussing the younger Ripley any longer, he turned back to AJ. "What else do you have?

"Luke Ripley has definitely been around the area."

Even knowing this already—or strongly suspecting at least—Caitlyn gasped, and her right hand covered her mouth.

Without looking at her, Matt reached over and grasped Caitlyn's left hand under the table and rested it on her thigh. He squeezed the limp digits until she turned her hand over and they intertwined their fingers. "How do you know for certain?" he asked.

"He had a hotel room at this flea-infested, rent-by-the-hour type of place, but he's been gone for a few days now. Turned in the key and everything."

Taken aback, Matt couldn't believe Ripley would be that stupid. "Did he use his name?"

"No. He used a false name and that motel, well, they don't care about matching an ID to a person if they can make a buck."

Hmm. If only he'd had the men before the gas leak, they'd have had this wrapped up nice and pretty with a fucking huge-ass bow on it for Caitlyn. "Where is he now?"

AJ cleared his throat and shifted. "We don't know. There's not another motel like that in the area, so I'm not sure where he's staying. But"—AJ grinned—"we did get the make, model, and license plate of the car he drives. That motel might not care about who rents from them, but they definitely care about the possibility of any damage. They have hidden cameras nearly everywhere."

"They just let you see their camera feed?"

"Of course not," Jake stated as if Matt had lost his mind.

"Dev?" Matt asked, already knowing his older brother probably hacked into the feed.

"Yeah. It wasn't easy for him to find the feed, not that he couldn't do it, but luckily we had a laptop that linked into the hotel's WIFI, and Dev somehow made a backdoor into it through that computer. At least that's what he called it."

Matt shook his head in disbelief at his brother's ability and the illegal shit he sometimes had to do for protection purposes. "Damn, he's a fucking genius."

The men nodded, but AJ spoke. "He can't do everything but somehow comes through when we need it. Could you imagine what he could control and how much money he could accumulate as a hacker? It's mind-boggling."

Realizing Caitlyn hadn't seen Devon since they'd been a couple back in the day, he turned to her. "Remember, he was in the CIA?" He furrowed his brow, trying to remember the last time she might've seen his brother. "Anyway, he was in it for a while and between that and his smarts, he can do just about anything with a computer. I mean, there are limits of course, but not that many where he's concerned."

She murmured, "Wow. I always thought he was a book-smart type of guy."

"And," Matt asked, "we weren't?"

Smiling, she chuckled. "No, I just saw the rest of you more of the brawn types of men compared to Devon."

"Anyhow," AJ said, probably saving them from an uncomfortable conversation, "I came to let you know we don't have eyes on Ripley, but the sheriff's department has a BOLO out on that car, assuming he doesn't dump it. It might even be where he's staying, and that helps us out a lot since everyone is looking for that vehicle."

Nodding, Matt asked a few more questions that AJ and Jake didn't have answers to, then noticed Caitlyn flagging in her chair. He squeezed her hand to remind her he was there with her.

"Thanks," Matt offered. "I think it's time for us to head to the house."

Seeming to understand, AJ and Jake stood. "We'll let you know if we find anything else helpful."

Matt wasn't sure what they'd learned today was helpful except the sheriff now had a specific car to keep an eye out for in the area. Assuming he didn't change the plates or steal a new one.

After saying goodnight to AJ and Jake, he led Caitlyn to the house with his hand on her lower back. Over the years, he hadn't realized how much he'd missed even that little contact with her.

Although it was early, he led a wilting Caitlyn to her bedroom. She appeared to be in great need of comfort. Maybe she'd expected the men to say they'd captured him and she'd be free. Maybe he shouldn't have let her sit in the meeting to gain hope and then lose it in the next breath. Maybe was a word that had lately begun to piss him the hell off.

"Are you okay?" He closed the bedroom door behind them. He was staying, and there were no ifs, ands, or buts about it. Well, if she said no, he'd leave. No question there. Thinking again, he turned back and locked it, knowing her concern about someone catching them together. Not that anyone couldn't actually get in the room—a shoulder to the door would do it—but to give him that last measure of safety.

She nodded, then looked at him. "Yeah." At the croaked sound of her voice, she cleared her throat. "Yeah, I'm okay. I just wish they'd captured him."

Closing the slight gap between them, he wrapped his arms around her while her head rested on his shoulder. "Soon. Just know that you're safe with me

230

and the men."

"I do feel safer than I've felt in years. It's just—"

When she broke off, he waited, thinking she needed to think through what she wanted to say. After what seemed like an interminable amount of time, he prompted, "Just what?"

"I want to send everyone away so no one else gets hurt. Melvin got hurt. You and some of the men could've died in this house." She looked up at him with watery eyes. "I don't want anyone to die protecting me, but I can't leave my dogs."

As if in tune with her, he realized there was more she needed to say, so he prompted her again, "And?"

"And I don't want any of your men to go because I do feel safe. It's so wrong of me to want people to put their lives on the line so I can have that safe feeling surrounding me. It's just wrong of me to wish it, but I can't stop."

Wiping at a tear sliding down her cheek with his thumb, he kissed her forehead. "First, putting our lives on the line is what we do, so you aren't asking us to do anything except our job." He kissed the tip of her nose. "And it's not wrong of you"—he kissed the left corner of her lips—"to want other people safe. Nor is it"—he pressed a light kiss to the right corner of her mouth—"wrong to want to feel safe." He scraped his teeth along her bottom lip.

A wave of need rushed over him, but he tamped it down before all logical thought escaped him. He couldn't push her, and tonight, he wanted to hold her and keep away all the dark thoughts and fears running through her mind. And they had to be there, swimming around, and while they submerged sometimes to ease her mind, right now they were jumping up to do a high dive and sending the ripples of anxiety through her.

"Let me help you undress," he offered. "Let's get you into some pajamas." He almost spat at the thought of her covered while they slept. "And we'll get you to bed."

Her large eyes shone brightly, and he knew he'd do whatever she asked, even if it meant leaving her alone for the night. Although he prayed that wasn't the case.

"Will you stay with me?" she asked quietly.

"Of course," he offered calmly. "I'll always stay with you." The words left his mouth before he could think straight.

His heart sank at the thought that he couldn't promise her that. No matter how much he wished it were so.

Chapter Twenty-Four

"You've had how many RSVPs?" Caitlyn gasped at Tonya. "This was a short notice event. I'm surprised people are attending." She'd expected some loyal to their cause, but most donors were booked out months in advance.

"I just took the list you marked people with serious donation potential and invited all of them, then added your possible donors to the list," Tonya said happily. "These are prior donors who have probably forgotten about us, and I think they'll make contributions this year. Now that we're back on their radar."

"I'm just…flabbergasted so many agreed to come." Turning her mind from the donors planning to attend the event, she asked, "Are you sure the area will be large enough?"

"Yes." Tonya touched Caitlyn's hand on the break room table. "Quit worrying. I've got this." Tonya beamed a large smile, and Caitlyn relaxed. A bit. She was still in awe.

And she still worried about a ton of things, but this was something she could count on her employee—and the closest thing to a best friend—to handle mostly without her. Tonya enjoyed doing public relations events like this little shindig they were putting on to separate people from their money—at least some of it.

Now, she needed to worry about what to wear. She

cringed at the thought and knew what Tonya would say before the words left her friend's mouth.

"I think you should wear the red dress."

The infamous form-fitting red dress with what looked to have a ladder on each sleeve. At least from her neck to mid-forearm, exposing her skin. It meant a bra was impossible to wear with it. She'd feel naked if she wore it. It'd been a pressure purchase while she'd been shopping with Tonya. Although she'd felt sexy trying it on and spinning around with the mirrors, she'd never dared to wear it anywhere. It had hung in her closet for nearly two years. Hell, it was probably out of style.

"It'll be perfect," Tonya continued.

If Tonya hadn't made the event casual, it wouldn't have worked because it wasn't a floor-length gown. Which probably helped their women's RSVP numbers since they didn't have to purchase a new gown. Most who attended these kinds of events had plenty of unworn dresses in their closets In hers, the red dress Tonya wanted her to wear stopped just above her knees. Another part of her that would be bare. Great. She'd almost be naked in front of everyone. The image of her wearing her shorts and a tied-up shirt in front of the men and staff flashed through her mind. No. That was different. She wasn't trying to coax money from them. Besides, she'd wanted to look sexy for Matt.

"I know you'll fight it, but I have a solution. I think a strapless bra will work, but just in case, I'll get you some of those breast-pasty things that allow you to feel covered when you can't wear a bra. In fact, I'll pick some up tonight. What size are you? Although I don't know if size matters."

Without thinking, she told Tonya while she was still internally screaming no. But wouldn't she wow Matt if she did wear it? Others would see her dressed like that, though. Did she feel that brave just to show off to Matt? Probably not.

"It's okay. I'll wear something else."

Waving a finger in an "Oh-no" gesture, Tonya narrowed her eyes. "You're wearing it if I have to come over there and dress you myself."

With impeccable timing, Matt entered the break room. He looked between the two women and must've decided they were done meeting. Technically, they were, and she wasn't in the mood to continue that conversation. "Ready for lunch?" he asked.

"Sure." She stood. "We just finished."

"What's the dress for your shindig?" he asked.

She looked at him questioningly. Had he heard her and Tonya talk about *the* dress? "What?"

Waving his hand as if to get his word across, he asked again, "Do I need to get a tux for your party?"

The image of Matt in a tuxedo played on a loop in her mind. He'd be so damn sexy that she wanted to tell him yes and make Tonya change the dress for the party. But she couldn't be that selfish. "No, it's casual. Do you have a suit or sports jacket?"

"It just so happens that I had something sent from my apartment in Baltimore for the occasion. So did my brother and the men. Just in case we were still here for the event. It always helps to be prepared." He had winked at her before his probing gaze made her wonder at his meaning.

Had he sent it for the event or to wear on a date with her? Not sure why her thoughts went there, she almost scoffed at the idea. Of course he hadn't. But a girl could wish....

Realizing he'd expected her to speak, she played back their conversation. He hadn't asked a question. "Okay." She figured that worked on many levels in conversation.

"Ready?" he asked.

She jumped. "Oh. Yeah." She turned to her employee. "Thanks, Tonya." As Matt led her to the back door, she heard Tonya say, "Red dress."

Outside, she turned to look at Matt, who was grinning. "What?"

"Do I want to see this red dress?"

Her face flamed. How could she be so embarrassed around him? They'd been intimate before, and things were the same. No, they were better.

Matt's phone rang and saved her from trying to explain about a way too-sexy dress that Tonya wanted her to wear. Secretly, she wanted to be brave enough to wear it.

With a terse greeting, he answered, but an emotion like relief flooded his face. Smiling down at her, he said, "I'll tell her." Then he ended the call and returned his phone in his jeans pocket.

Frightening her, he grabbed both of her forearms and held tight. "What?" she asked, worried.

"The sheriff's department spotted Ripley's car."

The sound of a sharp, indrawn breath was loud, even with the sounds of life all around them. It took her a moment to realize she'd made that noise. Her hand had crept up to her chest.

"He tried to elude them and led them on a high-speed chase."

"Oh, God, please tell me they caught him."

He nodded. "They believe Ripley's speed neared one hundred miles per hour. He was going too fast for a corner and wrecked his car. Wrapped it around a pole is more like it. Anyhow, he's in the hospital, on life support." He pulled her to him, and she numbly went into his arms.

Life support.

Matt rubbed his hands up and down her back soothingly, telling her it was over.

On life support? It was over.

Over, echoed in her mind. That would mean Matt would leave her. She sagged against him, and he held her from sliding down to the ground beneath her in a liquid puddle of relief and despair.

"Let me get you inside," Matt said, holding onto her tightly.

Caitlyn wanted to reach out and grab his arms to wrap around her again. She didn't want to do without it, but soon she would. Pulling all her resolve together, she stood straight and followed him into the house.

A smell caught her attention. Something that hadn't been there before. She made a point of sniffing the air where he could see. "Is that…chili I smell?"

With a smile and a nod, Matt beamed. "I put it in the crockpot this morning. Well, I cooked up the meat on the stove, but I cleaned that up. It should be ready now. Good and ready."

Her stomach must've agreed with the smell, because it took that moment to rumble. "Chili sounds great."

As they sat down at the dining table to his one Crock-Pot specialty, Caitlyn asked him, "Does this mean everyone is leaving?" *Or rather—are you leaving?* she wanted to ask, but wasn't brave enough yet since she knew the answer and didn't like it.

After stirring the chili in his bowl, he scooped some up with a spoon. After blowing on it, he nodded. "Yep." He put the overfilled spoon in his mouth for a huge mouthful.

Before she could ask him to be specific, Brad bounded into the room with a yawn. "Hey, brat, AJ says it's all over." He looked at their bowls. "Oh, Matt's chili." A smile reached his face. "I'm in." Ignoring the looks from Matt and Caitlyn saying they'd rather be alone, Brad served himself a bowl of chili and sat down.

Seeing the two of them together was always a little unsettling. They did look alike, and if you didn't know what to look for, you could easily confuse them. Besides the direction of the broken hump on their noses, their voices were different, as were the words that flowed from their mouths.

In her thinking, Matt had always been the more mature of the two. Not that Brad wasn't, but something changed him, and now he was angry most of the time. Pity. Brad was such a good guy, but it would take a strong woman to tangle the man he'd become. She wished she'd be around to see it, but she probably wouldn't see Brad again after the group left.

Left. Why did it keep coming back to that? She'd known that he wasn't staying. She'd been selfish in having him help her recover sexually. Not that she could see herself with another man, but still.

"I'm going to miss you, brat," Brad said once again using the nickname she hated. She wasn't that young woman he knew in college.

"I really wish you wouldn't call me that." She gave him her most pitiful eyes. At least she hoped. Hell, she could be coming onto him and not realizing it.

He shrugged. "Okay."

Just like that? That's all it took? How many times had she asked him not to call her that when they were in college? Maybe it was in the wording, or maybe he said that because he wouldn't interact with her much longer. She didn't see him taking a trip to Winchester just to visit.

"The men are coming in now," Brad announced.

She glanced at Matt who looked about to blow a gasket. Shouldn't he have been the one to pull the men back? He must've been trying to spend more time with her—alone. How sweet was that? Unless it had been to tell her goodbye, then it was all kinds of fucked up.

And then the guys who'd been outside, were armed like they were protecting the President in the Middle East. The bravado she'd been trying to hold onto slipped away.

"Matt's chili?" Ken asked before moving straight to the cabinet for a bowl and filling it. She'd hoped that large Crock-Pot would have plenty of leftovers. The thought of something Matt made left over—even if in her freezer—flipped something in her heart. However, with this group and the ones still sleeping, she could see an empty crockpot in no time. She wanted to run over and toss her hands over it, preventing any more from disappearing. That was Matt's chili.

"Thanks for letting us stay with you while we were here, ma'am," Ken said to her between bites.

She cocked her head. "Where else would you

stay?"

The men chuckled as if in on a private joke she'd been exempt from knowing.

"Well," Brad said, "you'd be surprised how many banish us to a hotel in town. It's much better if our resources are together should the shit ever hit the fan."

She blanched at what that might actually entail. Thank God she hadn't had to find out. "Has the…shit ever hit the fan?"

The men grimaced. Geez, it was like being an outsider to a private group. It sucked.

Matt spoke up this time. "Unfortunately, it has."

"Have you ever lost somebody?" Did she really want to know the answer to that question?

A heavy pause rested on the group, and they all looked down at their bowl of food. Her stomach revolted at what she expected to have been a heavy loss for these men.

Ken lifted his head first and spoke for the group. "Not someone we were hired to protect. But we did lose an innocent bystander on one mission. Jesse's wife's dog-sitter."

"Then," Matt added softly, "we lost one of ours, protecting Emily and her daughter."

Not sure what to say, she simply said, "Oh."

"Yeah, oh," Brad said sympathetically.

With her bowl empty, and unsure what else to say, she stood to wash it out, tempted to get more and keep it aside, but she decided that was just batshit crazy. It's something a stalker might do, and she wasn't a stalker, nor would she be. Although, she'd let Matt stalk her…and catch her.

Behind her, she heard the men talking about

packing and getting flights home. Tears welled in her eyes. She wasn't ready to say goodbye to Matt. Not for a second time in her life.

Chapter Twenty-Five

Watching his twin packing, Matt shook his head. "I don't know. My gut is screaming at me we're missing something."

Brad stopped folding his socks and turned to Matt. "Are you sure it's not because you want to stay with Caitlyn and that gives you a reason?"

His brother knew him well. "There's that"—no sense in denying it—"and there's this gnawing feeling that she's not out of danger yet."

"Luke Ripley is on life support. He's not coming to get her."

"I know, but what about the son?

"Matt, you've got to quit this. As far as we know, the son has done nothing. He's back in Water Valley."

"It's just—"

"What?" Brad asked irritably.

"Even though there's no evidence of it, I keep thinking there were two at Adam's house. Even he initially thought there might be two of them. It's the only way I can explain losing my senses. I think someone hit me from behind." He'd said this to the deputies and his brothers before, but there had been no evidence of someone helping Ripley. It had made him confused about what he thought had actually occurred.

"I don't know. What you say makes sense, but nothing supports it. We can't keep the men here on a feeling in your gut. Tell you what, if it will make you feel better, I can hang around for a while. But you have to decide how long you plan to stay around. And don't say you're not because you haven't packed a thing."

"I think it's smart that Jesse is chartering a plane so there are no problems with the weapons from 'point a' to 'point b.' And the idea to lease one makes even better sense since his and Dad's favors will only go so far."

"You're changing the subject. How long are you staying?" Brad asked.

"She's got a fundraiser I've agreed to escort her to. I know she'd let me out of it, but I'd like to support her. I really like what she's doing here."

"Then you're coming home?"

Matt rubbed his hand on the back of his neck. "Yeah. I guess."

"Do you want me to stay?"

"No. You're right. There's nothing that says she's in danger." Except his screaming gut, and Brad could be right that he was manufacturing the danger in his mind. Then again….

Brad dropped on the bed. "You want to stay permanently, don't you?"

Leaning against the wall, he sighed and admitted, "I do. I don't want to lose her again."

The two remained quiet for a moment, and Brad finally spoke. "Okay. Let's talk to Dev. He could probably hook up something for you out here. That way, you wouldn't have to fly in and out except for jobs. Hell, you don't even need to go on any of them unless Jesse schedules us up tight."

The idea had merit, and he hadn't been thinking

about it. But still…"I wouldn't be there to do the meetings and decide on jobs. I wouldn't be doing my share."

"Bullshit. We were ready to accept Trent living in Montana and still being a partner without the work that goes into it. Pity he declined, but I get where he's coming from."

That had been a monumental step in inviting their newfound half-brother to a partnership in the family business. And Brad was right. They had been going to offer it to where he didn't have to be there daily. Maybe it could work. "I'll talk to Dev."

Brad stood, picked up a shirt, and began to refold it for his duffel bag. "Yeah. He can do all that computer shit, and you can videoconference or something. Of course, it wouldn't be the same if you weren't there." Brad's voice had gone mournful as if he'd just lost his best friend. And that was what would happen if Matt didn't go back home. But hadn't he thought of this place as home? His home was with Caitlyn, wherever that place happened to be located.

Pushing off the wall, Matt grumbled, "See me before you go," and left the room.

He searched the entire house and no Caitlyn. How quickly she took off on her own boggled his mind. Shouldn't she still have a residual amount of fear? No, he reminded himself. Ripley was no longer a threat. Then why did he feel like there was still a threat to her? It had to be because he didn't want to leave her. While he had a few minutes alone, he dialed Jesse to talk to him about his new life…with Caitlyn.

****

Caitlyn smiled, joy filling her body as she watched

the veterans working with their soon-to-be service dogs. Learning to be a handler wasn't easy, but these men mastered the control faster than any other group they'd brought in for the training.

Proud of the job Tonya and Rick had done with these four dogs, she wanted to rush out and hug them. Instead, she continued observing them and mentally patting them on the back in recognition of an excellent job. When it was over, she'd find a way to reward them with something meaningful to them.

When they took a break, she joined the group, loving the dogs first—as always—then greeting their new handlers, who were curious about how things had resolved for her. These men—who didn't know her from Adam—had been willing to lay down their lives for her. The concept of help coming to them—in the form of a service dog—transformed the men into what appeared to be mentally and physically able men of society. Yet they were broken somehow, someway. Cooper, Bella, Sadie, and Gabe would fill that missing gap. At least as best as they could. It'd be up to the men to ensure their dogs remained sharp.

"Sorry I missed all of the fun," Mac added. He always did talk a bit too loudly. Of course, with his hearing loss and traumatic brain injury from when he'd gotten too close to a land mine, it was no wonder.

"I don't know if I'd call it fun," she said as sweetly as possible because she knew he didn't mean it like that. His humor just sucked. "But it's over." Saying it that time made the relief whoosh through her system. She'd said it already, but it finally sank in, releasing the pressure she'd been holding in because of the threat to her and, by association, her friends.

But being over also meant Matt would be leaving. He was probably packing right now. Knowing that was what he was doing, she couldn't be in the house. Before, she'd run him off. Now, she had nothing to offer him except herself. But she'd be nothing without the dogs and her friends and the vets she helped. Heck, once they got proper funding, she wanted to branch out and do something like Pups in Prison. Maybe for children with autism like she'd considered before. She'd definitely need more funds if she were going to keep and train a dog that long. It wasn't free, by any means.

In other words, she wouldn't follow him, even if he asked. She couldn't bring herself to leave her sanctuary. She'd gone over this in her mind a hundred times already. They had to say goodbye. There was nothing else for it. At least he'd said he was staying until after the fundraiser. Lying in his arms, she'd asked him to accompany her, because…well, because she'd still been scared. But also because she wanted him to be with her. She felt stronger and safer with him by her side.

Maybe she should wear the red dress. She could knock his socks off before he left, giving him something to remember her by. It was wrong of her to entice him to stay when he needed to return. But that didn't stop her from deciding she was wearing that damn dress.

Chapter Twenty-Six

The departing men huddled in the two rental vehicles and drove away to meet the private jet scheduled to land in the next hour, leaving her alone with Matt. It was quiet outside, and Caitlyn wondered how she'd never noticed. Living by herself, she'd always appreciated the quiet. Now, it turned into ominous silence spreading over the two of them. She shivered as she and Matt turned to go inside her home.

"Thank you for staying for the fundraiser," she told him as he secured the front door.

Turning back to her, he bobbed his head toward the kitchen. Figuring that meant he was hungry, she led the way and stepped to the refrigerator. "I'd offer you some of this awesome chili I tasted earlier, but alas, it's all gone." She laughed since she'd predicted none'd be left when the men dug into it. Matt must always win the chili cook-off award at any of their employee or community gatherings. "I do have some hamburger meat thawed if you want to make patties and toss them on the grill. I can cut up the lettuce, tomato, and onion."

In a microsecond, the breath left her as Matt snatched up her body, pressing it close to him and his massive chest. With his mouth hovering over hers, he whispered, "No onion. I plan to kiss you later." He wiggled his eyebrows in a playful gesture. "A lot of kisses, so definitely no onion."

"Well, that goes the same for you, mister," she teased, wanting to take her index finger and bounce it off his nose for fun, but her hands were caught between them.

As if to prove his point, his lips grazed hers. After only a brief kiss, he pulled away, then returned, dropping a light kiss on her lower lip and then upper lip, then each corner of her mouth with soft, gentle kisses before his tongue got wicked and washed across the seam of her mouth, trying to probe it open. When she didn't immediately respond to his entrance request, he nipped at her lower lip like she'd done to him before, and then his teeth closed over it, and a wave of heat washed over her body with immense intensity. She gasped, and her lips parted, offering the perfect opening for his demand. Playfully, his tongue entered and retreated, joining in with her tongue along the way.

His kisses made her feel like a beloved princess, all warm inside as butterflies danced in her belly, and heat coiled lower. It amazed her how he could do that to her with just his lips and tongue. On a low, feminine groan that might've sounded more like a whimper, she slid her arms from between them, landing them on his arms and pressing herself closer to him, trying to absorb his body heat as well.

In an instant, the whole tone of the kiss changed. Instead of flirty and soft, it became urgent and demanding. She loved that type of kiss also. It made her feel wanted...and desired beyond all means.

One of his hands slid up her back to around the back of her head, angling her so that he could deepen the kiss. His other hand slid down her back to her butt, and he pulled her lower body flush against him, showing her how much she affected him. Good, it wasn't just her and her racing heart and pounding pulse through her body that was enjoying this make-out session.

Exploring on her own, her hands slid up his arms and rested on his bulging biceps. The touch sent a jolt of electricity shooting through her veins.

When he broke the kiss, she attacked his neck since it was right there, beckoning her. Placing urgent kisses on his collarbone, shoulder, and then, sliding up on her tiptoes, the path behind his ear, she hit a spot where he visibly shivered. She halted and went back to it, nipping at it with her teeth. Again, he shivered. She'd long forgotten about his sensitivity in that spot.

He growled and pulled them apart with his hands on her biceps. "Enough, or we're going without dinner."

With a coy smile, she winked before she spun around and raced to the bedroom, hoping he understood the message and followed her. It'd suck if he didn't show. Maybe she should've told him. No, he had to have understood. He was a man after all.

In the bedroom, she stripped off her shirt and bra, toeing off her sneakers, then tackling the button on her jeans. She was hopping and nearly dancing in her rush to strip before he arrived in the room. He'd probably been sensible and put the meat back in the refrigerator before he followed her, and he'd obviously walked, not torn off like she had. If she could hurry, she could be in bed, waiting for him…and be ready.

She'd just hopped onto the bed when Matt joined her in the room. He didn't say a word. He just began stripping with his eyes glued to her. Playfully, she patted the space beside her. "I saved a spot for you."

She loved the sight of him without a shirt on. That broad expanse of a chest with enough curly hair to make playing in it fun but not so much that kissing on it choked a girl. Itching to reach out and touch his chest, and excited about how bold and brave she'd become, she decided to keep up her flirty mood and touched her own breasts instead to tease him. He always loved her touching herself. She moaned, and his hand froze on his pants. Oh, it felt good, but nothing compared to what his hands and mouth on her felt like.

That thought evoked a smile on her face, and warmth radiated through her limbs. She wanted his hands on her. She couldn't wait, so she jumped back out of bed and moved to a stunned Matt, who still had his hands on the button of his jeans. He stood transfixed by her little show, giving her a heady feeling of power.

****

Matt was in heaven, or the next best thing. Caitlyn was touching her breasts. The sight set his blood afire as it brought back many of the memories with her…even naked…especially naked and standing in front of him with a look like she was about to devour him whole. That might be nice, but he had bigger plans for them now that she could be intimate without anxiety. He'd like to let go fully, not worrying about anything other than her pleasure.

"Are you sore?" He wouldn't hurt her no matter how bad she made him want her.

She shook her head. "No."

"Well then, I could use some help here." He looked down at her and pointed to the button on his jeans. Really, he didn't need assistance, but it kept her hands off her breasts, which in turn kept him from drooling all over and then coming in his pants like a teenager getting to second base for the first time.

She smiled at him seductively, her eyes darkening, yet somehow sparkling.

As if belting out a love song, his pulse sang about their upcoming sex. She was free. He could see it in her eyes and her actions. Thank the fuck for that.

While she worked the button and zipper on his jeans, he placed both hands on her face and tilted her up to him. His heart pounded, beating against his chest as if trying to gain freedom from the constraints. At first, he and Caitlyn simply gazed at each other with a fiery intensity that should've seared them both. They'd had that before anything had happened to her. So much passed between them like this. Lust...love...trust.

The trust was in her eyes, and that meant no holding back.

Matt leaned down and took her mouth in a searing kiss. His intention had been to go slowly and gently, but fuck...she had his mind so muddled he couldn't imagine what would come out of his brain while reminding him the steps to having sex. Thankfully, he figured he could do it all without that coaching from within.

Once she'd finished her chore of unfastening his jeans, he moved his hands down to her arms before she could wrap them around him. Frustratingly, he broke the kiss and leaned his forehead against hers. "Get in the bed." His demand didn't have the power behind it he wanted because he was gasping to catch his breath. "I'm right behind you."

When she didn't move, he spun her around to

where she was facing the bed. Since she still wouldn't move, Matt swatted her on a perfect butt cheek to get her forward momentum going.

"Ow," she said, rubbing her hand on the spot where his red handprint was already showing. Fuck. That couldn't have hurt her. He didn't swat hard. A shot of remorse hit him for potentially harming her.

Caitlyn turned around pouting and with an intensity in her eyes that almost knocked him over. "You're going to have to kiss it and make it better."

A chuckle escaped him. Hell, he planned to kiss her entire body again anyway. A shiver of anticipation plowed through his veins at the thought. Sex had been good between them when they were younger, but now…it wasn't that it was better necessarily, but it was that emotional part that threw him for a loop.

He removed his shoes. Shoving down his pants and underwear, he tried recounting football stats to help him slow down the thinking in his pants.

Once his attire was crumpled up where he'd initially stood, he made haste to the bed. Caitlyn lay there with only a sheet covering her from the waist down. All the ground of distance he'd gained while recalling stats was lost when she pulled the cover off her in invitation.

Damn, she was beautiful…and sexy…and *his* woman. Even more so than when they'd been a happy couple. That halted him in his tracks. Could they be another happy couple, or were they doomed to a short love affair?

"You can take it off." She sank to her knees on the bed and pointed to his prosthesis.

"Are you sure?"

"Yes. Go ahead."

With her blessing, he shrugged and sat on the edge of the bed. Then, he pulled the compression sleeve off, leaving it draped on the artificial limb. Then he did the remaining steps to free what remained of his leg. All that time, he felt her warm breath near his ear while she observed.

"How long have you had it?" she asked when he'd finished.

"A little over five years." Years he'd wanted her by his side, and when that hadn't happened—hell, she probably hadn't heard—all he'd wanted to do was crawl into a hole and die. Thankfully his father and brothers had helped keep him sane. Surprisingly, Brad had been the one to find the place in Memphis to get the custom-fitted limb.

The more he was around other amputees, the quicker his pain and regret seeped away so he could function as he was. He'd worked doubly hard on strengthening his legs. It was weird working out without the prosthetic, but luckily there were other amputees there to motivate him to recovery.

"I love the scene painted on the artificial limb."

He was so used to it that it didn't even occur to him she might find it interesting. "It was there the last time you saw it."

"Yeah, but I didn't want to ruin a perfectly good moment"—she bit her bottom lip—"like I am now."

"You're not ruining anything. As for the design, it's just the American flag waving in the background, and an eagle, and my SEAL team badge and trident." His SEAL tattoo had been on his calf. The one he'd lost, so he only saw it fitting it belonged on his prosthetic.

"It's a work of art."

He didn't want this to turn into him or anything to do with his only having half a leg, so he shifted and swung his stump on the bed, then used his other foot and hands to help propel him back on the bed. With his hands behind him, he scooted the rest of the way until there was enough room for the two of them to move, because as far as he was concerned, staying in one spot didn't work unless you were a teenage kid working with a one-minute window of sex. And he planned for it to be a hell of a lot longer than that.

Matt turned to his side, propping his head up with his hand, elbow sinking into the mattress. Similar to what she'd done earlier, he patted the space next to him with his free hand and gave her an expectant look.

Raking his gaze over her again, he wondered how he'd gotten so lucky to find her again after all this time. She was the entire package—beautiful inside and out—and she was his. He wouldn't walk away from her again. He'd be staying—somehow, some way. Devon would work it out. He had to. Matt couldn't accept any other answer than being with Caitlyn.

With a giggle, she plopped down on the bed on her back, her arms and legs spread wide. Well, one arm hit him in the chest, so not so wide. By allowing this, she still felt she was in control somehow. "Take me, I'm yours," she said dramatically.

She didn't have to tell him twice. He didn't even need a map for the playground she provided. It was still seared into his brain—something to never be forgotten.

Now, he had to decide where to start. Hell, he'd—

"Just remember," she broke into his thoughts, "fair

play." Her seductive tone shot goosebumps skittering along his body.

Even though she'd opened herself up, he didn't think climbing on top of her right away was the way to go, just in case. However, she didn't seem bothered by it when he'd flipped them before. Then again, she had also been in the throes of an orgasm, so she might not have been aware of his actions.

So, he'd start with what was level with his mouth, and it wasn't hers.

Chapter Twenty-Seven

Caitlyn sighed in pleasure. She should've known he'd start with her breasts. That had been typical of him when they'd been together in the past. She wouldn't complain because the sensations she underwent when he kissed her body were off the charts.

She supposed she should've been nervous, maybe even fearful about opening her body up to Matt as she had, but she trusted him to make love to her. With him, the fear of being intimate had resolved itself. When they'd made love before and he'd climbed on top of her, if she hadn't been so sated, she feared she'd have reacted differently. Well, at least reacted. Thankfully, he'd moved before her brain could go from a top-of-the-world orgasm to cowering in fright. A small part of her wondered if she'd had Matt alongside her all these years, would she have been normal with sex?

With his mouth on one nipple and his free hand fondling the other peaked nub, her blood flowed hot through her veins, and the heat below simmered, ready to boil into an orgasm that she knew he'd make sure she had.

Matt's tongue flicked her pert nipple, and she caught his heated gaze boring into her. Placing her hand on his head, her fingers absently ran through his hair. Locked in each other's gaze, his hand tightened his hold on her breast and squeezed, and then moved slowly down her body.

Caitlyn's breaths sped up, knowing what pleasure was sure to come. He kissed her on the mouth; his lips worked their way slowly down her body. The warm, damp kisses carved a path of desire over her chest, down around her belly button, sending goosebumps running over her skin. Then he moved to her core, where his hot breath on her sex sent a shiver of delight running through her body. It was all so much pleasure she could barely contain it.

Moving his body to position himself between her legs with his mouth even with her mound, Matt spoke softly to her. "Anytime you want me to stop, just say so."

Jokingly, she asked, "Do we need safe words?"

He cocked his head to the side and raised an eyebrow. "Not unless there's something you're not telling me."

She couldn't tell if he was jesting with her or thought it to be the truth. "No. I still don't know what vanilla means, so 'stop' works for me." However, she didn't plan on using the word tonight.

After a deep, soul-searching gaze, Matt nodded and chuckled. "Okay. Now, I need to taste you again."

Oh, she wouldn't shy away. She wanted him to taste her also. Matt was a master at oral sex—always bringing her to orgasm in almost no time whatsoever. Big, strong orgasms were always a guarantee once his tongue touched her so intimately.

As her hands played with the top of his head—all she could reach in this position—anticipation raked through her. When his tongue touched her clit for the first time, she nearly came off the bed. Damn the man.

She heard a chuckle from him at her response.

Running a finger down the seam of her wet folds, he split them, and his tongue slid down her center. She couldn't bite back the moan that escaped from her chest.

"Damn, you taste like perfection," Matt said before his lips went to her clit and sucked on it.

An electric shock zipped through her, but he wasn't done torturing her to ecstasy. Torturing because his finger inside her and his lips on her felt damn good, but he wouldn't allow her to come until he decided it was time to bring her to that pleasurable peak. Oh, he'd get her there, but on his own timetable. She wanted to come.

A second finger glided inside her, and she grew wetter.

His voice rumbled over her sex. "I know you want me to hurry, but you have no idea how much you've been driving me crazy. I've imagined doing this to you all day. Savoring you. And with your shirt today as thin as it was, I saw when your nipples peaked when we were in the cold air conditioner. I swore you were teasing me until I realized you had no idea."

His fingers remained in place, tormenting her with their movements, and his mouth went back to her clit, using his tongue, as he flicked her sensitive nub. She craved…no needed him inside her.

"So wet," Matt murmured.

She arched her back and tipped her hips forward, moaning in bliss and not trying to hide her frustration. "Please, Matt. I want to come."

He stopped his movement and lifted his head to her. "That's all you had to say."

With his fingers and mouth teasing her flesh, an orgasm began to ride her.

"I'm so close," she cried out. Her breath came in pants, and her body was on fire.

Matt said something against her clit, but she couldn't make it out. The intense work of his fingers and mouth were almost too much to handle. "Let go. I've got you," he breathed.

Her heart beat overtime at his words. When his mouth went back to her clit, she exploded with a million balls of fire radiating through her body in extreme ecstasy. She floated and hated that she needed to come back to herself. To find safety. But with Matt kissing his way back up her body, but shifting his mass off her, it could wait while she enjoyed the remnants of the immense orgasm he gave her.

****

Although he wanted to drive his cock into her, Matt kissed his way back up her body, keeping his aside until she said it was okay for him to be on top, even though the movements weren't necessarily easy with his partial leg. Still, since it was a below the knee amputation, he had more usage than if it were otherwise.

It was possible that his being on top of her would never happen again. Part of him chastised himself for taking advantage of her the first time. The other part decided he might be helping her in slow bits.

If she never allowed him on top, they'd learn to deal with it. She'd made such great strides already, and even though he said earlier he wouldn't hold back, he loved her and refused to push her before she was ready. Although he wasn't sure he could still do some of the positions they'd used to, he'd give it his damnedest.

He took her earlobe between his lips and sucked, trying to fight off the pain in his erect cock. He wanted to plunge deep inside her so badly that it hurt, but she needed to lead the way. He just hoped their lovemaking hadn't ended for the night.

With her eyes still closed and her arms out to the side where she'd grabbed hold of the covers when she came, Caitlyn whispered, "I want you inside me...on top."

Yeah, he wanted it too, but.... "Are you sure? It's okay if you're on top again." More than okay in his mind. He'd get to watch those tempting breasts bounce around with her movements.

She bit her lip, and his heart sank a little. She wasn't truly ready. "How about you start on top, and then we'll flip?" he offered.

"No. I'm ready."

She still hadn't looked at him, so he couldn't tell what her eyes were telling him. "Look at me, Caitlyn."

It took a moment, but she opened her gorgeous eyes and turned to him. "Please," she begged.

Now, he was nervous like the first time he'd ever made love to her in college. He'd known then she was the woman for him. That hadn't changed. He nodded once. "Okay."

She turned back to look at the ceiling. It was almost like she was out as an offering.

Well fuck. "Please don't be afraid of me. We'll take it slowly," he said with his gaze hungrily glued on her lips. "You tell me to stop anytime you want. Okay?" He looked up into her gaze now focused on him. It swam with understanding and love.

She nodded her answer and gave him a soft smile.

Slowly, Matt moved his body fully over hers, injured leg straining, but he was strong enough for this. Damn, it felt good to be in this position. So what if it was the missionary position. It fucking rocked when it was with Caitlyn.

Reaching to the bedside table, he tore and unwrapped a condom, then gritted his teeth when he rolled it down his hard length before he moved to her.

The first thing he did when he hovering over her was kiss her passionately. Heat seared their lips and desire raced through as their tongues intertwined and dueled with purpose. So much could go into a moment like this, and so much coaxing could come out of one.

He reached down to make sure she was still wet. He barely held back his groan when he discovered how wet she was. It must've been some orgasm that rocked her. A smile tugged at his lips, loving he'd done that to her.

Breaking apart their lips, he attacked the area between her jaw and collarbone, along with her silky throat. "You're so wet."

"Um hmm," she hummed.

He grasped his cock and notched it against her core, sliding it around her wet folds to have her juices coat him before he entered her. Settled and ready, he looked up in her eyes. "Look at me, Caitlyn. I want to see you when I push inside you."

Her lust-filled gaze stared back at him with eyes where the blue darkened over the green.

The tip of his cock slid inside her, and he halted. She may have said she was ready, and they may have made love already, but he wouldn't take anything for granted.

"You're so damn tight," he groaned. How could he have forgotten that little bit of information in such a short time?

"I want all of you, Matt."

He held his breath and slid inside her in one swift thrust. When she gasped, he froze. "Shit. Did I hurt you?

She shook her head back and forth on the pillow. "No. The fullness just surprised me."

Thank God. Slowly, he began to move, sliding out to the tip of his cock and then gliding back inside.

Damn, he had to be in heaven, because nothing should feel that good. The only thing he imagined would feel better was bareback. It'd probably knock his socks off.

When she wrapped her legs around his waist, allowing him to push deeper inside her, any thoughts of her having fear washed away, so did his resolve to go slow. Accelerating his thrusts brought a moan out of Caitlyn. She closed her eyes, and her head fell back.

"I want you to come again, Caitlyn."

She shook her head. "I can't."

"Yes, you can. Touch yourself. Make yourself come with my cock inside you. I want to feel you clench my cock. If you don't, then I will, but you're faster at it, and I can't hold out much longer." When they'd first been learning to pleasure each other, they'd shown the other by pleasing themselves. It was so fucking hot they'd kept it in their lovemaking. It was time to bring it back.

Caitlyn looked at him and then eased her hand down between them to her clit. Just the idea of her touching herself had him wanting to explode.

Her head fell back again, and she moaned in ecstasy at the combined efforts of her and him getting her to orgasm. "Faster, Matt," she demanded.

He happily obliged, sliding in and out with force. With the hastened movements, he gritted his teeth while he held back from coming.

"I'm close," she breathed.

Thank the fuck for that. His restraint was only so strong.

"I'm…I'm…" she gasped out. The next minute, she was moaning and writhing beneath him and clenching his cock so tightly he almost couldn't move it in and out of her.

The sight of her gasping her rapid breaths and the flush in her face did it for him. Satisfied she'd come a second time, Matt let go and jerked as an orgasm to beat all orgasms ripped through his body, leaving him physically drained. He collapsed on her body, then swiftly moved off her, before ensuring he wrapped an arm around her waist and pulled her to him.

After he'd caught his breath, he moved. "I need to get rid of the condom."

"Hmm. Wait, do you need me to do it?"

Sitting on the side of the bed, he welcomed the calm resting within him that she had wanted to support him…care for him.

"No, there's what's called a bed-to-bath method that will make it quick. Nothing to use long term, but it'll work." He leaned over and kissed her lightly on the lips. "I love you, Caitlyn Robinson."

With a smile, she returned his sentiment. "I love you, Matthew Hamilton."

Hell, he hadn't been called Matthew in longer than he could remember. And he loved it coming from her lips.

Things would work out with them. He knew it would. Whatever it took, he'd be by her side and protect her forever.

Chapter Twenty-Eight

Caitlyn and Tonya scooted off to Caitlyn's room to dress for the fundraiser. Tonya had a lovely periwinkle blue dress to wear that Caitlyn imagined would look fabulous on her friend. Before dressing, Tonya's task had apparently been to get Caitlyn to wear that damned red dress. Admittedly, she'd felt beautiful when she'd tried it on at the shop, but wearing it in front of other people seemed almost as difficult as going naked in front of them, and the dress wasn't really that bad considering other attire she'd seen at these types of events.

"I am not wearing that red ladder dress," she stated firmly as she crossed her arms over her chest.

With her arm held high and the hanger holding said dress, Tonya countered, "Yes, you should wear it. I picked up the pasties, but looking at it now, it's not as low-cut as I thought, so you could probably wear a strapless bra with it." She turned from the dress to Caitlyn. "And I know you have one of those." She shook her head. "I can't believe we didn't just check first before I bought those things."

Caitlyn thought she could wear a strapless bra during every conversation about her wearing the dress. She'd always kept mum on the topic, hoping Tonya would let it go. Considering Tonya's tenacity, that had been a silly notion. Tonya wanted her to wear the seductive dress. Yes, she called it seductive because of the openings on her arm, the clinginess of the fabric, and the plunging neckline in front and back that made her feel wonderful. Due to their different standards, Tonya might not call the neckline plunging, but she did.

As if reading her mind, Tonya broke into her thoughts and the excuses she had prepared. "It's not too revealing for the event if you plan to use that as an excuse. When I set the attire, making it casual versus formal, I imagined you wearing that dress to the event. So don't disappoint me and chicken out." She shook the clothes hanger, and the dress swayed with the movement.

Changing the subject, Caitlyn asked, "I saw the RSVP list. You did a great job, Tonya. I hadn't expected many to make it since it was short notice." Then she realized they'd already discussed that and tried to think of something else to talk about besides her attire for the event.

Tonya shrugged. "We couldn't grab some of those who I think would be big contributors because they were booked. But"—she grinned—"they want us to throw another one where they can see the dogs and what they do."

Caitlyn wanted to jump off the edge of her bed and hug the woman for such a creative idea to get donors, but she wouldn't because Tonya still held the cursed dress aloft.

"Well, if there will be more of these small fundraisers, maybe I should save the dress for next time," she tried.

"No. I'm telling you as your employee, friend, and fashion guru, this is the dress to wear tonight. Besides," she said with a noticeable twinkle in her gaze, "don't you want to look good for your man?" Tonya shook the dress with the corner of her lips twitching to emphasize her point.

When Caitlyn didn't respond, Tonya took the dress off the hanger and laid it on the bed beside Caitlyn. It took all her willpower not to jump away and put space between the inanimate object and herself. She knew she was being silly, but she just didn't know if she could pull it off.

"I'm not listening to you any longer on what I should purchase. I wouldn't have even looked at it had you not been there," Caitlyn said jokingly.

"Humph." Tonya turned to her dress she had hung on the back of the closet door. While sleeveless, Tonya's dress covered to nearly her neck. Caitlyn wouldn't balk at that dress to wear. She admitted to herself that she shouldn't balk about the one Tonya was pushing her to wear either. She really did want to look good for Matt.

A girlish giggle almost burst from her. She'd have eye-candy with her all night. Then her laughter died. Damn. There would be a bunch of rich women—single rich women—at the event that Caitlyn didn't trust to not try to steal him off for the night.

To keep his attention away from them, she'd wear that damn dress. There. Decision made. No more excuses. She wouldn't have to hear any more about it. "I'll wear it." Her voice held conviction. With a smile from Tonya, Caitlyn went to the bathroom to put on her makeup, her thoughts running in and out about how she should wear her hair. Up or down? If up, then how? No, she'd go with down. Matt liked it that way.

Caitlyn was nearly finished with her makeup when Tonya settled her makeup bag down on the "his" side counter on the his-and-hers sinks. "I'm glad things are safe, but I miss those men hanging around."

Caitlyn's hand halted while brushing on mascara. "Any particular one you're missing?" she fished.

Tonya's flustered state amused Caitlyn. "Yes. No. I mean, they were all good men."

Sticking the mascara wand back in the tube and screwing it closed, Caitlyn held back her laugh. "I noticed you talked to Ken a lot."

"Yeah. Well…." Tonya applied powder on her face with a huge brush. "He's nice, but he doesn't live here."

Caitlyn's heart sank to her stomach with that simple statement. She didn't want to worry about her and Matt's relationship, but what Tonya said summed it up. They lived in different parts of the country. *No,* she told herself forcefully, *I won't let anything ruin tonight—my last night with Matt.*

"If it's meant to be…." She trailed off, not even being able to be positive of that.

The two women chatted about the fundraiser as they continued preparing. All four veterans had agreed to come and proudly show off their dogs. Caitlyn could barely contain her excitement over it. They'd each be near a corner in the room and allow people to greet the dog and show them a few simple tasks the dog did that made the difference to the veteran. With them spread out, there shouldn't be a large group huddled around a single veteran and dog, which pleased her because two of the veterans had problems with large crowds, but they'd assured her that having the dog there would help.

As the two women slipped into their heels, Caitlyn

said, "I hope we can get more donations. After this ends, I'm hiring one of the two grant writers I found to help us. If you have the right submission, there's a lot of money to grab."

"Have you...had the books audited recently?" Tonya's nervous voice surprised her.

"No. Rick does a great job on them."

Tonya bit her lip as if contemplating her answer. Keeping her gaze on Matt and Rick, who were at the open bedroom door, she said, "I think you should have them audited. It's the smart business thing to do." She turned and left a stunned Caitlyn in her wake. By the time she left her stupor, Tonya was chatting with the two guys, who'd been waiting so they could all walk over together.

What had she meant by her statement? Was Rick not as experienced as she'd believed? Maybe it's too much over his head. That had to be it. She'd been wrong to tease him into the position with more pay. Maybe his errors could be good in their favor. Her heart sank at the thought it could be worse.

Whatever the reason, it had to wait because they had to get the show on the road. Whether their bank balance was higher or lower due to potential accounting errors, they still needed more money to get through the remainder of the year.

She stood in front of the full-length mirror in her bedroom, ensuring she looked all right. A groan escaped. Maybe she shouldn't be wearing this dress. It felt more like date-wear versus open-your-wallet-wear. Then again, she and Matt could be considered on a date for the evening.

Liking that, she nodded to herself and turned from

the mirror only to almost run smack into Matt, who'd walked into her room without her notice. When she stepped back, she lost her balance both mentally and physically, but Matt's hands grabbed her before she fell on her backside.

Wow was an excellent word to describe Matt. Clean-shaven—she missed his perpetual five o'clock shadow—he wore a charcoal gray suit that did not hide his bulging biceps, topped off with a red tie. Holy crap, his tie matched her dress. Surely he hadn't known what she'd planned to wear. Heck, even she hadn't. But still, he looked like he belonged in a boardroom giving orders. He exuded strength and raw masculine sexuality. Holy crap, the women would be all over him tonight.

"Are you okay?" He still held her, steadying her.

With her faint nod, he released her. "You look great." He could've worn almost anything to attend the event, but this was above and beyond in her book.

He smiled. "Thanks."

She appreciated the hell out of it his going the extra mile to look good tonight, but she'd have to stick with him to keep any barracuda teeth from latching onto his yummy body.

"You look beautiful, Caitlyn." He leaned toward her, but she edged out of his reach.

"It took long enough to get this makeup on, and you won't mess it up." She grinned, pleased he'd complimented her outfit. Score one for Tonya.

"Then expect me to mess it up at the night's end." He held out his arm, and she looped hers through it and smiled. Her stomach fluttered, considering the evening to come. She definitely would allow him to do whatever he wanted.

Her heart pounded, and her pulse rate increased at the thought. Tonight. Their last night. She'd enjoy every second of it.

****

Damn. Caitlyn looked smokin' hot in that dress. With the way it fell around her perfectly shaped body, she took sexy to a whole new level. One Matt definitely appreciated. How the hell was he to remain vigilant—because his gut still churned they'd missed something or someone—when his dick just wanted to pant after her all evening like a lusty schoolboy?

The short walk from the house to where they held the fundraiser went by quietly. She seemed lost in thought. Maybe she was getting into the right mindset to ask for money. He sure as hell knew requesting it would be a tough job to handle, and he was in awe that she could do it so well. True, he'd only seen her work with Hart, and she'd explained that was a different case due to the amount of money, but she was confident, passionate, knowledgeable, and not afraid to talk about funding.

No sooner had they entered, Hart attached himself to Caitlyn's other side. The man explained that most of the people in the room appeared to know each other, and he knew no one, so he was glad Caitlyn had arrived when she had.

Scanning the room, Matt had to agree many had clustered in small circles. Only about twenty people had already arrived. For the meal, the chef and helpers had taken over Caitlyn's kitchen and the small work area in the training facility—but most potential donors were watching the dogs and the veterans. Matt had thought that the dressed-up rich people would prefer to stay away from the dogs and dog hair, but it appeared Caitlyn knew her audience well.

Everyone greeted her, and Matt—not being introduced as her fiancé, which surely pleased Hart—remained steady by her side, receiving quite a few winks, either from some secret he'd missed or in flirtation. He hoped not flirtation because the women were too old for him and the men were…well, men. He held nothing against someone who swung that way, but he loved women. Not all women, just his Caitlyn.

As she worked the room, more and more people arrived. She'd explained that only half of them were actual donors, the others were their plus-one, and some had their own large pocketbook. That made him equally ecstatic for Caitlyn's purpose and uncomfortable with how he'd keep her safe. If only Hart would quit sticking to her, he'd feel better. There was no doubt in his mind that when it came to Hart, it was 100 percent jealousy. Would this man swoop in while he was in Baltimore closing up his life there while he prepared to move to Winchester? *No,* he assured himself. Caitlyn loved him. She wouldn't turn to another man when Matt was out of sight. He knew better than to even think like that. Caitlyn had been through a lot, and he'd been the one to help her recover. Oh, she hadn't recovered fully—probably never would—but she'd opened herself to him.

A catering employee whispered in Caitlyn's ear, and she nodded. "It's time to eat. Would you both excuse me so I can announce it to everyone else?" She pointed to a table on the opposite side of the room. "Tate, your table is over there."

How had she known that off-hand? Surely she'd reviewed the seating charts, but to remember where the man sat stuck in Matt's craw. Maybe his jealousy wasn't unfounded because she'd set him across the room from her.

"I'd love to sit with you," Tate nearly gushed like a schoolgirl.

Caitlyn shook her head, her hair flowing around her to perfectly frame her beautiful face. "I'm sorry. Seating has already been assigned, and my table is full."

Hart looked over her head at Matt and gave him a "watch your fucking back" look. It took a good amount of his resolve not to punch the prick right in his face. He didn't want her party ruined over the bloodshed of a potential donor.

Matt wondered why the dickwad hadn't donated yet. He'd talked to everyone on staff and watched plenty of training. He best not be stringing her along, hoping for a hookup with Caitlyn as part of his reward. Matt would have to kill the fucker if that were the case. Tonight, they'd have to ensure they tried to firm up his donation.

Turning to Matt, Caitlyn placed a hand on his chest and quietly told him to sit, and she'd be right there. He didn't like it, but their table was front and center anyway, so he could watch her closely. When he arrived at the table with Rick and his partner, along with Tonya and her plus one—a not-so-bad-looking man even though he didn't rate other men, a snort almost escaped at the memory of when he was in high school telling Brad how handsome he was because it meant his twin—himself—would also be handsome.

It'd been vain, but he'd been a teenager, and a girl had said he was ugly. Of course, that'd been right after the twins had broken each other's nose. He probably hadn't looked that ruggedly handsome.

Vivian Blanche, who had to be in her seventies, rounded out the table of eight with a young, muscular man doting on her. The man blushed when Vivian introduced him as her date for the evening. Later, Matt learned from the man that he was a nurse in the group caring for Vivian. She might act like a spry spring chicken, but she was sicker than she wanted people to notice. For some reason, that wholeheartedly included not worrying Caitlyn with the fact.

Already being briefed on Vivian from Caitlyn— how the woman sent them ten thousand dollars a year except for the last couple of years—it was easy to see she cared for the older woman. That pleased him that the feeling was mutual. Caitlyn didn't need to be hurt by anyone.

Caitlyn announced dinner was served, and those still loitering turned to find their tables. After standing and helping Caitlyn in the chair on his left, he sat and turned to Tonya on his right. "This is incredible. You did great, Tonya. There aren't any empty seats."

The woman blushed at his compliment. "It was nothing. I got help along the way, like managing all the vehicles when there really isn't a parking lot."

"But you did it," he said, thinking of how professionally staged the vehicles were on the drive and in part of the yard.

"Oh, a valet from town and an off-duty deputy sheriff volunteered to take over that daunting challenge."

He chuckled. "You are smart to know when to hand stuff off. I've heard that many party planners keep a tight hold on things until everyone hates to work for them." Where he gained that knowledge escaped him, but he'd heard it somewhere before, probably from one of his sisters-in-law.

"I won't lie. This is the first time I've handed anything off. But we haven't had an event here. Usually, the hotel takes care of almost everything. Besides, plenty of people in this community will do whatever they can to support what Caitlyn has built. She just doesn't realize the depth of the conviction to Helping Paws."

He was seeing the draw to her place from those in attendance. Hadn't he heard several people flew in for this shindig? They had to have, because he couldn't see much money in town alone. It wasn't that they couldn't make that much money; it was just a smaller place than Baltimore.

Caitlyn ate maybe two bites from her citrus salmon dinner. He imagined it had to be nerves since she was expected to give a short speech. In an attempt to soothe her, he held her hand under the table once it was apparent she wouldn't eat another bite. He'd devoured his filet with a crabmeat topping and the loaded potato side. The roasted asparagus was left untouched. Oh, he liked his vegetables, but asparagus hadn't made the cut since they made his pee stink.

When dessert was served, he released Caitlyn's hand hoping she'd at least nibble on some of the mini-cheesecake sampler placed before her. He didn't hold back. It was fantastic, and again, like the size of the filet, he wished for more. He couldn't complain. The same sizes would've been served to him in a fancy restaurant, but when he liked to cook, he'd prepare more to fuel his large frame.

Tonya leaned in close to Matt. "I need to talk with you." The urgent whisper in her voice had the hair rising at the nape of his neck. He covertly glanced around as best he could. He hated that he hadn't checked their seating assignments at the table early since now he couldn't see everyone without turning his head, which made it obvious. He liked to see the entire room, plain and simple, and he'd been so green with jealousy of Hart that he hadn't left Caitlyn's side long enough to ensure he had the best seating.

Giving his attention to Tonya, he swallowed hard, and the delicious dinner roiled in his stomach.

The woman looked almost green. "Can we slip away a second after Caitlyn leaves the stage and does her walk around for committed donations that she didn't receive earlier? I'd prefer you didn't tell her or…Rick about it."

Sensing the importance of this—at least to Tonya—he nodded slowly. "Is she in danger?" he whispered.

"No."

Relief wooshed through him at that. No way did he want to leave her alone, but he'd make sure they were somewhere he could at least watch her. He'd been informed that while she walked the group before the event, that was more of a welcome, even though some confirmed contributions. It was after the event that she had to work the room to gain those commitments of funds.

Caitlyn leaned into him as she placed her cloth

napkin on the table. "Wish me luck."

Without a thought, he kissed her lightly on the mouth so as not to mess up her makeup as she'd asked, and whispered, "Good luck," against her slightly parted lips.

Her smile grew, and she stepped up to the makeshift stage and microphone. Mesmerized is what he could call the people in the audience. Before she finished, she had them eating out of her hands.

God, he was so proud of her. Sure, what she'd accomplished with building Helping Paws was commendable, but not allowing what had happened to her to prevent her from doing this—something like asking for money—was damn amazing. And by surviving tonight, she'd enjoy the other fruits of her labor and her dogs. There was a graduation ceremony for Cooper, Bella, Sadie, and Gabe tomorrow, and she'd invited everyone present. It wouldn't be anything fancy, but it'd be a changing of the guard, so to speak.

Once she stepped down, donors swarmed her, and Matt wanted to rush to her side and protect her. But these people weren't a threat to anything but her time, and she'd give it to them whether they donated or not.

The people at his table began to stand, and he followed suit. Once they'd moved away, Tonya placed one hand on his arm. "Now, please?"

He nodded, and they walked to the back of the room and into a corner. Tonya wanted to go outside, but he informed her that he wasn't losing track of Caitlyn.

Seeming somewhat appeased, Tonya informed him she hadn't had the heart to tell Caitlyn, but she couldn't wait another moment to share her suspicions. She then went ahead to tell him a story that made his blood boil to the level he wanted to throttle someone. That someone had been hurting Caitlyn, whether she'd known it or not.

Chapter Twenty-Nine

Matt almost ignored his vibrating phone. Good sense had him reaching into his pocket and pulling it out. Devon's name flashed on the screen, so he connected the call. "Yeah."

"I hear that I need to set you up remotely," his brother stated.

Barely able to hear the call over the noise in the room, he moved near an empty spot where he could still watch everything, especially Caitlyn mingling. "Yeah. If she'll have me."

"I remember when you dated way back when. She'll have you."

"Think it'll be a problem?"

Seeming to understand his vague question, Devon added, "It'll be fine. We'll just have to get used to calling you up when we meet. Besides, it's not very often we're all here together."

He smiled at that. While the group of brothers decided cases, workloads, pay, etc., they allowed Jesse to be the figurehead and final decision-maker. There were too many times they needed one direct response without waiting, and Jesse provided that. When he wasn't available, Devon stood in his stead. Brad had always told them, "Age before beauty."

"Also, as you know, Jesse wants us to discuss leasing a plane or finding a share in one that we can use to help us get to jobs faster. It makes sense since so many are at the last minute with little time to lose—like a kidnapped kid."

"I can't imagine they're cheap, but if we can afford it," Matt agreed, "I think we should do it. That could really help with the weapons issues also." Sometimes, they were limited with what they could take on a commercial flight—even in the locked, hard-sided container required for an unloaded weapon. Airport security generally worked with them, but sometimes airline policy didn't. He didn't even want to get started on shipping the rifles.

"Yep. Okay, I called about that name you made me look into. I couldn't find a Tate Hart that meets your description. If he's planning to donate one million dollars, I can't find where from. I tried a couple of variations on his first name, even though Tate isn't really short for anything I know exists. But, nothing. Sorry, man."

His temper flared. That asshole had been leading her on with the promise of something to benefit her organization. "Son of a bitch!" Matt sounded. He scanned the room, looking for where Caitlyn was. "I've got to go, but I need your help on another matter. Check out bank accounts for Rick Marsh. I think his name is Richard. I think he's skimming off the donations submitted via check to Caitlyn's foundation. Get Em involved. Tonya, her other employee, noticed separate deposit slips when he did a bank run, so try Caitlyn's bank first."

Without waiting for a response from Devon, he ended the call and pushed through the small crowd to get to the opposite side of the room where Hart was trying to lead Caitlyn toward an exit. Since they'd seen him in her company earlier, several of those in attendance tried to stop Matt and chat about Caitlyn and Helping Paws. She'd have to forgive him for being rude to her potential donors, but whether she realized it or not, she needed him. Hart was up to something. But what?

After what seemed like an interminable amount of time, he reached the exit he'd seen them slip through. What could Caitlyn have been thinking? He quickly reminded himself that she didn't consider Hart a threat. More of an annoyance. In her mind, the danger to her life was lying up in a hospitable bed.

Stepping out the door, he took a moment to allow his eyesight to adjust. His heart pounded in fear for Caitlyn, and fear he wouldn't be there when she needed him…like before.

Hearing a muffled squeal, he quickly moved in that direction while his gaze took in the entire area, trying to locate Caitlyn and the asshole who might die tonight if he hurt her. Zeroing in on them, he charged toward them, raging anger filling him and flowing in each heavy step. Seeing Caitlyn struggling in Hart's embrace froze his blood. Oh, hell no!

Matt pulled his weapon from beneath his jacket and pointed it at Hart's back, not wanting Caitlyn in danger from one of his bullets. "Let her go," he asserted.

Hart froze and slowly turned to Matt with a smirk on his face. Seeing the weapon in Matt's hand, his smirk dropped, and he narrowed his eyes. After a moment, he slowly lifted his hands. "What's the problem? Jealous of a little competition?"

Ignoring the questions, Matt's eyes never left Hart, but his voice softened for Caitlyn. "Come here, Caitlyn."

She scooted around Hart and hid behind Matt.

Thank the fuck she didn't argue. The asshole had been trying to kiss her. He'd had her in an unwelcome embrace. Matt would love to shoot out the fucker's balls, but that would cause too much trouble for him. "I want you to leave and never come back here."

"Matt?" Caitlyn questioned quietly. Her shaking hand rested on his shoulder. This incident must have freaked her out, but she seemed to be holding it together. "He just tried to kiss me. I'm sure we can clear up the misunderstanding."

His grip on his weapon tightened. Misunderstanding? God, she had a big heart. "Caitlyn, he's a fraud. He doesn't exist. Devon tried to find any trace of him and the money he keeps talking about. He's here because he wants you."

Quizzically, she looked around Matt at Hart. "Tate?"

"I'll just leave now. We could've been good together, Caitlyn." Tate walked backward from them until he reached the front yard. Then he turned and strode to the valet for his vehicle.

While Hart—or whatever the hell his name was—waited for his car to be delivered, Matt lowered his weapon and put it away. He reached around him—not taking his eyes off Hart—and pulled Caitlyn into his arms. He still wanted to punch the motherfucker, but he had Caitlyn to worry about. She shook and squeezed tightly around his waist, her face buried in his chest.

"Thank you." The weakness in her voice didn't

match the ferocity of her grip on him.

He tightened his hold on her, and once Hart was gone, Matt dropped his head into her hair and closed his eyes. "I'm sorry I was late to protect you." Anguish laced his voice. She shook her head, and he couldn't care less that she was probably leaving makeup all over his suit jacket, tie, and shirt as long as she was safe. That was all that mattered. What had that asshole planned? Would he have forced her away? Surely not. There was a sheriff's deputy near the vehicles. A mental shudder went through him at the thought of her being taken against her will once again.

"He just tried to kiss me. That's all."

"That's too much without your permission." He rubbed his hands up and down her back in a soothing gesture. Way too much spun in his mind. He imagined it was in her mind also, but she was trying to be brave. He just knew she did it to help him relax. "I'm sorry."

Caitlyn pulled her head back and looked at him with tears in her eyes. "What did you mean he's a fraud?"

"Oh, honey, he's using a fake name for some reason. He doesn't have money. I really think he fell in love with you at first sight and said whatever he needed to get close to you." That at least sounded logical. Whether it was the truth was a different matter. If Matt hadn't known that Caitlyn needed his comfort after extracting her from Hart, he'd have detained the man to find out why. He just prayed that was the last they saw of whatever his true name was. Maybe he'd see if he could find some prints and ID the bastard so that she could get a restraining order.

When a tear slid down her face, he wiped it off

with his thumb. He prayed she wore that waterproof makeup shit women sometimes chose because there were a lot of potential tears floating in the rims of her bright eyes. Sure enough, the next second, she broke down crying. He placed his palm on her head and guided her back into his chest. Fuck whether his coat absorbed her tears and makeup.

"At first"—she hiccupped—"I thought I was back there. In Oxford. When—"

"Shh, sweetheart, you're safe. Ripley can't get to you anymore. Neither can Hart."

That statement stuck with Matt for the remainder of the evening. After Caitlyn had freshened up, she returned to her potential donors, and Matt watched her expertly gain commitments of hundreds of thousands of dollars for Helping Paws.

Now, he had to tell her an employee she trusted had been stealing from her. Fuck if his heart didn't ache for the pile of shit being thrown her way. Enough was enough.

Chapter Thirty

Caitlyn rested on her side, her head propped on a hand while she studied a relaxed and sleeping Matt. The night before, he'd been her knight in shining armor, saving her from Tate and whatever he'd planned. She shuddered at the thought. She'd been fooled by the man like everyone else had.

Matt had also been the perfect date for her benefit. He'd been polite and helped keep conversations on Helping Paws and its future. He'd even led some old-time donors she hoped would donate again to one of the veterans and their dogs. A little show and tell went a long way for the evening. She knew begging for money wasn't his forte, but no one would ever have known it. And, he'd left her side when she'd needed to work the room alone. Granted, that had left her unprotected, but she couldn't have predicted what Tate had planned when he asked to speak with her privately about his donation. He must've been able to tell she was tired of listening to what he intended to donate, and told her that he had the check ready but didn't want to give it in front of the other donors.

What a fool she'd been.

For her, receiving a check in front of other donors would go a long way to people anteing up now versus committing and sometimes forgetting to mail the check. She knew all would not come through with their donations, but assuming the general amount of people who didn't send their donation, they'd brought in enough money to take them through the year and beyond. Joy filled her. It'd been the most successful night they'd ever had, and she planned to do something nice for Tonya to repay her for the brilliant idea and event.

The arm holding her head began to fall asleep, so she shifted. Wow, Matt had a serious bedhead going on. His dark, short hair stood up in all directions, except the edge of the left side, where it lay flat against his head. Obviously, he'd been turned toward her most of the night. Remembering the night, she smiled. He'd been so gentle the first time they'd made love. He was still hesitant with her. Little did he know, he'd come very close to erasing those memories by overwriting them with special ones of the two of them. To include a rough and hot tumble at about two in the morning when she'd woken him and insisted he take her hard from behind. He'd scoffed at first, but—her smile widened—she'd convinced him.

Wanting to make Matt breakfast, she was just able to contain the minx in her that wanted her to reach out and play with the smattering of dark hair on his chest and then follow it down to the V she knew existed low on his belly. They'd never get out of bed if she did that.

Quietly, she slid from between the covers and, from her closet, pulled out a pair of jeans and a T-shirt. She'd worry about a bra and panties later. Besides, Matt liked it when she went commando. It drove him insane with lust, and she wanted him like that since it turned her into a lusty woman.

In the kitchen, she filled the countertop with the

fixings for breakfast. She wanted to serve him eggs, bacon, fried potatoes, sausage, grits, and biscuits. Sure it was the same breakfast he'd been eating, down to the homemade biscuits. Maybe she should make pancakes? Not finding an open spot on the counter for the mix, she nixed it. There would be enough food already. This time, she'd even bring out the jellies and jams she'd made, not the store-bought ones. Until now, she'd been embarrassed. What if they had turned out terrible? After testing each one—strawberry, peach, and blackberry— she found them tasty enough to serve without worry, but she still saved them for special occasions. Today felt like one.

While the oven was heated, Caitlyn mixed the biscuit dough and then cut it into acceptable-sized circles to bake. Cleaning her hands of the sticky dough, she found she'd been humming. She'd never thought she'd be this happy again in her life. It was all Matt. Today would not be their last day together. She'd find a way for them to live with each other even if she had to beg. She'd never expected to say that but knew she couldn't live without him.

Leaning over the sink to watch the birds in the front yard on the bird feeder, she smiled when she felt the presence of someone else. Somehow, she'd known that Matt wouldn't sleep long enough for her to finish the breakfast to surprise him.

When he got close, she almost turned but liked when he held her with her back to his front, so she remained still, anticipating his touch. An arm slipped across her belly, and she knew something was wrong before a hand covered her mouth. Her pulse rate soared with fear laced in it. She began to buck and fight against the tight hold. She'd been pulled back from any weapon she could've found on the counter. Why was this happening to her? Not again.

"Keep quiet." Tate! Tate Hart was attacking her. Why? She couldn't speak to ask the question out loud.

She couldn't tell if he had a weapon. He did, however, have her arms pinned to her sides under his tight hold.

Her stomach roiled with a sense of dread that she could be a victim again. Being raped once in a lifetime is one time too many, so she kept up the wiggling and trying to kick back with her bare feet—the only weapon she had available to her. As frightened as she was, she wouldn't be docile as a lamb to the slaughter. She could call out to Matt if she could get his hand free of her mouth. Tate's grip was too tight. Her foot landed squarely on his knee on one attempt to break the hold. He grunted and his hold around her waist loosened, and while she couldn't wrench free, her arms were no longer plastered to her side. She clawed at the hand on her mouth, but it held tight.

****

The incessant buzzing of his cell phone woke Matt from a heavy sleep. Before opening his eyes, he knew he was alone in bed. He felt the loss of her body heat. Last night, he'd been able to explore the desire between him and Caitlyn to his heart's content.

She'd recovered well enough after Hart—or whatever his name was—basically attacked her. While it'd only been a kiss he'd tried to press upon her, Matt knew he'd also just gotten started. He knew the asshole would've taken it further. The idiot was besotted with Caitlyn.

They'd ousted him as a fake millionaire, which should embarrass him enough not to show his face again.

Matt took a long, languid stretch with muscles he and Caitlyn had worked hard. It was like old days, making every second count. He chuckled to himself. Plus, having enough condoms to meet their explosive need was a bonus.

He couldn't wait to tell her that Devon would set him up here. Christ, he'd best ask instead of just assuming, but she couldn't fake her feelings for him. They still loved each other.

The phone began buzzing again, signaling a call, not the expected ping of a voice mail. His senses perked up. Someone was intent on getting his attention. Rolling over, he picked up the phone and pulled it to his ear while he wiped a hand down his face to wake himself up fully.

He didn't even look at the caller ID. He just accepted the call and greeted whoever was on the other end with, "What?" It might've come out shorter than he'd meant, but he wouldn't worry about that. If it were one of his brothers, they'd understand and then get their ass kicked for bothering him so damn early.

Without acknowledging his attitude, Devon pressed forward. "You've got a problem."

At those words, Matt sat up and looked around. Where was she? He had to find Caitlyn. "What's the problem?"

"Tate Hart."

That fucker. He'd kill him if he got his hands on him again. "I thought you said he didn't exist."

"He doesn't, but a James Tate Ripley does. J.T.

289

Ripley. We knew his first name was James, but his middle name never appeared in conversation."

Oh, holy fuck. His heart rate spiked, and he stripped the covers off him and swung his legs over the edge of the bed to attach his prosthetic. Where had Caitlyn fucking gone?

"But he'd checked in with his probation officer. Fuck!" He wanted to slap himself for being so stupid. "Hart only came up here on occasion. He could've checked in and still come back here." If Devon's news was accurate—and it always was—then Caitlyn needed to know who the man really was so she wouldn't be fooled if he came sniffing back around begging for forgiveness.

"Since you were insistent something wasn't right about him, I did more digging. At three o'clock in the morning, the thought of Ripley's son hit me. Brad looked at his photo and confirmed he saw him speaking with you and Caitlyn one day about her organization."

Fuck. Fuck. And double fuck. "But he was here when we arrived from Mississippi. Luke hadn't learned her location when I chased him away from Adam's house."

"Remember when you said you felt like you'd suddenly been knocked senseless from behind?"

"Yeah. It was like—"

Devon finished his sentence since they'd all heard it enough times from Matt, then asked a question. "Someone else was there. What if his son found the information while his uncle tortured Adam and tried to move in to help his uncle grab her by pretending to be a donor and get close to her without anyone thinking anything was untoward? But, then, you came into the picture."

"Let me put you on speaker so I can dress. I don't know where Caitlyn is, and I have to find her." He selected the speaker function and laid the phone on the bed beside him. He went to work getting the prosthetic bed-to-bath feature on. He could pull on the compression sock and such later. Right now, he needed to see Caitlyn to ensure she was all right.

While he collected himself, he spoke to Devon. "The asshole tried to molest her last night. I'm guessing that cruelty runs in the fucking family."

Standing, Matt gathered his balance and ended the call with his brother. After reaching into the bedside drawer, he pulled out his Glock and went in search of the woman he loved, praying he wouldn't need the weapon he gripped tightly.

Hearing scuffling in the kitchen, his heart skipped a beat, and he moved straight in that direction. Peeking around the corner, he saw J.T. Ripley working to retain a struggling Caitlyn. His blood boiled, but he leveled it with the calmness he needed. If Ripley would take his hand from her mouth, it'd be easier, but she'd also be able to call out.

Matt entered the room, pointing his Glock at Ripley, but unfortunately, Caitlyn blocked any clean shot he had. "Hey, Ripley. Why don't you pick on someone your own size?" It was a stupid cliché, but it seemed appropriate to this situation.

Caitlyn's wide, fear-filled eyes ate at Matt's heart. He just wanted to gather her and whisk her to safety. She didn't deserve to deal with this…again. Twice now he'd allowed this maniac near her without protection…like he had the father.

"Took you long enough to figure it out," Ripley sneered. He dropped his hand from Caitlyn's mouth and grabbed her by the neck, pulling her closer with her back to his front.

"Let her go," Matt demanded, moving slowly around the room, hoping to get a better line of sight to Tate fucking Ripley. He bit back hard, wanting to punish the son for the father's offenses to Caitlyn, but he knew he couldn't. The asshole had his own crimes, which included putting his fucking hands on her.

How the hell was he going to extricate her safely? The HIS teams were gone, and Rick and Tonya had the day off. Not that they'd necessarily come to the house looking for them. Then, an idea hit him. It was risky, but so was their current standoff. Ripley didn't appear to have a weapon, so he was willing to try it.

"Caitlyn, do you remember how to sing?" He knew it sounded like an odd question, but Caitlyn had told him after the rape she'd taken self-defense courses but feared she'd forget them when the time came. Except one. She'd watched *Miss Congeniality* many times, and he knew just jogging her memory would help her realize she could take the upper hand. Hell, he definitely couldn't shoot because Ripley used her as a shield, and he couldn't risk hitting her by mistake.

Of course, if Ripley'd had a weapon, he'd never ask her to do something so risky. He just needed some space to subdue the man before he could abscond with Caitlyn.

His question seemed to transform her from the frightened woman in an attacker's arms to a confident woman who wouldn't allow some jerk to abuse her.

With a slow nod of confidence, she focused while

Matt kept his weapon ready if she failed. But he knew she could get away from him long enough for Matt to take control.

"Solar plexus," she said, elbowing Ripley hard with her free arm.

Ripley grunted at the contact she made but didn't release his grip.

"Instep," she said as she stomped on his instep. Granted, her bare feet weren't bringing the entire pain that step could've done, but Ripley grunted again and listed to the side where she'd begun her torture. She hobbled a bit, showing she'd hit him hard enough to impact her foot.

Keep it up, Caitlyn. He's weakening.

"Nose." Only hearing the word should've alerted Ripley that she was about to bring her fist up and connect with his nose.

Ripley dropped his hands off her to grab his bloody nose. Caitlyn didn't have a lot of strength behind it, but it still was a touchy spot when hit.

She turned and raised her knee. "Groin." Matt winced and almost grabbed his package at the ferocity of her attack on Ripley's groin.

Opening his free arm, Matt grabbed her tight against him when she raced into it. His other held his weapon and remained steadily trained on Ripley. "Are you okay?" he asked her while holding her tightly.

"Yes. I did it," she said excitedly. "I saved myself." She kissed him on the cheek. "Thank you. I wouldn't have thought of the SING method. I was too frightened."

With Ripley on his knees, one hand holding his package and the other his bloody nose, Matt looked down at her and smiled. "I knew you could do it. Now, I need to subdue him before he can walk again. Do you have something we can tie him up with until the sheriff's department can arrive?" Releasing Caitlyn, he closed in on Tate and issued an order. "Down on the ground."

Tate looked ready to bolt or fight—who knew with that lunatic—when he noticed Matt still pointed his weapon at him.

"Hands behind your back," Matt instructed. As he accepted a long zip tie from Caitlyn, he raised an eyebrow.

"For the computer cables. I've heard they can also be used to cuff someone."

He didn't have the heart to tell her they were so thin they might not work. But she was so damn proud of herself for helping. "They can, but those are too short for someone this size. But, if you zip three together, I can use that since it's only temporary."

As Caitlyn worked, Ripley became belligerent. "That bitch can't keep my dad in jail."

"So, what? You were bringing her to your father?"

"No," Ripley spat. "I was going to kidnap her so she wouldn't testify at my dad's next parole hearing. Without her, they'll let him out. My uncle and I weren't sure exactly what we would do to her after that. Maybe give her to my dad as a 'Get out of jail' present."

Caitlyn covered her mouth over a gasp. Matt noticed the slight tremble in her body, and he wanted to engulf her in his arms and make her feel safe.

Matt couldn't stop what spewed from this fucker's mouth without knocking him senseless, which he might've done before he cuffed him, but not after.

With the flimsy zip ties secured, Matt opened his arms to Caitlyn and held her with all the strength he could muster. He probably held her too tight, but she didn't complain. She just snuggled in closer.

Dropping his head beside her ear, he whispered, "We need to call the sheriff's department."

She released a heavy sigh. "Do we have to do it now? You feel so good."

A smile split his face. "The sooner they're here, the sooner he's out of here, and you can finish making me breakfast."

If he hadn't known better, he'd have thought she'd been ripped from his arms. She moved so quickly to pick up a phone. He chuckled. That was the woman he loved with all his heart and soul.

Chapter Thirty-One

"How are you feeling?" Matt asked Caitlyn as she walked into her living room. After dealing with the sheriff's department and Caitlyn having a good cry, Matt had held her until she'd fallen asleep. Once the reality of what had happened hit her, it'd been too much for her to handle. It had evoked those memories he'd wanted to replace. There was still time for him to give her new ones that would hopefully wipe her horrors from her mind as much as possible.

His heart pounded hard in equal parts fear and relief. If Devon hadn't woken him this morning, Ripley could've gotten away with kidnapping her. He worried once Ripley was free, he might try again. The man had been screwed up, probably from growing up with a screwed-up father. But he wouldn't tell Caitlyn of his fear. He'd be here to protect her whether she agreed or not. A smile tugged at the corner of his mouth. She'd agree. She'd have to understand how his job could sometimes take him away. Until Ripley was back in jail for violating parole, he wouldn't leave her side, but after…he liked what he did for a living. He might not have been accepted with only one good leg if it hadn't been for his brothers. Most people assumed a disability as a weakness. Not his family. He'd sure miss seeing them almost daily.

"I'm fine," Caitlyn said, breaking into his wayward

thoughts.

"Come here." He reached out from his position on the couch.

Without hesitation, she slipped onto his lap. "Is it finally over?" she asked into his shoulder.

Mindlessly rubbing her back, he thought for a moment and gave her his hope, not reality. "Yes. Father and son are in jail, and uncle isn't a threat. You're safe." When the bastard was released, he'd learn he couldn't mess with Caitlyn.

"What if he gets out?" she asked weakly.

He'd never been able to get anything past her. She was too damn smart. "If he does, I'll be here to protect you." *Plus the entire Hamilton clan,* he left off.

She looked up at him with her beautiful eyes. "You will?"

It was as good a time as any to get this conversation over with. Devon had confirmed everything would be ready for him to telecommute. It would still feel odd, but it gave him Caitlyn, so he'd take that oddity, because life with Caitlyn was a win.

Brushing his thumb lightly across her jaw, he leaned down and kissed her softly. "Yes, if you'll have me."

"What do you mean?"

"I mean that I could live here—with you—and still work with HIS. Don't get me wrong, I'd love to learn how to train the dogs to be helpful here, but Dev is setting me up to work from afar. My brothers and I have always had our picks of the missions, so when you need me, I'll be here."

"Am I dreaming?"

Matt chuckled. "No, sweetheart, you're not." He

cocked his head, a small sense of foreboding sitting with him. "Is that okay?" Christ, he'd thought they were on the same wavelength. He couldn't stand it if she said no.

Relief soared through him as she threw her arms around him, banishing all his worried emotions. "Matt, I'll take you any way I can get you. We have a lot of years to make up for. Years where I split us—"

Matt slid a finger over her lips, cutting off her words. "We're past that. It's our future and us. And, one day, I hope you'll consider marrying me." It wasn't a romantic proposal like the first time when he'd been down on one knee, but he'd figure out something proper when the time came.

Pressing her lips to Matt's, Caitlyn whispered, "I love you, Matt."

His heart swelled with love at that simple statement. At one time, it'd been something he thought he'd never hear again from her lips. Now, he'd never hear it enough.

"I love you, too." He'd never get tired of telling her those true words.

Done with the chaste kisses, Matt used one hand to hold her head, moving her lips in place while he laid his upon hers and began to show her how much he loved her…how much he loved that she'd let him live here…how much he was glad she was truly on her way to recovery.

His tongue wanted to be inside her mouth, making love to it, so he nipped at her bottom lip, and when she gasped, he surged inside, tasting her while they dueled for domination of the kiss. She should've remembered he was always the stronger one in that foreplay and led the merry chase to the bedroom.

He froze for a moment. He wanted to take her to bed, but not right now. And if they kept kissing like they were, he'd end up tossing her over his shoulder and hauling her into the room and beat his chest or something stupid like that.

Softening the kiss briefly, he broke it and leaned his forehead to hers as they both gasped for air. "I want you, and if we don't stop, I will carry you to the bedroom and have my way with you."

Damn his forgetfulness around Caitlyn. He couldn't get off track any longer.

Caitlyn laid her head on his shoulder and sighed in what he prayed was pleasure. "You really want to learn to train the dogs?" she questioned, absently brushing her hand over his chest.

Turning the conversation back to Helping Paws reminded him of the unpleasant conversation he needed to have with her. Granted, it was suspicion since Devon hadn't got back to him on that topic, but that was where most problems began.

He cleared his throat. "I do, but we need to talk about something important."

At that statement, her hand froze, and she looked up at him, still cuddled in his lap. "What's wrong?"

"It's come to my attention that Rick might be embezzling from the foundation."

Drawing her brow down, she responded, "What do you mean?"

Undoubtedly, this would be hard for her to hear and believe, but he had to protect her. He'd almost confronted Rick, but he didn't want to overstep any bounds they'd created. "Tonya noticed that when Rick took the donations to the bank he'd filled out two deposit slips. She only glimpsed them, but she couldn't be certain."

"Why didn't she say anything to me?"

Tonya had hurt her feelings by not speaking with her directly, but hadn't she said something? She'd told him she had. "She never said anything?"

Keeping those brows pulled down in thought, she finally remembered. "She said I should have an audit. But that's it."

He rubbed her back. "She'd planned to tell you everything, but with the event, she didn't want more on your mind. When she realized how close we were, she told me so that I could tell you about Rick after the fundraisers."

"Two deposit tickets?"

"Yeah, I can see it. Remember when you told me that Vivian would double her donation to twenty thousand dollars, yet she'd only donated nine thousand and not ten? If Rick is doing this—which Dev is looking into his accounts and we should have something soon—then he's just skimming off any donations that he has to take to the bank."

Shock floated in her eyes. "I can't believe it. He wouldn't." As Matt allowed the reality to sink in, he knew anger would flow from her next. It hit her faster than he'd expected when she bounded from his lap and began pacing the living room.

"Son of a bitch. How could he do that? I want an audit right this minute. Who can I call? Why am I asking you? You don't know the local accountants. But there must be one who's available on the weekend...."

Matt sat silently while she went through her tirade.

Being in the Hamilton family meant the Hamiltons had each other's back for anything and everything. "Um, honey." He tried to gain her attention. When she stopped both her pacing and ranting, he smiled. God, he loved her. "I know someone who will audit your accounts for you, even this Saturday and Sunday, and any other day needed."

Hope washed over her face. "Who?" she asked eagerly.

"Em."

Disbelief flashed across her features. "You said she's an accountant, but Emily's too young to know this."

Laughing, he stood and walked to her, pulling her into his arms. "You're remembering the girl. The woman is not only an accountant, but a kickass forensic accountant."

"And she'd do this to help me?"

"For you, the love of my life, she would."

Epilogue

Seven months later

"Are you sure you need to go?" Caitlyn asked Matt as he packed a bag to leave for an unspecified amount of time.

He knew she was worried. He'd taken short assignments since he'd moved in with her, but never when he didn't know when he'd be back nor what he would be up against.

Life had evolved for them. His working for HIS from afar had been a transition, and it had taken everything within him to leave her that first time. Once she'd helped him forgive himself for what happened all those years ago, his soul had been freed, and their relationship was stronger, and he'd trusted being parted from her. Hell no, he'd never forget, but Matt was at peace now…and so was Caitlyn.

This happened to be another time he'd rather stay home, but it was Brad. "Need to? No. Want to? Yes." He shoved another black T-shirt into his bag. "It's Rylee's sister who's in trouble, but Brad has taken it upon himself to protect her." He stopped shoving the socks in his bag and looked at her. "She and Brad have a somewhat volatile history, so we're a little up in arms about his decision." He didn't plan to share that he knew the two had spent the night together when Devon and Rylee had their second wedding ceremony in Vegas. He also didn't want to share the fighting the two had engaged in when Rylee had been in trouble, and Brad had been charged with keeping Madison safe.

"Are you okay with me leaving?" Christ, he was leaving her alone with the twins she carried. Love burned through him at the thought of her carrying their first children. Thank goodness he'd married her immediately after he'd decided to live in Kentucky with her. As soon as her father had been 100 percent, they'd held a small ceremony, and everyone in the family had traveled to them.

Placing a hand over her tiny baby bump, she smiled. "We'll be okay. Tonya said she'd stay with me if needed. Are you sure you don't know how long you'll be gone?"

He moved to her and pulled her close, rubbing his hand down her back in a soothing gesture. "No, but if you need me home, just let me know and I'll be here without delay. Brad may need me—whether he realizes it or not—but you are my priority." He kissed the top of her head. "When I get back, we'll go back for another ultrasound. I hope the kids cooperate to find out the sexes."

She absently nodded. "With my weird cravings, I think they must be boys. My stomach gets queasy just looking at a salad." They laughed at that as he'd witnessed it firsthand and had thought she'd toss her cookies when he tried adding more vegetables into her diet. Him actually adding vegetables. He shuddered at the concept.

If someone had told him a year ago that he'd be back with the woman he'd loved since he'd met her in college and would soon be a proud papa, he'd have laughed at them. No, he'd have probably slugged them for giving him false hope.

A knock on the front door split them apart. Not expecting anyone, they strode to the door together. When they opened it, Tonya looked apologetic. She'd been that way since they'd hauled Rick away for embezzlement. His mother lived in a long-term care facility, and the bills had been adding up to a total he couldn't find a way to pay. He'd hoped the small amounts he'd been taking would go unnoticed by anyone.

Tonya told them that she should've noticed it sooner since Rick talked about finally being able to pay the doctor's bills, and she knew what they made at Helping Paws. In Matt's mind, she'd redeemed herself when she'd found a phenomenal grant writer for the organization. "I'm sorry, but this man insists he speak with you immediately."

"Lionel Brookes." The short, stout man in a nice suit held out his hand. He may have been only about five feet five or six, but he packed a lot into the hand Matt shook.

"Matt and Caitlyn Hamilton." He loved saying that. Christ, he sounded like a girl. "How can we help you?" The fidgeting the man was doing pushed an unwelcome curiosity through him. He'd rather have been holding his wife before he had to leave.

"I'm with Brookes, Campbell, and Associates, a law firm in Lexington. May we speak privately?"

His interest was definitely piqued. "Thank you, Tonya," Matt said dismissally. The woman seemed relieved she didn't have to be part of anything legal.

Pulling Caitlyn to his side, they opened the door wider for Lionel to enter.

"Would you like me to take your jacket?" Caitlyn asked.

Appearing relieved, the man pulled off his long coat and handed it to her. As she hung it, Matt took control. "We don't have an office in the house, so if the living room would be okay, we'll meet there." Since the bitter wind had been kicking, Matt imagined the man didn't want to brave it again until he had to.

Matt and Caitlyn settled on the couch, side by side, holding hands that rested in Caitlyn's lap. Lionel sat in an armchair and brought his briefcase to his lap. "First of all"—he pulled a stack of papers from his briefcase—"congratulations on your marriage. My client was pleased to hear about it. She cared a great deal for you, Caitlyn."

"Who is your client?" she asked softly…hesitantly.

Matt had noted the past tense in the attorney's words and wondered if Caitlyn chose to ignore them in her question or didn't grasp that this would be one of those good and bad meetings.

"My client was Vivian Blanche."

Caitlyn tensed and squeezed his hand, telling him she probably caught the "was" in that statement.

"Vivian passed away last week. Most people don't know that she was a person with epilepsy. She had a seizure, and when she fell, she hit her head wrong and died instantly."

With a gasp, Caitlyn's free hand flew to her mouth. After several deep swallows, she told them, "She and I talked about branching out the program for dogs who partner with people with epilepsy and can help them know when they are about to seize so they can go to a safe place. I explained it wasn't in the budget then, but I'd consider it. Oh, Matt"—she turned her head into his chest—"if only I'd done it, she might be alive."

"Shh, you know how long it takes to train a dog. You can't know that you'd have one ready in time."

"Vivian talked to me about donating to Helping Paws so you could begin the program. She wasn't looking for a dog herself. She just saw the good it could do for others."

"She what?" Caitlyn asked, raising her face to look at Lionel.

"She came to me a couple of days before she passed away to set up something for you. Unfortunately, there wasn't time to prepare the paperwork before her accident."

Matt knew there had to be something for an attorney—wearing what was probably a thousand-dollar suit—to visit them personally. "Are you just here to tell us this or is there another purpose to your visit?" He knew he sounded close to an asshole, but this was tearing up Caitlyn, and he was done with it. They'd received the bad news, so there'd best goddamn be some good news.

"Yes. There is a purpose to my visit. I'll read this to you, but I'm going to give you the gist of it right off the bat. Vivian left the bulk of her estate to Helping Paws in the hope you could train dogs for epileptic people."

Caitlyn sucked in a breath and tightened her hold on his hand. "Wait, did she donate the land?"

The attorney smiled slyly. "Anything is possible." With a serious expression, he cleared his throat before he continued. "As for the estate, when all is said and done, Helping Paws will receive around four-point-six million."

Whether it was from her condition or the unexpected news, Matt was prepared when his wife fainted, slumping down on the couch. He picked her up and carried her to their bedroom, with an "I'll be back" to the shocked attorney.

Not long after he had Caitlyn settled on their bed, she woke, confused.

Sliding his hand along her forehead, he brushed away stray strands. "Hey," he said softly, catching her gaze.

"What happened?"

Matt leaned in and gave her a light kiss on the lips. Pulling back, he smiled. "You fainted."

"I…what?"

"Fainted. I figured you'd want to wake up in here rather than in front of that attorney."

She scrunched up her forehead, appearing deep in thought. "Vivian," she whispered.

"I'd say she loved you and what you did here," Matt assured her.

"Is the attorney still here?" she asked.

He nodded. "Yes."

Caitlyn tried to get up, but Matt held her down. "Rest. I'll deal with this for you."

"But you have to leave."

"I've told you more than once, you are my priority." He looked at her stomach and raised his eyebrows. "You and our babies. Let me do this for you."

"Okay, but call me if you need me."

He kissed her on her forehead. "Okay." He wouldn't call her for anything. He figured she had to sign some stuff, but the attorney would have to return when his wife felt better.

He looked at his watch as he left their bedroom. Just enough time to finish this and bail his brother out of whatever the hell he'd gotten himself into.

A Note From Sheila

Thank you for reading *His Heart*! If you enjoyed reading Matt and Caitlyn's story, I would appreciate it if you would help others enjoy this book, too. You can recommend it to friends, readers' groups, and discussion boards. It will mean a great deal to me if you'd take a moment to write a review and share how you feel about my story so others may find my work. Honest reviews help bring my books to the attention of other readers. Best news, only a few words are needed.

A word about the author…

Sheila Kell writes about romantic men who leave women's hearts pounding with a happily ever after built on memorable, adrenaline-pumping stories. Her debut novel, His Desire (HIS Series #1), launched as an Amazon #1 romantic suspense bestseller, later winning the Readers' Favorite award for best romantic suspense novel.

As a Southern girl who has left behind her days with the U.S. Air Force and as a University Vice President, she can usually be found on the Mississippi Gulf Coast, where she lives with her cats and all the strays that magically find her front door. When she isn't writing, she has her nose in a good book, is dealing with the woodland critters who enjoy her back porch, or wishes she had a genie to do her bidding.

Ways to connect
https://www.sheilakell.com
facebook.com/sheilakellbooks
goodreads.com/sheilakellbooks
bookbub.com/authors/sheila-kell
I'd love to hear directly from you, too. Please feel free to email me at sheila@sheilakell.com.

Don't miss out on new releases, exclusive excerpts, and giveaways!

Join my newsletter:
www.SheilaKell.com/subscribe